IN THE SANCTUM
OF ENTROPY

ALDRIC J SAUCIER

ISBN: 0615646484

ISBN-13: 9780615646480

Library of Congress Control Number: 2012940406

Entropy's Espresso
Superior, Colorado

This book is a work of fiction. Names, characters, places and incidents either are the product of the author's imagination or are used fictitiously, and any resemblance to actual persons, living or dead, businesses, companies, organizations, events or locales, is entirely coincidental.

For Ever

CHAPTER 1

THE WILDERNESS OF ETERNITY

———

A hush swept across the empty highway, hollow and deep, like a faint draft emanating from a mountain cavern. It carried a certain sadness, a feeling of desolation, as if there were nothing left to hope for. A man stepped out of his car and into the emptiness. He carried within him a deep depression, the weight of which had forced him to pull over and rest for a while. An insatiable longing for happiness gnawed at his gut, gradually eroding his soul. The struggle to keep going exhausted him. He sat down in the middle of the highway and closed his eyes. His shoulders slumped as he drew his knees up to his frail body and folded his thin arms around them. The warmth of the sun embraced him with affection, comforting him. He sat still under it, his mind churning through his anguish. His thoughts drifted back to the beginning...

At first, when it happened, the cable news shows, Internet blogs, and media outlets strained to convey what was going on. Something was happening on the other side of the world, in faraway Kyrgyzstan, at some place no one had ever heard of called Inylchek. A howling thing was crying out in the night from deep within the surrounding mountains. It took time for the media to arrive at the remote location, and when they did, a strange interference prevented live transmission from the site. With scarce details available, the various expert personalities floated naive theories based on their own analysis of a phenomenon they knew nothing about, latching on to its dramatic potential like ticks digging into a fresh meal. As pictures emerged, the realization of what was happening sunk in. A pit had opened up. An abyssal trench with no bottom. A thing beyond man's ability to control was damaging the world in a way that could not be fixed. The world was ending.

There was an expectation, a dogmatic conviction, that the final moments of the world would be swift and immediate. Across the globe a fervid anticipation grew for the sweeping death the destruction of the planet would bring. Yet, as the day dragged on and the sun held steady in the sky, unmoved, it became apparent that something was wrong. Scientists desperately tried to explain to the anxious public that the Earth was experiencing time dilation. The passage of time had slowed, prolonging the end of the world for an unknown duration, possibly an eternity. Somehow, instead of passing through time, people were now observing it without being affected by it. They were helpless spectators, condemned to an everlasting life, caught in the instant of planetary death. The lack of immediate explanations for why this was happening was blasted by celebrity pundits. Fear and panic was sensationalized by a media hype machine that was less interested in preparing the public for the end than winning the final ratings race.

The public had been raised on a steady diet of sound bites. Short attention spans had been trained to quickly migrate from one subject to the next without ever pausing to contemplate a deeper meaning. Viewers consumed information with the same frivolous interest as they would a summer action film. Worldwide social upheaval initially provided thrilling entertainment, but after the riots, the political unrest, and mass suicides peaked, the ratings started to decline. The public hungered for the next new thing to focus on, and when they found none they turned back to their own interests as if oblivious to the crisis at hand. As astounding as it was, and as offensive as many enlightened people found it, the public grew bored.

Even the destruction of the planet could no longer hold the attention of a society enthralled with self-infatuation. The medium of social networks had provided individuals with a false sense of importance. The magnitude of the event before them failed to register through the everyday trivial distractions that so readily filled their lives. Even though the world was ending, it was not ending for them. It was that thing that was happening somewhere *else*. The general view in the United States was that unless the world was ending at their doorstep it was not worth thinking about. The slow pace of the creeping abyss diminished its danger. By the time it crossed the ocean, *America* would have a solution. For those where it was ending, the public shared heartfelt sympathies through a status update. Fast-food empathy delivered at the click of a button by a spoiled society too jaded to contemplate putting anything before their own petty interests. Who cared *those* people were dying? Those people were always dying.

The response from a media desperate for an audience was to ratchet up the message of Armageddon until it could no longer be ignored. It was the end, and everyone needed to pay attention to it. The onslaught of coverage across every device and every method of broadcasting trapped people in an inescapable hysteria. The message was persistent and demanded viewers to stay tuned, lest they miss a second of valuable content. And the reason? There was money to be made and enough of an economy left to buy those desired things before they disappeared forever. A billion deaths were not enough to deter marketing firms from racing to discover what this final generation would buy and convincing them that they needed it.

The government was slow to react to public outcry, and by the time it did, the lawyers were ready. They tied the courts up in litigation, knowing the government's resources were stretched thin with more important matters to attend to. The bombardment continued unabated. Boredom was ruthlessly driven out of the public consciousness, and in its place came an unrelenting desperation for some form of escape.

It was into this environment that a new game was launched. It promised total escapism for the general public. Its name was *Conundrum,* and it could be played anywhere and any time. It could run on any device, connect to all social networks, and most importantly, filter out everything you no longer wanted to acknowledge in the real world in a manner more complete than anything that had come before. It was not just a fantasy game; it was complete emancipation from life itself. It promised total immersion through a revolutionary combination of biofeedback and an adaptive artificial inspiration algorithm that mimicked imagination. It could read emotions and build whatever the heart desired, at whim, giving new meaning to instant gratification. The game was many things to many different people, all at the same time. This was its advantage. A vast new world unwittingly created by the people who populated it to be everything they had always wanted. The game quickly took over the lives of millions desperate to shut out the real world around them.

Civil unrest in the face of the end of the world had been the government's greatest challenge. *Conundrum* became the answer to this problem. The Defense Advanced Research Projects Agency (DARPA) stepped in and began funding the game's development in conjunction with major pharmaceutical companies. At first they tied the distribution of mood-altering pills to in-game social events in order to enhance the experience. This eventually evolved into every player being sent his or her own pill dispenser, which could issue a customized psychoactive dose that matched whatever circumstances the player encountered or imagined. The effects were wide ranging, and the addiction was immediate. In real life players became docile and withdrawn, while in *Conundrum* they became masters of their own fantastic destiny. Popular consumption of the pills quickly expanded outside the game to become the accepted new normal. Vast swaths of society disappeared overnight, leaving behind them a dying world they no longer wanted to live in.

The man sitting in the middle of the empty highway curled himself up tighter.

"Denying reality has always been the oldest of comfort foods," he said bitterly as he continued to reminisce.

He knew this all too well. The constant deaths, overpowering fear, and burden of carrying a sane perspective in an unhinged world eventually broke him. Despair had overtaken him, destroying his health, what little faith he had, and any remaining ambition. Like so many people around him, he stopped going to work. He considered suicide, but not realistically. The riots, the murders, the insanity of a world that had lost all hope of finding a way to live any longer cast a weight on his body that threatened to suffocate his very being. There was nowhere to go. He settled into his apartment with the shades drawn shut and began playing video games. They demanded his attention and distracted him from thinking about what might be happening outside his self-made bunker. He tried every game that came out, but none could fulfill the promise of complete escape. Then came *Conundrum*, the single greatest game ever created. He bought it, logged on, and created for himself the life he had never had, but had always wanted. He embraced the fantasy. He even changed his name to that of the character he played. When he finally awoke from his many adventures, several hundred years had passed, and yet everything he had tried so hard to escape from was still there waiting for him.

A distant crack of thunder interrupted his thoughts and caused the man to look up. He watched the highway carefully, but there was nothing. He was alone.

"Damn Cayenne," he seethed, thinking about her, remembering how he woke up from *Conundrum*.

He had not left willingly. Had he not been drawn into a strange place he called "the white room," he might never have stopped playing. He remembered the first time it happened, the people he met, and the girl whose name would forever stir feelings within him. It was funny how a few words with strangers had changed his life forever.

After the white room, he found he could no longer enjoy the game. He guessed it was easier for him to let go than for most people since he had never indulged in the pills. He had witnessed the effects of pills early on and had sworn never to take them no matter how bad things got. For him, the recurring bouts of depression were a reminder that things were not right in the world, or his life.

He remembered walking outside his apartment for the first time in years. He had canceled his government-subsidized automated food deliveries, and decided to go down to the corner store to buy food in person. His excitement was tempered by the first dead body he encountered. His neighbor had hung himself in the stairwell just outside the lobby door. It was disturbingly real, without the protection of distance technology provided, and it left him numb for days afterward. He decided to stay in his self-made bunker for a little while longer, until he grew used to the sight of it.

When he finally did leave the building, he immediately noticed the sky. Waves moved through the atmosphere as if the bright blue sky had been turned into an ocean above him. He looked at the streets around him, which were devoid of people, and realized that before him was a world unlike anything he could have ever imagined. And it was real. The media storm had passed with the destruction of the East Coast. What was left of the country had grown quiet, as if it had given into the inevitable and was waiting patiently for the end. He took only a few things from his apartment; most of it he left behind, knowing he would never return. He set out to look for something. What that was, he did not know. He had only vague ideas and all the time in the world to figure them out.

Time to think? Time to live? But am I living? Is this still life? Was it ever? All these thoughts plagued his mind. He let out a forced sigh that growled at the end. His hands clenched into angry fists.

He felt the intensity of his depression lifting. He stared down the highway wondering where he was going and if he even had a destination. His soul was sapped of motivation, and his body was weary from his fruitless search. Somewhere out there, in what remained of the world, was an answer, and he was determined to find it. He had to keep moving.

"Just another day at the office," he said, standing up to stretch as if throwing off a blanket. He stood still for a moment, listening, but he heard nothing beyond his own breath. He sat down in the driver's seat of his car and stared into his own tired eyes through the rearview mirror.

"Man, I look like shit," he said aloud.

He felt like it, too.

CHAPTER 2

RUBBER BAND

———

It was as if he had fallen and caught himself suddenly. That was how he had arrived here. It was at some point in the past, a couple hundred years ago at least. He kept his eyes closed, waiting for everything to come back into focus. His mouth tingled and tasted metallic. It always reminded him of the sensation of licking a nine-volt battery. It was a familiar flavor…the flavor of time travel.

"Rubber band!" a woman shouted out from somewhere behind him.

He slowly opened his eyes. He was in a bank, standing in line for a cashier. The frontal lobe of his brain felt heavy, making his eyes feel tired. He knew it was because of his ongoing depression and had nothing to do with this situation. His face hid the depth of trouble he was in under the same bitter scowl he always wore. Most of the time he hated people, and the rest of the time he just didn't like them. This was his barrier to keep people away. There was always a good reason to avoid the general population. The person to his right was one of those reasons.

"I ain't gots time for no rubber band!" a fat man said loudly as if expecting the untamable forces of entropy to stop based solely on his complaints. He put his hands on his hips. "I just gots me a puppy, and I gots to feed it."

"You should just put it out of its misery. I mean, that would be the right thing to do," said the depressed man.

"Just who the hell do you think you are telling me to go kill my puppy dog?"

"My name is Echo, Echo Gain, and I don't think I'm anybody. In fact, I'm a nobody. I know that much for sure. Why keep a puppy when it can never grow up? It has no future."

"Man, none of us gots any future." the fat man snarled, looking at Echo, trying to remember him. "Do I know you from somewhere? Man, I can't be sure if we've met before or not."

"We must have met at least once before. My name is Echo."

"Yeah, yeah, you told me already. I go by Riboflavin."

"That's pretty cool. Good game name."

"You play?"

"Not so much anymore."

"Huh. That's too bad. You look like a smart guy, like the type of guy that gots everything figured out three steps ahead of everyone else."

Echo half-laughed. "Sometimes."

"You gots family?"

"It's just me."

"That's a hard way to live these days."

"I get by…"

Echo said it so casually that it belittled how difficult things were for him. Evanescent memories haunted him like whispers in the dark, faded shadows of people he once knew, taken forever by the passage of time. He could not mourn whom he could not remember, but he also could not replace who was forgotten. He felt tormented by emptiness, yet comforted by solitude, and found no peace between the two extremes.

At least I still have my hair, he mused.

He looked around again. The bank was filled with about a dozen seemingly random people. Bank employees and customers with nothing in common, except this one event that had caused them all to be snapped back in time. Many people still looked bewildered. It was hard to tell who had arrived first. The only thing they all knew for sure was that they were there to relive a traumatic event. Something they all wished had stayed forgotten.

Riboflavin's arm suddenly jerked forward to grab a deposit slip. "Ack! Man, I can't stand that! It feels like my arm's asleep. I can't control it."

Echo moved up in the line for the cashier with two strange lurches. He was tired of explaining things. "It's a rubber band. Everything that happened before will happen again, and there is nothing we can do to change it."

"You ever tried to?" Riboflavin's arm relaxed. He rubbed it.

"To what?"

"Change the past?"

"You can't. It's just like your arm. You filled out a slip before in the past, so you fill one out now. It already happened one way, and now that's the only way it can ever happen. All you can do is wait it out."

"Man, that's crap. There gots to be a way, some kind of shortcut."

Echo shook his head as if amused by Riboflavin. He knew there was no such thing as a shortcut. There was no easy way out. It was all just wishful thinking. He watched as the people around him struggled against the inevitability of the history they had created. Bodies moved awkwardly around the bank; arms and legs jerked about as if tugged by the invisible strings of puppeteers. Quiet conversations investigating why they had snapped back to this bank were rudely interrupted by their own mouths repeating what they had said centuries ago. Echo knew why they were there—he remembered—but he thought it best to keep it to himself.

He and Riboflavin moved up in line again. It was taking too long, Echo thought. He worried about how much time was passing in the present. There was nothing he could do about it. Things had to play out at the same pace as they had originally. He needed a distraction to occupy his mind. He decided to agitate Riboflavin with sarcasm.

"It can't grow up into a dog. It's stuck. Think how it must be suffering."

"Man, why do you give a shit about my puppy dog? It ain't none of your business!"

"Don't you care?"

"I don't care what no dog thinks. I gots me a puppy, so *I* feel better, not so it—"

His sentence was halted by the arrival of the event that had brought them all back to the bank. It was a robbery. Echo let out a sigh of relief at the sight of the robber. Things would progress more quickly now. The rubber band had recovered the memory from his mind with the subtlety of a punch to the gut. He remembered it well, especially the outcome. The man who had just entered the bank would be shot dead in less than ten minutes.

"I'm alive...again? But I'm dead!" the robber whispered. He looked over at the security guard by the door. This was the man who had killed him, and would kill him again. The robber shuddered and shook his head.

"I don't want to die. Please don't kill me again...aaagghh!"

The robber's mouth contorted uncontrollably as words welled up inside him like a sickness to be vomited out. Sweat began pouring from his face as he struggled to stop his hand from reaching inside his coat for the gun. His mouth drooled as his lips curled into the words that would be his death sentence. There was nothing he could do to stop himself.

"Nobody move!" he yelled.

"Oh god, no!" the robber shouted, his mouth dispensing criminal rants and repentant calls for forgiveness in the same shared breath. His past and present self were fighting for control over the conversation, like two separate people trying to speak over one another.

"This is a robbery!"

"No! No, it's not! I didn't mean it. I take it back—"

"If anyone moves, I'm going to blow their fucking head off!"

"It's a second chance! It can be different! I didn't mean to do this! Please, believe me!"

Everyone raised their hands just as they had done before. All of them bore a mixed expression of the fear they felt in the past, boredom from having to relive it again, and anger at the robber whom everyone held responsible for causing the rubber band. The truth was, no one knew what a rubber band was. They happened randomly every few years, just like jury duty. It would be over soon enough, and a man would be dead. Echo seemed decidedly relaxed in the midst of it all. He watched the robber try in vain to resist his body from walking toward the cashier counter. Sneakers squeaked across the floor in a foot-dragging contorted dance that culminated in the pistol-whipping of some old man who just happened to be in his way.

"No!"

"Outta my way, old man! You should have killed yourself a hundred years ago."

"I'm sorry, I don't really mean that!" the robber sobbed between insane shouts. It was clear that coming back from the dead to inevitably die, painfully, all over again, was tearing the mind of the man apart. He quietly sobbed between screaming profanities at anyone he thought was moving behind him. He waved the gun around erratically in the air as if swatting at invisible flies. The movement was an exaggeration of years ago, amplified by the robber's attempts to control his own actions.

"Stop me, stop me. Please stop me!" he pleaded.

Riboflavin grit his teeth angrily. "Did you see that? That mother-fucker hit that poor old man!"

Echo slowly nodded. "That's nothing to get upset about. When this ends, everyone will snap back safe and sound…well, more or less."

"More or less?"

"Nobody can predict these things, right? Nobody knows when they will occur, or with who, or even how. All I can tell you is what I've experienced before, and that's that time continues on in the present even while we are here in the past. That's why they call it a rubber band. We are in two places at once, just temporally stretched out."

The robber continued screaming. Riboflavin cracked his knuckles. "Man! I've never gotten used to this shit."

"People make their own problems."

"Damn right they do. Then they go and use the end of the world as their excuse."

"The world has been ending for so long I don't think that even qualifies as an excuse anymore. Look at that guy." Echo gestured at the robber. "He did this for the thrill because he was bored, or aspiring to be a celebrity. People used to do this all the time. Just flip out and hope they were exciting enough to get picked up for a pilot. That guy was probably desperate to not be forgotten, never considering the consequences of being remembered. It's just more stupid people doing stupid things."

His mind suddenly wandered off to any number of stupid things he had done. The word *dumbass* came to mind. "Besides, I have bigger problems than this."

Riboflavin chuckled loudly. "You think *you* gots problems? God-damn. My bitch is stuck permanently on the rag. She keeps coming at me, like she's in heat. She tells me, it ain't no thing, just keep my eyes closed, and I'm like, I love you baby, but——"

"*Bigger* problems than that," Echo interrupted as quickly as he could. "Just before I snapped back, I was speeding down the highway like a fool, and like a fool I was driving with my knees so I could snack on pistachios."

"Didn't you say something about time moving here and back there at the same time or whatever? Don't that mean you are driving still?"

"Great, isn't it? I mean, basically, I'm speeding down the highway screwed in a Honda Civic."

Riboflavin laughed at him. "You drive a Civic?" Then he suddenly stopped to think. "If time is still going, that means my puppy is starving, don't it?"

Echo shrugged. "Maybe not. I mean, who knows? It could be eating your face off while you are lying there catatonic, right?"

"I ain't gots time for this shit!" Riboflavin yelled.

Echo paused to consider the context of the word *time* given their cir-cumstances. His palms were sweating. This was taking too long, and that highway he was on was filled with abandoned vehicles. He could snap back and die. The last time he experienced a rubber band, he burned a pancake. This time he could end up smeared across several miles of deserted asphalt without any hope of rescue. He needed to speed this up somehow, but time was linear; there was no way to change the past. Though he wondered if the inevitable outcome could be sped up.

"You know, Ribo, that robber guy is looking really stressed out."

Riboflavin looked at the maniacal eyes of the robber. "Yeah, he is. Looks like he might blow up any second."

"Time is linear, you can't change that. But maybe if the robber died sooner, this would all end quicker. I mean, it would still be the same outcome at the end of the day, right?"

"You think?"

"Doesn't hurt to try."

Riboflavin cupped his hands over his mouth and yelled across the bank. "You're already dead, motherfucker! Save us the trouble, and put a bullet right through your head. Man, I gots things to do! I gotta feed my puppy dog!"

The robber jerked his head around, with his gun waving wildly in the face of the cashier. Anxiety was driving a knife in his gut causing him to wince between his words as the sweat trickled off his brow like a leaky faucet. His mouth struggled against the words he wanted to say and the words he had already said.

"Fuck off!"

"Put all the money in the bag, bitch. And don't forget the pills."

"Can't you respect a man's last moments?"

"Move it, lady. I haven't got all day."

"Respect?" Riboflavin looked at Echo. "Goddamn bank robber wants us to respect him? Can you believe this shit?" Riboflavin laughed. Echo joined in with him, but only because he felt he had no other choice. In truth, he could not stand Riboflavin.

Echo loathed the presence of other people. They irritated him in a way that he felt was deep and justified. When the world ended, it was as if society collectively gave up. Nothing mattered anymore. It was complete mayhem. It was liberating to watch the wealthy elite implode, industrialized mass production falter, and politicians flee their posts. It was liberating all right, for the first month; then everyone woke up to the reality of time dilation. *The last day of the end of the world would take thousands of years to pass.* Society wasn't perfect, but it worked well enough, and the choice was either to self-destruct or hold it together the best they could until the end. It was to be a long, hard road of gradual decline, social atrophy, and the onset of widespread mental illnesses.

"It's never simple," Echo sighed, "It just never is. We make our own problems. People make each other miserable."

"I hear they make a pill for that shit," said Riboflavin.

"The government makes a pill for everything these days."

"Damn right. Everything, 'cept these rubber bands. I bet that's because they made them, too. They're trying to time travel to fix things, but it's gone all wrong. They fucked up. That's why things are weird and stupid. Can't trust those motherfuckers! Man! I never should have paid my taxes!"

Riboflavin reached in his pocket, pulled out a prescription bottle, and popped three pills in his mouth. Echo cringed. He watched Riboflavin's eyes relax as the medicinal agents took effect. Echo wondered how much time had passed in the present and how close he was to dying a fiery death. Time seemed to crawl at the bank. He felt trapped.

"I have got to get back to the present. I mean, I don't want to crash."

"Man! That would be pretty fucked up to die in a Civic."

Echo smirked as he planted the setup. "Too bad about your puppy. I bet it's really hungry."

He waited. He did not know these people and, chances were, would never see them again. Nothing he said here mattered.

"I'm really curious if this will end sooner if that guy dies faster."

Riboflavin snorted. "Let's find out." He licked his lips and yelled as loudly as he could. "Hey, motherfucker! Why don't you try putting that gun in your mouth? Maybe if you die now, the rest of us can go home."

Somebody shouted, "Yeah!" from the far back of the bank.

The robber heaved his body around and pointed the gun at Riboflavin and Echo.

"Maybe if I shoot one of you, and you die instead of me, maybe the universe will be appeased, and I can live in your place! Maybe all we need is a sacri—"

"I want the money and the pills from the other drawer, too. Move it, bitch!"

"What we need is a sacrifice."

The robber struggled to take aim at the two of them. Echo wanted to duck down, but his legs were planted in place by the rubber band effect. He wanted to run, but there was no way he could. People began to scream as the gun waived in their direction. A cashier behind the counter demanded that Echo and Riboflavin stop provoking the robber. To the cashier's horror, Riboflavin continued to egg the robber on.

"Sacrifice? That's sounds like some goddamn old-time religion to me!" Riboflavin glanced at Echo and gave him a nod. Sweat broke out across Echo's body. Riboflavin laughed at the robber.

"You want a sacrifice, motherfucker? Put that gun in your mouth and kill yourself. Don't keep us here, man. We done nothing wrong. You made your choice. You fucked up. You're done. You been done. Nobody knows your goddamn name, and nobody cares. Fuck you and the horse that you popped out of, you ugly motherfucker!"

An impatient heckle came from the back of the bank. "Just shut the hell up and die, you selfish asshole!"

Riboflavin applauded the heckler. Echo worried about what might happen next; he wasn't sure anymore. Even though he knew for certain that time was linear and the past could not be changed, he suddenly feared that he could be wrong.

The robber shook with rage. There was no sympathy in this crowd of strangers, and he should never have expected any in this day and age. He grabbed his gun with both hands and aimed it at Echo, believing he was the heckler. Echo ducked down, but his feet were planted in place exactly where he had stood in the past. He heard the pull of the trigger.

Click! Nothing. The robber let out a mental-breaking gasp. He put the gun in his mouth. A woman screamed. He pulled the trigger repeatedly. *Click! Click! Click! Click!* Still nothing.

"Nah-ha!" Riboflavin laughed. "You can't change the past, stupid motherfucker!"

Echo watched in disbelief as several other people pointed at the robber and called him names. The robber began to cry in high-pitched sobs. Echo thought he should feel bad for the crook, but he felt nothing. He looked at the way the people were acting. He thought he should hate them, but felt nothing for them, too. There was nothing for him to feel at all. None of it mattered to him, and he was not sure if it should.

"Leave me alone! Just leave me alone!" the robber howled. His mental decay was culminating in a full-blown breakdown. He screamed nonsensical noises that frightened everyone. It was as if he were possessed by a demon speaking in tongues. It wasn't supernatural: it was the collapse of a man who knew the conclusion of his future and was rapidly speeding toward it. Hope had left him, and they had witnessed it. The bank was silent as the robber grabbed the bag of loot and walked toward the exit. He no longer struggled against the pull of time. He was broken. His face was full of tears and sweat. He looked at the security guard poised to shoot him, bit his lower lip and whispered some form of forgiveness toward the man. The security guard returned a bored groan. His task of shooting the robber dead held no more importance to him than folding laundry. The guard's indifferent gaze caused the thief to utter a sudden, involuntary yelp.

The robber reached the door and spun around with vigor ready to shout his last words, but his timing was off, and the security guard shot him three times. His voice crumbled midway through the exhale of his last breath leaving the words his lips were forming without the sound to speak them. The robber fell over dead. Blood poured out of his mouth and eyes and mixed with the tears and sweat. Riboflavin stared at the fresh corpse, satisfied.

"Man, Echo! Why'd you go duck down like that? If you knew the past couldn't change, why'd you think that motherfucker could shoot you?"

"Well, you never really can be sure, can you?"

Riboflavin gave Echo a foul look. "You're just some fucking coward, ain't you?"

"Why don't you take some more pills, you ignorant asshole! See if—"

And just like that, Riboflavin was gone. Taken by time back to wherever he had come from. It irritated Echo greatly that he had not had the last word. He took a deep breath, tried to let his anger go, then let it out. The rubber band was over, and the reality of it began fading.

His mouth tingled. The present was coming, but not fast enough. Echo began closing and opening his eyes trying to speed up the process. He was not sure if what he was doing would have any effect at all. When he returned, he could find himself dead in the ruins of his vehicle, or if he died in the present while in the past, he could be trapped in the past living in his old self, with years of memories of future events that may or may not happen ever again. Could the worst of what he had forgotten become an inevitable future he would have to live through again? He hated that possibility and that there were no answers for anything.

He closed his eyes once more. "Come on. Come on!" he urged.

He began to feel an odd sensation, as if he could hear music in another room, being played low, but he knew the tune. It was the melody of the present. The buzzing four-cylinder engine of his car, the crunching of pistachios in his mouth, the wind rushing by at 110 miles per hour through an open window. Then it was as if the door to the other room was suddenly thrust open, and the volume turned up in a startling manner. He was back in the present, speeding down the highway. He did not even remember closing his eyes during the transition. A sudden bump in the road caused him to focus. *What the hell was going on? Where was the car going?* It was veering toward the right, accelerating head-on toward an abandoned vehicle.

CHAPTER 3

PHENOMENTHON

———

The battered old Honda Civic dropped off the right side of the highway, kicking up handfuls of rocks into the wheel wells as it raced toward the back of an abandoned SUV. Echo's hands gripped the steering wheel tightly. His instinct was to yank it hard to the left—a panic-driven move that would wreck the car.

"Nope, wrong! Think, dumbass! Don't be a moron," he yelled at himself, spitting half-chewed pistachios across the dashboard.

He took his foot off the gas pedal and very slowly turned the wheel to the left. The car smoothly veered back onto the highway, avoiding the abandoned SUV and potential catastrophe. He took a deep breath, felt the anger burning inside him, and let the breath out. He kept his foot off the gas, letting the car slow down. He had been driving too fast and had been completely unprepared for the rubber band.

There was no telling how long he had been in the past or why the time he'd spent there moved at a different rate than the present. He wished for a clock that could give him some reliable measurement, but clocks were notoriously unreliable these days. They ran at vastly different speeds depending on their proximity with the event horizon. About the only thing clocks were still good for was cooking. Local time was generally stable, but leaving the house for a quick drive somewhere could result in any amount of time passing. Those were the perils of time dilation. It was safer to always move forward and never look back, which suited Echo just fine.

He reached into his bag of pistachios, slouching down in the seat to position his knees on the steering wheel again. He knew it wasn't safe, but it would be a year, at least, before another rubber band occurred. Possibly longer. He also knew there would be no one on the road for miles. The highway was deserted. Very few people traveled through the restricted zone surrounding the abyss due to the danger of undiscovered time distortions. Only FedEx braved such journeys, and more than one truck had never come back. Echo knew the risks, but there was something about the zone that appealed to him. It was a good place to think. He cracked a nutshell and ate the freed pistachio. He brushed some of the mess he had made off the dashboard. The interior of his car started to fill with a very bright white light. He looked out ahead. A bolt of lightning was blocking the right lane.

"Great. Where did that come from?" he quipped, taking control of the car again. He squinted against the glare of the jagged stalk of superheated plasma. What little he knew about lightning stalks had come from a urine-soaked pamphlet he had picked up off the floor of a gas station bathroom. It had been a fascinating read filled with unsubstantiated theories based on rumor, luck, and hearsay, but it was the only thing he had ever read that even attempted to address the mind-bending hazard of a lightning stalk.

Lightning stalks could appear as fast as normal lightning, but they lingered for days, frozen in place, caught in their own bubble of time. Getting near one was a death sentence because of the bubble. The bubble itself was invisible. Anything that entered it would slow down to the infinitesimal speed within the bubble and be vaporized by the lightning. The best advice was to completely avoid the phenomenon by a wide margin. However, if it appeared in front of a moving vehicle and could not be avoided, as was happening to Echo, there was one theory on how to survive it. Because a bubble's effect was presumably confined to a small radius, it was possible to skirt the outer edge of it and survive. The theory stated that if only part of the vehicle entered the bubble, the rest of the vehicle would hold anchor in the present, preventing the vehicle from being trapped by the slower time.

"Gamble my life on a hypothesis I found in a bathroom? Hey, why not?" Echo said cynically. "What could go wrong? I mean, it had correct grammar, right?" He gnashed his teeth angrily. "Fucking shit!" He was not really angry; he was actually very nervous, but the ranting helped ease the tension.

Speed was the key. The faster he went, the more likely he would be able to push past the bubble. He slammed the gas pedal down, hard. The old four-cylinder engine waited two seconds to respond then revved loudly. He had always hated that slight delay, but it had never been a sports car. The Civic sped toward the lightning stalk, with the engine redlining.

"Not fast enough! I'm going to get stuck in that thing and fucking die!" he raged. It had taken what seemed to be fifteen minutes to get the car up to 110 miles per hour previously. There was not enough space between him and the lightning stalk to max out the speed again. He switched to the left lane, where only a few jagged strands of the stalk lingered, and hoped for the best.

The car shuddered from a soft impact. It had hit the bubble and was proceeding through at a slow, yet constant speed, as if it were motoring through warm caramel. The molten bright-white plasma of the lightning stalk pulsated just outside the car like a strobe light. Echo reached into the glove box and put on his sunglasses. It felt like the car was on rails. There was no use trying to steer. He'd have to ride it out. A pungent burning rubber smell began to fill the car. It concerned him greatly, but not as much as the crackling deep fryer sounds coming from underneath the vehicle. Electrical tentacles sprouted off of the stalk, making contact with the exterior of the car, burning the paint off the hood and warping the passenger-side windows with heat.

"Like a car wash from hell!" Echo yelled, pushing against the steering wheel as if he were pushing the car itself forward. "Faster! Got to move! Going to die here!" The back window shattered. The passenger seat caught fire. He quickly dumped the open bottle of water he usually had by his side on it. The heat evaporated the water, which steamed up the windshield. After a sharp bump, it was over. The Civic broke free of the bubble. The engine buzzed obnoxiously, pulling the car down the road at full speed. Half the car was smoking. Small flames danced on the hood, but they were superficial, and the car did not appear to actually be on fire. Echo looked back at the lightning stalk. Grinning proudly, he gave it a salute good-bye.

"Well, that was easy," he said with a laugh. He turned around to the fogged over windshield and used his hand to clear off a spot so he could see out. He saw a dark object on the road. It was a turtle. He instinctively jerked the wheel to the right.

"No No! No! No! What are you doing, you idiot? We're dead! We're dead!" The Civic turned sharply; the overheated tires exploded under the strain, sending the vehicle flipping end over end. Glass burst all around Echo. The side airbags deployed in time to catch the shattered glass, keeping the shards inside the vehicle as it tumbled. He held tight to the steering wheel while trying to avoid being thrown into the path of the glass fragments flying around the cabin. The car landed on its roof and slid upside down for half a mile before coming to a stop.

Echo wiped the blood from his forehead; there wasn't much—just enough to keep him angry. He unbuckled the seatbelt and crawled out the window over the shattered glass as quickly as he could. He feared an explosion and forced himself to move faster until he had dragged himself out. He stumbled away from the car, watching for fire. The Civic was dead. Echo sat down on the road, shaking his head, then lay down on his back and stared up at the sky. The sun was stuck permanently at 3:00 p.m. The sky maintained the same light-blue tint it had had for as long as Echo could remember. He watched the rhythmic rolling of waves move across the sky. It was like staring up at a bright blue ocean. People theorized that the waves were created by distortions in gravity rippling from the abyss beyond the horizon. Nobody knew for sure, but after so much time had passed, the sight of waves in the sky had become the norm, and to a degree, soothing. He watched them until he felt relaxed. Time passed, but he was unsure of exactly how much. He sat up slowly.

"Well, that sucked." He checked himself for broken bones or hanging flesh. "Looks all right—both arms, both legs, both feet. Guess I'm lucky." Then he looked at his destroyed car and the few meager belongings he owned scattered across the highway. The sight of his mangled things bothered him. In the end they were just things, but they were *his* things. He took a deep breath, then said, "Maybe not so lucky."

In the distant past, he would have used a cell phone to call for help. They were useless now. Something in the air distorted the signals to such a degree that the devices no longer functioned. Satellites suffered from similar problems, while aircraft were known to simply disappear. The waves were the cause. Everyone knew it, everyone said it, yet it couldn't be proven without the scientists. The scientists were gone. The world was collapsing. Everything everywhere was in decline. He looked at his half-burned beat-up Civic as further confirmation of this fact. The car rested upside down on its roof, with the wheels pointed toward the sky like a dead insect. A faithful friend now destroyed beyond repair. He could see his laptop up the road mixed in with the debris-ridden trail of his things. Computer guts hung out of its casing, a fatal injury he could not mend. He had no desire to walk over for a closer look.

"Oh well," he sighed. "I guess this is one of those moments I can categorize as cleansing." The car suddenly made a metal popping sound. He ducked for cover, as if it might explode. The car began to rattle loudly. He could see no fire. The strange noises grew louder, like metal twisting. He stared from a distance worried about what might be happening. The car started to slide backward. All his exploded belongings that were strewn across the road also started to slide. The sight of everything moving on its own brought about primal, supernatural fears of ghosts and goblins, which caused his neck hairs to stand up.

"What now?" he griped. "What the hell is it this time? Is it the frogs or the locusts? Because I've lost track of what plague we're on."

The sliding car started to gain momentum. A part flew back on, a dent popped out, the pistachios dropped back into the bag. He started to walk after the car.

"It's like a marathon of phenomenons—a phenomenthon," he joked, wincing from pain as he did. He knew he had brought these problems on himself. Traveling this close to the edge of the abyss, even though he was too far away to see it, was an invitation for the unexplained.

Then everything clicked.

"Wait, is this…instant replay?" he asked himself.

He had never experienced instant replay firsthand. It was one of the many things he had read about online in the forums of *Conundrum*. Supposedly an event could reverse itself back to the point where it began. But it had to be a sudden event of significant impact. Especially one with emotional consequences. Echo regarded this idea as bullshit perpetuated by the absence of scientists. Superstition, myths, and religion filled the vacuum they had left behind. The government had taken ownership of science in the name of national security. They had gathered up all scientists and sequestered them inside military-run compounds called ThinkTanks. The rumor was that they were working on a solution to the "end of the world" problem. One rumor floating in a sea of conspiracies.

"Okay, enough thinking. Let's try paying attention here, have to focus."

The car was sliding away faster now. He had to jog to keep up. Jogging made him aware that his knee was injured. A sharp pain stabbed him with each step he took, but he kept pace by limping. His belongings flew back into the trunk. The car flipped right side up, the tires re-inflated, and even the black rubber streaks on the road lifted up off the pavement. The engine banged and turned over buzzing again at full throttle. A new danger occurred to Echo as the engine roared. If he did not get back in the car before the replay finished, chances were that the car would end up speeding down the road without a driver, and wreck again. He had to get behind the wheel before time moved forward, but he had no idea how much longer the replay would last. He started to run, overriding the stabbing pain with the fear of blowing this second chance.

"Move your ass, damn it! Get in there!"

A chunk of the car flew across the road to rejoin with the door. It swept under Echo's legs, knocking him down. He cursed at himself angrily and got back up. It felt like jagged razor blades had replaced the cartilage in his knee, clawing him as he ran. He grit his teeth, angry with himself for being so weak. He had always been so weak. The car started to slow. The replay must almost be finished, he thought. He was close. He reached out for the door handle and missed. He reached again and still missed. "Damn you!" he screamed at himself. He grabbed the handle, opened the door, and jumped inside. He was so angry at himself, but he had to forget that. He had to pay attention.

The car jerked twice. Backward. Forward. Back again. The engine revved. He held onto the steering wheel with both hands. He wiped the bloody sweat off his forehead with a shirtsleeve so his vision would not be impaired. He had been given a second chance to not wreck the car. This time he would make a better choice, he thought, as his mind flooded with ideas about fate, destiny, and permanence. He shook all the stray thoughts out of his mind, and focused. The car quaked, and the engine revved again. Then it lurched forward with wheels squealing as if it had been hurled onto a drag strip. Echo was flung back into the seat. He gently applied the brakes, being careful not to panic. He felt a bump. Then he heard a sound. *Ka-runch!*

"What's left?" he wondered, but he knew what it was. It was the turtle. In the rush, he had forgotten about it. He stayed focused on slowing the car down, until it finally came to a complete stop. He opened the door to inspect the damage. Half the car had melted. Most of the paint had burned away. The tires looked questionable, but drivable. All the windows were smashed; somehow their rejuvenation had not been included in the instant replay. Echo was grateful for the repairs he had been given. He opened the trunk and found everything intact. He followed a moist tire tread stain back to where the turtle lay. Its shell had caved in, its eyes were bugging out of its head, and a little piece of something from its insides was dangling from its mouth.

He looked back at the lightning stalk, then up at the sky, and finally down at the dead turtle. He felt exhausted. He wanted to not feel bad about running it over. It was just a stupid animal crossing the road. He had tried to avoid it the first time and almost killed himself. Now he no longer cared. He told himself this, but he didn't entirely believe it. The turtle had caused no harm. It had no malice. It wanted only to get to where it had been going. A place that now it would never see. He wondered, what had it been looking for? What had brought it out onto the highway? Echo told himself he really didn't care. But staring at it was enough to stir something inside him. Something he was not entirely comfortable with.

"I bet you were lonely…"

He dug a shallow grave and tossed the turtle in it. By the time he got back to the car, he had concluded it had been the right thing to do. He felt a little bit better than he had the day before, but he knew it wouldn't last.

CHAPTER 4

THE PARADOX OF SANITY

———

Echo found himself lost in thought. He watched as two strangers he had met only an hour ago examined his car. The locals had recommended them. They were supposedly the best mechanics in town. They were also supposedly the last remaining firemen in the city. Whoever they were, Echo was now stuck with them. The Civic had barely made it to the firehouse and had abruptly died while pulling into the garage. He stood off to the side, out of their way, while he watched them tinker with it.

A muscular young man who went by the name Purge stuffed a handful of nacho-chocolate-flavored potato chips into his mouth, piling them on top of the half-chewed mush already filling his cheeks. When he spoke, his lazy beach bum voice showered the immediate area in front him with food particles.

"So, like, dude, I always thought that when I retired, like, when I reached old, like, old man old, I'd buy this house and just start filling it with cats." He chewed a little, pointed out something wrong with engine to the other man, coughed, and swallowed.

"Like those people on TV. They call them 'collectors,' because, they collect things. Dude, I want to have, like, sixty-two cats in my house. I'd be all old and angry because my hair was gray or something. The hot mom neighbors would totally call me the cat-man, and be, like, curious and all that stuff. Because I had lots of cats."

"Don't listen to him. Guy's full of shit," said the man named Turducken. He spoke in a curt, direct manner, with a growling voice and had the habit of enunciating every syllable. He slammed the hood down on the burnt Civic and wiped his forehead with an old pair of silk panties he used as a rag.

"Can't do squat for this thing. Goddamn horse broke all four legs. Doesn't sound scientific. No way around it. Your car is fucked."

"Great," grumbled Echo. He stretched his head back to stare at the ceiling of the firehouse. He had nowhere to go specifically and was in no hurry to get there, but he knew he wouldn't find anything standing still. He could just steal another car; that was what most people did in his situation. There were so many abandoned these days.

"Do you think I can rent a room until I find another car? I can pay cash," said Echo.

"Cash? Goddamn worthless. Don't take that crap out here. We got plenty of pills too. Welcome to stay. Need to pull your own weight, though."

"Well, I can do the dishes or clean or—"

"No way, dude! Batshit does the dishes," Purge said, throwing the empty bag of chips away. "Dude, Batshit is OCD, and he won't eat unless he cleans the dishes. I mean, there's totally a reason why he's called Batshit."

Echo looked bemused. "Okay, so what do you want me to do then? Name it. I'm open to bartering, or whatever needs getting done, barring anything, you know, perverse."

Turducken picked up some of his tools from the floor and began haphazardly tossing them into his toolbox, one at a time, like he couldn't care less. He cleared his throat.

"Want to find a new car? Could find another beige econo-coffin down some street. Better choice is I give you a nicer car from the back. Custom salvaged. Custom restored. With my own goddamn hands. Have to work for it, though."

Echo held the bridge of his nose. "Work? You mean as a fireman? But you guys are not really firemen. I mean, your fire engine is a tank." He pointed at the intimidating machine parked behind Turducken.

The vehicle had eight wheels, an armored wedge-shaped front end, a large troop-carrying door at the rear, and was about one and a half Civics long. The original paint scheme was olive drab, but it had been haphazardly hand painted over with flat red to better resemble a fire engine. The paint was chipping off in various locations, giving the machine a slightly festive red and green flavor. Lights scavenged from police vehicles had been strapped to flat angles along the sides using duct tape, and a pile of assorted speakers powered by a 10,000-watt amplifier were held in place on the hood by knotted floral patterned bed sheets.

Purge spoke defiantly. "Whoa! *That* is not a tank."

Echo looked at the overly decorated armored monstrosity with a grin. "You're right, it's a fucking parade float."

"That's wrong, dude." Purge checked to make sure the coast was clear. "And, like, don't let Batshit hear you call it a float. He's real sensitive about that." He walked over to the vehicle and patted it lovingly. "It's an M1126 Stryker, an armored fighting vehicle, and it's totally not a tank. See, it has tires. Wheels make it a vehicle, a totally awesome—"

"Shut up for a minute," Turducken barked. Purge ignored him and began to explain how they played recorded siren sounds, and sometimes excerpts from old Van Halen concerts over the hood-mounted speakers. Turducken interrupted him.

"Want to know why his name is Purge?"

This stopped Purge immediately. He folded his arms, waiting for the humiliation. Turducken didn't lose a beat.

"See all those muscles? He works out for two hours a day. He used to take protein supplements. That awful powder they sell in huge tubs? He was drinking pounds of that stuff to put on weight. Wanted to be a big man. A superstar pro wrestler. Was doing it for months. Living off dust and water. One day it had been two and a half goddamn weeks since he'd last moved a bowel. Thought he'd die impacted, like Elvis. Had to take him to the hospital." Turducken gave a disgusted laugh. "What a mess."

"Okay, dude, he gets the picture. You get the picture, right?" Purge asked.

Echo thought they were crazy, but he grinned anyway. "I can connect the dots. Purge, that's clever. Look, you guys seem pretty cool, but I heard you leveled an entire building just to put out one fire. I mean, what the hell is that?"

"Dude! Nothing snuffs out a fire like a big explosion."

Turducken sighed. "Can't use water for two reasons: One, not enough pressure left in the system. Two, not enough people to put out big fires." He combed his hand through his long gray hair. "Denver is pretty much abandoned. Most people went to Salt Lake. Government runs that city. Like a daycare for babies. Could always skip it and go to California. End the day relaxing on the beach. People keep going west. Trying to stay ahead of the horizon. East keeps getting closer. Land keeps getting smaller. Not a whole lot of options. I figure I'd just stay here. Goddamn it. I grew up here. This is home. Still got time before the end. Thousands of years, they say."

Echo ran his hand across the heat-warped door of his car. "I used to be kind of a shut-in, played a lot of video games, or I guess *the* video game. You know, *Conundrum*. Now I'm looking for something. I just don't know where to find it. I'd like to stay and help you guys, but I want to keep moving, and I don't want to spend years working off a car."

"Years?" Turducken looked at Echo as if personally offended. "Cars are not worth shit. Hundreds abandoned all over the place. There is no value to them. Good cars are hard to find. The fancy ones. We pick them up when we see them. Take them back here. Clean out the filth. Just like new. That's all you owe. Time spent cleaning them up. I'll make you a deal. We're shorthanded this week. Our friends are in Salt Lake for supplies. Ran out of suppositories. Want to help out for just a few days? Just until they get back? Won't be easy work. It's good work. Help people all over town. You interested?"

The last thing Echo wanted to do was stick around. He could easily find a new car on his own, but it would take a couple of days, and he would have to drag his things around with him.

"Let me see if you have anything interesting back there," he said.

"Only the best. Guaranteed." Turducken tucked the panty rag in his back pocket. Echo tried to ignore it.

They walked out the back door of the garage into a parking lot behind the firehouse. Echo scrutinized the four-story red-brick encased firehouse and thought it reminded him of a tombstone. One of the corroded window frames unexpectedly squeaked open. A man stuck his head outside and shouted, "Who the fuck is this?"

It was Batshit. His long black hair was parted by the oversized sunglasses he wore over a perpetually frowning forehead that made him appear insanely angry.

"Oh, heh…the new guy." Batshit's words were punctuated by a mischievous snicker, "Hey, don't fuck this up!"

The window slammed shut. Purge told Echo he was harmless. Echo stared up at the window.

Four cars were parked in the back lot behind the firehouse, each covered with a protective cloth sheet. Turducken positioned Echo in front of them and introduced each vehicle like a game show host. Purge gripped the sheet of the first car tightly, waiting for Turducken to introduce it.

"And the first car is…" Turducken sang. Purge threw back the sheet. He made gestures with his hands as if caressing the quality of the vehicle as

Turducken spoke. "An Audi S4. Sprint blue. Has a 3.0-liter supercharged V6. All-wheel drive. Gaudy LED headlights. Explore the wasteland in style."

Echo nodded his approval. They walked over to the next vehicle. Purge waited for his cue from Turducken and threw back the sheet. "A Porsche Cayenne Turbo."

"No," Echo said.

Purge and Turducken looked at each other, puzzled. Turducken stepped toward Echo. "Not your color?"

"Just, no." Echo wanted the subject dropped. "Look, guys. That car is not for me. It's the name, Cayenne—it just bugs me."

"The name bugs him," Turducken growled. He impatiently snapped his fingers, ordering Purge to cover it back up. They moved on to the next car.

"Maybe this then." The cover was thrown off the third car. "A rare Mercedes S600. Has a V12, 510 horsepower. Big. Silver. Obnoxious. Oil baron gold membership. Nicer than the Audi. Not as nice as the Porsche. But you don't want the Porsche."

Finally, they came to the last car covered up on the lot. Turducken put his hands on his hips. "A goddamn MINI Cooper," he said without fanfare.

Purge lifted the cover just enough for a peek that revealed a Union Jack flag painted on the hood. Turducken had nothing but contempt for the little car.

"Small. Quick. Built for ladies, like a Kotex. If you like it, there's no shame. No prejudices here. You are what you are. Or are not what you are not. Easy to park. Don't fart in it. Turns into a rolling hotbox for hours."

The joke escaped Echo. He walked between the different vehicles as he looked at them. He practically lived out of his car. One of these could be his new home. He wasn't sure about any of the choices.

"Do you have any normal cars?"

Turducken took a step back, insulted. "Like a Camry? Is that normal? End of the goddamn world. No more cars being made. No more cars ever going to be made. Germany gone. Japan gone. Never coming back. Fine automobiles are rare. Could always go downtown. Jimmy open a beige sedan from Executive Rental. Rental lots are always full. Full of boring. Monster trucks run over beige sedans. Makes them more exciting. You don't want normal. You were a shut-in. You were beige. Never got out there. Goddamn it, Echo. You were dead and beige. Pick a car with color. Any car here. Live. Get out there. Enjoy the time that's left."

"I miss my Civic. It was a good car and…it got great gas mileage," Echo whined a little before realizing he was whining.

"Holy dog shit!" said Turducken. "No car needs fuel anymore. Thermodynamics are broken. Time paradoxes are inside the goddamn engine. Drive for miles and miles without stopping. Never ever fill the gas tank up with gas. Nobody knows why. Nobody knows how. Nobody cares. It just is. Make up all the excuses you want. Live under a rock behind a locked door. The world will keep living without you. Don't be scared about 'what if.' What could be or what will. Think about what *is*. This, right now. Pick one, live life. Find happiness. Drive. Really drive for the first time. Get to where you need be. Where you want to be."

Find happiness? Echo thought. *Get to where he wanted to be?* It seemed so simple, yet completely unattainable.

The Civic was all he had ever known, and it was difficult to let go of it. He was afraid of change, but he had no other choice. He had to make a decision, and there was something about the color blue he liked.

"I'll take the Audi."

Turducken looked pleased. "Good car. Stay for a week?"

"Let me check my schedule." Echo looked to his left. Then looked back. "Yeah, I'm free."

"An asshole, eh?" Turducken laughed. "As long as you're an agreeable asshole, everything is cool."

They shook hands; it was a done deal. Turducken wrote down their agreement on a notepad and had Echo sign it.

"You start tomorrow. Get a good night's sleep."

Echo thought this was an odd thing to say, since the sun never moved in the sky, and the day remained forever frozen in place, but he understood the sentiment. He watched as Turducken tucked the signed sheet of paper under the windshield wiper of the Audi. Purge offered to show him to a room he could stay in. Echo wondered what he had gotten himself into.

CHAPTER 5

A WORLD WITHOUT BIRTHDAYS

———————

Echo lay awake in the spare room on the second floor of the firehouse. The windows had been tinted to make the never-ending daylight feel like dusk. Everything in the room was bathed in a dim blue-violet hue. The idea was to get the body in the mood for sleep by stimulating its natural circadian rhythm. Doctors, with the help of the government, had enforced the twenty-four-hour day. Without the measurement of hours, days, and weeks, the amount of actual time that passed would be imperceptible. With some form of measurement, even if it were not entirely accurate, businesses could have hours they were open and hours they were closed, and holidays could cycle through the year. This helped give people something to look forward to and a way to organize in a world where time had essentially stopped.

Sleeping under eternal daylight was impossible to get used to. Windows could be blackened, sleep masks worn, and a multitude of pills taken to find rest. Yet it was never quite the same. It was never tomorrow. Deep down this was known in some hidden part of the human psyche. It drove many people mad. Depression reigned. Despair flowed freely through the air like an incurable plague. Over the thousand years that passed, many people broke, and could not be fixed. These things used to weigh heavily on Echo, but he had eaten it all up, chewed the pieces that were bitter, and swallowed them whole, where they became a part of his soul. Everything bothered him and nothing bothered him.

He closed his eyes. Purge knocked on his door.

"Time to get up, dude. Meet us downstairs in, like, fifteen minutes." The flip-flops clapped down the hall as Purge retreated.

Echo sat up in his bed. Had he slept? It was hard to tell. It never felt like sleep. It was never more than a nap. He felt it was late at night. If he allowed himself to focus on that odd feeling, he knew it would be the end of him. He could hear the others talking outside his door. He hated being in a strange place with strange people.

A half-hour later, the Stryker rumbled through the vacant streets of downtown Denver. The city was not completely empty. There were small groups of people who still lived there, but they were spread out. A couple parts of the city were social hubs where people congregated like animals around a desert watering hole. One of these hubs was a place called the 16th Street Mall. It was a double-wide street that had been converted into a tree-lined pedestrian plaza. It was filled with a variety of stores, dive bars, and specialty shops. Countless government-sponsored pharmaceutical vending machines stood on every corner beckoning people to take pills, to help stave off the depression. On every other block was a street performer quietly playing a guitar, and on every block in between was an artist commenting on the times by painting an extravagant mural on the sidewalk. It was a busy area, but far from crowded.

They ate breakfast at a small restaurant that had opened shortly after the end of the world. It was a trendy place called Doldrummer, where it seemed all the local hipsters hung out. Torn nautical sails and kites tied down with bricks decorated the walls in a vain attempt at expressing its stagnant wind namesake. The food was supposedly Mexican fusion. Echo had allowed Turducken to order for him. What arrived was a bowl of sauce with a soggy burrito swimming in it. The appearance carried with it a scent that warned Echo of a terrible aftermath should he eat it.

Turducken saw the look on Echo's face. "Unpleasant looking? Looks weird, I agree. But trust me. The food is very good."

Echo remained hesitant to eat the concoction. Turducken became frustrated.

"Ever eat fancy? The big fancy restaurants? People call you 'sir' even when you're rude. Food comes out. Looks good. Pretty, like a painting. Should taste good, too. It doesn't. Hardly ever does. Tastes like beige. Bland like hospital crackers. Chef spends more time being artsy than cooking. Here is the opposite. Chef spends more time on taste. No time left to make it art. Taste is more important. Looks weird. Tastes great. Give it a try. Trust Turducken. Bad restaurants die quickly these days."

Batshit leaned uncomfortably close to Echo. He was eating a strawberry Pop-Tart that he had brought with him.

"Eat…heh. Eat that, eat something else, you better eat. You don't know what crazy shit we might see out there today…heh. You might not have an appetite to eat tonight." He spoke with an intensity that suggested he could begin screaming at any moment.

Echo calmly pushed Batshit back to his seat. "I've seen my share of stuff, things I don't want to think about."

"You have no idea." Purge coughed a little. He gathered up another fork-load of his salad. The lettuce strongly resembled chips of dyed green Styrofoam.

"Dude, last week we get this call, I mean, like, we call them calls, but nobody uses the phone, people come and tell us." He coughed again. "So, this family, they had kids, and you know how kids don't grow up because of, like, you know, because of how it is, right? So, the parents locked themselves in a closet with the kids, and just, I mean they just totally set themselves on fire." He shifted in his seat, uneasy. "All we found were bodies, and, like, a note about how the kids had no future. I mean they were kids dude, just kids, and, you know…there are not many of those left."

Purge lost his appetite. He stood up and walked outside to get some fresh air.

Batshit slammed his fist on the table. "It was *fucked up!*" he screamed. Some dishes crashed somewhere in the restaurant. "Heh…"

Turducken held his hand to his mouth as if to say "Shhhh," in order to quiet Batshit before they were asked to leave. "A fireman sees the worst of people. The worst of humanity."

Echo absently took a bite of his food. His neck straightened. It was surprisingly good. "So why do it then? You guys are just volunteers, right? I mean, you could just walk away, ask the government for help."

"The government," Turducken scoffed. "All pulled out of this area. Still have some police. Don't see them much. Except for parking tickets. People make the difference. People like us. We help people."

"By blowing up buildings?" Echo asked.

Turducken grinned. "Let me tell you a story. Long ago. Before the end. In ancient Japan. In a time when Tokyo was called Edo and ruled by the Shogun. Buildings were packed together. Tightly. Almost on top of one another. Made of wood. Paper. Origami. All kinds of fire-starting material. A tiny fire could spread quick. Only firemen could stop the spread. Firemen back then were groups of criminals. Spent all day drinking. Sometimes stealing. Until there was a fire. Then they became heroes. Hydrants hadn't been invented yet. Water took too long to gather for a fire. Too long to put a fire out. Buildings had to be destroyed instead. Firemen ran inside burning buildings to tear them down. Only criminals were brave enough to do this. Feared as criminals. Revered as firemen. Nothing to lose. Everything to gain. Like us. Have to put fires out quickly. Nothing quicker than a bomb. Not an easy thing to do sober."

Batshit growled. "Heh…moonshine…liquid courage kidney failure."

"Batshit brews his own beer," said Turducken. "Always a case in the Stryker. For emergencies. Help out with the difficult calls. Therapy in a bottle." Turducken paused and collected his thoughts. "Buildings blow up to save lives. Over half the city is empty. Quarter of it half empty. Lots of abandoned buildings. One fire could spread out of control. Burn down most of the city. This is my home. Won't let it go down like Pittsburgh. Whole place was gutted. Time works for us sometimes. Fire can burn forward like normal. Most times it does that. Fire can also burn backward. Put itself out. Pretty rare. Lucky when it happens." He shook his head. "We don't blow up things for fun. Only for fires." He chuckled. "One day closer to the end, it can be fun. Finally take down that goddamn courthouse. Fucking parking tickets."

Echo licked his teeth trying to get what seemed to be a wood chip unstuck from between them. He looked inside the burrito. "Just what the hell is in this thing?"

"Fiber," Turducken said, pulling out a splinter from his mouth. "That's what they told me."

Batshit snickered. "Heh…vegan is a code word for sawdust."

Echo pushed the food away. "Great. What kind of restaurant serves landfill? I mean, what's in the flan? Drywall?"

Turducken was annoyed with Echo. "Think there would be an eternal supply of food? Wonder why water these days tastes tangy and bitter?"

"Well, I thought they were adding a twist of lime to keep it exciting."

"A nice lie to cling to. Drinking water is saturated with urine. Filters can't remove all the impurities anymore."

Purge rushed back to the table. "Dude! Some dude just told me some other dude is going to, like, totally burn down a tree, and I was like, no way!"

Turducken stood up. His posture suggested he heard the sound of trumpets calling him to gallantly ride to the rescue. "Where?"

"Way over in Cherry Creek North, in, like, the art district. The dude I spoke to rode his bike here, so it may already be on fire, or may not. We totally need to hurry."

Batshit ran out the door to start the Stryker. Echo was slow to rise. "What's the rush, Purge? It's just a tree, right?"

Turducken leaned over the table, using two fingers to poke Echo in the forehead as he spoke, as if to drive what he was saying into Echo's head.

"Think about it. Trees took hundreds of years to grow. Trees don't grow anymore. If some asshole burns one down once a year, trees won't exist in a thousand years. All that's left is what we have now. Won't ever be any more. Ever."

Echo picked another wood chip out of his mouth. "Haven't you ever seen a forest?"

"Seen pictures," Turducken growled.

"There are far more than a thousand trees out there."

"Not in the city. That's what matters. Let's go."

Turducken tossed a bottle of pills on the table as payment and charged out the door. Echo ran after him. They rushed to save a tree, but when they arrived, it was not a tree that had been set on fire. It was a human being. Purge had misunderstood what the guy had told him, or it was the guy who had misunderstood the man as he walked toward the tree with a gas can in hand and a lighter. He had sat down in the street under the never-moving shadow of the tree, doused himself with gasoline until his clothes were soaked through, and lit himself on fire. By the time they arrived, only a charred human form remained, engulfed by tall flames and the sound of crackling body fat. Turducken looked disgusted and saddened at the same time.

"Rather the tree had burned."

Echo grabbed the fire extinguisher from the back of the Stryker. Purge stopped him.

"Don't bother, dude. Better save that for when we need it," he said. "This dude is totally toasted."

Echo had not seen such a thing before, except in history books when monks had set themselves on fire to protest the war in Vietnam. They wore a calm expression as they burned, the same as this man. He sat upright, on fire, baked into his seated position. Echo walked too close and caught a whiff. He gagged and wanted to throw up. Batshit jerked him away from the fumes. Turducken walked over to have a look at the dead man.

"The coppery smell is blood burning. That bitter smell. Like burnt liver? That's internal organs. Been cooking for a while. Had he just started, it would smell like charcoal." His mind pondered the moment. "Bet we taste like goddamn pork. Makes sense in a way. People are kind of close to pigs. Anatomically. Don't *smell* like pork when we burn though…"

Echo stared at the burning body. Turducken patted him on the shoulder. "Looks like another artist," he told him pointing to the other side of the street. The sidewalk was covered with neatly arranged painted canvases and sketchbooks. A sign said "free," with arrows pointed at the art, and one especially large arrow pointed at the spot where the burning man was sitting.

"Artists live around here. Probably didn't even scream. Nobody screams. Not when they reach this point."

"We…always thought we had a future." Batshit seethed. "This is the peak of our civilization…heh…we…just never realized it until it was over. Heh…irony."

Purge walked the perimeter, speaking to the handful of people who had not run from the horrific sight. He handed them coupons for special medications they could redeem at any pharmaceutical vending machine should they feel depressed about what they had seen. It was standard procedure in the government's "end days" manual. They were all grateful for the free meds, and within a minute, had already forgotten about the man. They began to argue over who should get the free art. The petty bickering ended when Batshit walked over and broke the canvases over his knee, destroying them.

Batshit made an angry fist at the crowd. "Modern society thrives on misery." He tore up the sketch books. "All there is, is nothing. This barbeque…heh…this was for a nobody trying to leave a mark…so he'd be remembered, and you heathens don't fucking care…do you?" The people stared at him, coolly, and slowly wandered away.

The flames died down, and Turducken threw a blanket over the charred corpse to smother the rest. "Echo, get a body bag."

"Shouldn't we wait for the police?"

Turducken shook his head to tell him there would be no police. "They call us firemen. We should be called garbage men. Get me a beer…and a spatula. Going to need a spatula for this one."

Echo half laughed. "You're joking, right?"

Turducken tried to move the body with a grunt. "Body's on there pretty good."

Echo's grin faded. "I guess it was too much to hope that he sat on a pat of butter."

"Not a lot of hope left in this world. Even less butter." Turducken knew it made no sense, and he did not care.

They ended up using a shovel to remove the body from the road. The charred corpse wouldn't fit into the body bag in its seated position. They had to hammer it with a pair of rubber mallets until it was prostrate. Echo held the bag open, trying his best not to watch. They rushed to get it over with, picking up the parts that fell off as they worked. None of them spoke as they carried the mass over to a Dumpster and unceremoniously tossed it in.

"He made his choice," Turducken said, slamming the Dumpster close.

Purge pointed out the blackened ash stain baked into the street. "I guess that dude left a mark after all."

No one said anything. The crowd had dissipated to a few bystanders. The rest had gone home and were almost certainly swimming blissfully in the best antidepressants medicinal chemistry had to offer.

Echo wiped his hands on his shirt. "I feel strange...I feel, I feel disturbed."

Turducken cleaned his hands with the same old panty rag he seemed to always carry. He looked at Echo, said nothing, then looked down at his hands and picked the dirt off. Ash was stuck deep under his fingernails. He glanced at Echo again.

"Don't go to pieces over that. There is a hell of a lot worse than that."

Worse than that? Echo thought about the story Purge had told. He felt nauseous. He wanted to leave, but he knew he had to stay. He really wanted the car. He told himself the car would be worth it. That it was blue and fast. He took a deep breath and caught a whiff of the body in the air. He quickly let it out, with a hack. He had seen so many people die over the years. Seeing it mattered the most, and mattered the least. Watching a person die in front of him carried no more weight than a video game character getting blown to pieces. He was desensitized to the sight, but not the smell, not the complete reality. The smell made it too real. It invaded his mind in a way he could not shut out. He felt tired.

Turducken handed him a med coupon. "Take one of these."

Echo frowned. "I've never taken drugs. I don't care how depressed I get, I will never take any of those pills."

"Why not? It's designed to make you feel better."

"I don't want anything to *make* me feel better. I want to live in what little reality we have left. Things are too weird already for me to wonder if what I am experiencing is some undocumented side effect. Yes, I'm depressed, just like everyone else, but I get by."

"Doesn't have to be that way. Things are not going to get any better."

White light flashed in the sky several times. Thunder boomed down from above in an unnatural-sounding rapid pulsation that rattled the nerves. Everyone stood still, waiting. Their vision seemed to double, then triple. A strange glowing aura surrounded everything. Then the glow faded away, and things seemed to return to normal.

"Is it over? Dude, are we synced?" Purge asked.

Batshit looked at his hand. He waved it around. "I *hate* time lightning!"

Echo hated it, too. "They don't make a pill for that."

Turducken looked a little insulted. He raised his hand to make a point, when the deep thump of an explosion erupted. The sound ricocheted off the flat faces of all the buildings, making it impossible to tell which direction it had come from. Turducken climbed on top of the Stryker.

"Everyone look for smoke. Look for smoke."

They watched the sky. Purge checked down several adjacent streets, but he saw nothing. Turducken ordered everyone into the Stryker. They began to drive slowly. Turducken rode outside the main top hatch, with binoculars. He spotted something. Batshit hit the gas, jolting the vehicle forward. He turned the siren on. Then he took a beer bottle out of the cooler, broke the neck off, and poured the contents in his mouth. He turned on some vintage Metallica and screamed. Purge head-banged to the pounding music and urged Echo to get into it. Echo held his ears.

Rounding the corner, they saw flames consuming the bottom floor of a doughnut bakery. A man stumbled about outside it with his arm on fire. He seemed dazed. The Stryker raced right at the man and screeched to a stop within inches of hitting him. Turducken ran over with a fire extinguisher to put the man's burning arm out. Batshit threw the empty beer bottle over the side of the Stryker and jumped out. He stared at the fire, convulsed, flexed his arms, and screamed. The air smelled like burning doughnuts. Batshit cocked his head to one side.

"Heh…grease fire."

Echo grabbed Turducken by the arm and asked him what to do.

"Wait here. Don't follow," said Turducken. "It's too goddamn dangerous." He handed Echo the fire extinguisher, put on a fireman helmet, and ran inside the burning building.

Batshit pulled a large brown paper bag from out of a metal box in the back of the Stryker. He took another beer out of the cooler, broke the neck off, and chugged the entire bottle. He picked up the paper bag and raced after Turducken straight into the wall of flames. After a few minutes, they raced back. The paper bag was missing. Purge grabbed Echo and the injured man, and pulled them behind the Stryker. Echo heard several puff sounds, then a muffled explosion. *Phump!* It was not loud enough to hurt his ears. It reminded him of the sound heavy boots make when dropped on a carpeted floor. He waited for the building to fall, for the dust to cover him, but nothing happened.

Echo was disappointed. "I thought you blew up buildings to put out fires?"

Turducken walked over, his hair singed and clothes still smoking. "Just did. Doesn't always have to fall over. Fire's out. Job's done."

Batshit sat by the front wheel of the Stryker and applied burn cream to his hands. "First degree," he mumbled bitterly. "Bullshit."

The bottom floor of the building had been gutted. Parts of the automated fryer lay in the street, and doughnuts were everywhere. Purge picked a pink frosted one off the side of the Stryker, blew on it to clear the ash off, and ate it. The man they had rescued appeared to be the owner of the business judging by the doughnut-patterned apron he was wearing. He was in a state of shock. Turducken checked the man's vitals. He cut the scorched sleeve off the man's shirt and sprayed the exposed bright red skin with an ointment that sizzled on contact. Through it all, the man made no sound. Purge waved his hand in front of the man's face.

"Dude's not synced up. He must have gotten caught between flashes."

Batshit blew on his hands. "Heh…I hate time lightning."

Purge wrapped Batshit's hands up in bandages. "Dude, do you think, like, the lightning started the fire?"

"It doesn't strike. It's not a bolt. Can't start a fire." Turducken couldn't seem to find a way to explain it.

The worst part about time lightning was that nobody knew what it was. It was a series of flashes that people called lightning. Time seemed to vibrate; it echoed, and caused people to see multiple images of the same thing—like a gong had been struck. No one knew what it meant when they saw multiple images of the same thing. Was it the past, present, and future being seen at the same time? Alternate realities? Saying that things came out of sync was just a term people used to describe what was really not understood. Making up an explanation was the only way people could deal with the fear of not knowing what was happening to them. It was clear time lightning was a bad thing, but how bad was anyone's guess. People had decided it was best to stay still until everything felt synchronized again, lest they fall out of sync with the present. Which may have been what happened to the injured man.

Turducken lifted the man into the back of the Stryker. "Need to get him to the hospital. Before he snaps out of this. Before he feels the pain. Arm injury like that might not heal for a hundred years. Could heal in an hour. Can't predict it."

"What about the fire?" Echo asked. "Don't you want to know how it happened?"

"No. Not interested. No time for interest. It's out. Get moving before this guy wakes up."

Purge had to drive while Batshit rested his hands in the back with the injured man. They had moved only a few blocks when the man woke up full of piss and hate. The filth that came out of his mouth caused all of them to regret their rescue effort. Turducken spoke to him evenly, but nothing he could say would calm the man down. The man accused them of kidnapping, of holding him for a ransom of doughnuts that could no longer be made, and other nonsense. Purge drove as fast as he could to the last operational hospital in the city, but the man's anger boiled over. He became physically violent, thrashing about the vehicle. Echo and Turducken tried to hold him down without touching his burnt arm. The man kicked and screamed. He broke a first aid kit, which made Turducken angry. The man punched Echo in the chest, knocking the wind out of him. Finally, Batshit had seen enough. He pushed Turducken and Echo out of the way, lifted his leg, and stomped on the man's head repeatedly until the man lost consciousness. Even Turducken was shocked by the brutality. A large red boot mark swelled on one side of the man's face. When they arrived at the hospital, Turducken listed the man's injuries for the staff. He included the possibility of a concussion. Then they left and never spoke of it again.

CHAPTER 6

CONFLAGRATION

———

The following morning, Echo woke up to find Batshit sitting in his room. He wore the oversized sunglasses he never removed even though the tinted windows made the room dark. His hands appeared to be fully healed. He sat in a chair close to the side of Echo's bed. Echo made no sudden movements. He did not want to provoke the maniac into action.

"I collect pictures of…sunsets," Batshit said menacingly, yet calmly. "They remind me of things…heh…when things were different." He slouched in the chair. "I say they remind me, but I can't remember… I just know these things existed…things long ago." His jaw clenched. "We…deserved this. We…are just, heh, animals. We…lie to ourselves that we're not." His teeth could be heard grinding in the dark, his jaw chewing through his thoughts. "I thought…I thought I would come here and tell you…heh…I am not a violent man…but, heh…I thought about it last night, and I realized…I realized I *am* a violent man." He slowly stood up, his leather boots creaking, and left the room.

Echo stayed in bed and considered his options. He felt the need to flee at first, but that made no sense without a car. He wished he had not been so foolish with his Civic. Then he remembered he really had little choice in the events that led to its eventual destruction. He felt trapped. These problems were exactly why he avoided people, but he had to interact with them. He couldn't stand living in isolation any longer. Anxiety settled in his stomach. He wondered how he would make it through the next few days. Would things get better? Would they get worse? What would happen if they did? He couldn't run. He hated that all his things were piled up in the garage and that he had so many things. Without them he could run away. He took a deep breath and calmed himself down, putting the few days he would spend here in perspective with the next thousand years. He let the breath out. None of this mattered.

It was still early to get up, but he could no longer sleep following the visit from Batshit. After getting dressed, he went downstairs to find Purge loading up the Stryker for the day. Purge saw Echo and smiled.

"Morning, dude! Pretty crazy yesterday, right? It's not usually that busy. Most days we just drive around with nothing to do."

"I woke up and Batshit was in my room. He told me he's a violent man."

Purge paused for a second. "Did he talk about, like, alien abduction?"

"What? What the hell? Are you…I mean, no, he didn't."

"Dude, I've known Batshit for almost thirty years. I know it may seem shocking to, like, wake up and have a dude in your room talking about how violent he is, but that's how he opens up to people. He's kind of shy. He has, like, zero interpersonal skills."

"But is he a violent man?"

Purge bobbed his head with a yes nod. "Hell, yeah. You better believe it. Dude, his name is Batshit. Think about it." He restocked the cooler with beer. "He never talks about who he was before everything went bananas. We saw a family photo in his wallet once. Didn't even look like him. Like a totally different dude. We guess something must have happened to them. Maybe they got killed, like, when all the riots and stuff happened."

"Everyone lost something back then…"

"When they announced the world was ending, who knew it would take this long, right? I think we handled it better than, like, the Europeans did. I think it's because we were so far away from, like, where it began or whatever."

"It helped we got stuck in the daylight."

"Yeah, dude, it was night all the time for them, right? We could've handled that, we would've been like, so what? Because we're Americans, right? Dude, as long as I can totally order pizza, a cool beer, and watch the Super Bowl, who cares that the world is ending?"

Echo groaned under his breath. "The government has done an amazing job holding things together." He really didn't believe that.

"Streets are totally empty, like, we even ran out of looters."

"We ran out of people."

"Yeah!" Purge exclaimed. Then his voice got quieter as he considered the implications. "Yeah, I guess we did run out of people."

Turducken yelled at them from upstairs, "Need ten more minutes! Batshit is checking the goddamn mash."

"Dude! We brew our own beer!"

Echo nodded. "So I've heard."

Purge opened the cooler to pull out a beer and showed Echo that the bottle had Batshit's name crudely painted on it with a homemade stencil.

"Yeah, calling it Batshit seems a little crazy, but dude, this stuff has a kick to it. We're not sure exactly what Batshit puts in it. I asked him once and he was like—"

Purge frowned and deepened his voice to impersonate Batshit. *"Uppers, downers, bunch of caffeine pills, corn, oatmeal, beef-like substitute, nutmeg, touch of bleach."* Purge returned to his own voice and made a sickened face.

"…And that's why I only ever sipped this shit. Most of the time we give these to real hard luck cases, right? You know those dudes that are about to blaze up their own bodies or whatever. If we can find them ahead of time, we give them, like, a six-pack."

"Great idea," Echo said, cynically. "I guess putting people into a coma is better than putting them in a Dumpster."

He'd rather drink liquid Drano than that swill. He imagined them asking him to have a sip; he'd refuse, then Batshit would stomp on his face for the insult.

Turducken jumped down the stairs. "All good now. Start it up. Time to see what's going on out there." He smiled at Echo. "It will be quieter today. We can go to the zoo."

Purge shook his head, touching his nose. Turducken instantly remembered. "Goddamn it! Forgot. There is no more zoo. Couple years ago there was a barbeque. We—"

He seemed ashamed and said, quickly, "—and we ate the animals." He cleared his throat. "Every September there is this culinary festival: "*A Taste of Colorado.*" We decided to enter it. Looked everywhere for fresh meat. Other chefs used dog food. We wanted to win. Thought we could steal one critter. Word got out. Everyone went to the zoo. Weekend festival turned into month-long barbeque. Big feast. Elephant steaks. Giraffe hoof soup. Penguin pudding. Red panda stir-fry. Even ate those mudskipper fish. Battered them right up. So many flavors. Mind blowing. Went nuts with recipes. Soon the zoo was empty. Ran out of critters. Goddamn legacy of humanity!" Turducken wiped his forehead with the panty rag. "Managed to come in third place."

"I'm sure it was worth it," Echo said sarcastically. He knew hysteria could spread quickly and make even the craziest ideas seem reasonable, especially during a cooking festival, but there was no excuse for what happened. They would never see animals like that again. Lost forever. Driven into permanent extinction in order to make a gourmet snack. It was the apex of hypocrisy. It was only a matter of time before these criminals found a reason to justify cutting down all the trees too. He could not wait to leave.

Batshit clumped down the stairs. "Heh…it brews. Let's go."

The Stryker drove far north into an industrial area of the city, where they stopped to check on a large oil refinery. The gate to the place had been crushed, and the plant seemed abandoned. There was no longer any value to the fuel, but the refinery was a potential powder keg of dangerous chemicals. The police had asked them to keep an eye on it at some point in the distant past, and they had been doing it for so long now, it had become routine. Echo walked with the others slowly canvassing the huge complex of pipes and towers. It was quiet. There were no noises from the machines, though they appeared to be operating. The thick pungent odor of oil vapor filled his nose.

"What are we looking for here, again?" Echo asked.

Batshit snarled. "Vagrants…and assholes."

Turducken checked a door to make sure it was still locked. "Imagine if this place caught fire. What would we do? What the hell would we do? Need to make sure this is secure. No funny business going on."

Echo saw a laptop computer lying on the ground connected to a camera on a tripod. "What's that?"

Purge rushed over. "Dude! That's mine! Don't touch it! Just don't go near it."

"Okay, but what is it?"

"It's, like, my science experiment." Purge typed into the computer and pulled up some pictures that had apparently been taken by the camera. "I set this up to take pictures of the burn-off tower over there." He pointed at a tall tower jutting out of the complex with a flame at the top. "See how the flame never moves? Like it's frozen, right? Only it's not. Look at this, dude."

Purge compared a picture taken twenty years ago to one taken a month ago. There was a slight difference that showed the flame was still burning, but at a speed so slow, it was barely visible to anything but a camera.

Echo pretended to be interested. He had seen pictures like this before online. Some people had taken pictures for hundreds of years to show the same result; time was still moving forward, albeit at an imperceptible crawl.

"Huh, so even though I can't see the flame burning, it really is, eh?"

"It's crazy, dude!"

"So how come this flame is burning so slow, but that guy who set himself on fire yesterday burned so fast?" Echo asked. Purge stumbled over possible explanations, but Echo knew there was no answer. No one knew what was really going on, and chances were no one ever would.

A car horn beeped twice at the gate. Two men waved at Turducken, urgently. He ran over and spoke to them. The entire conversation could be seen in his reactions. These were good friends with bad news. He pulled out the old panty rag to wipe the sweat off his forehead. The car pulled away. Turducken ran back over.

"Have to leave! Have to go now. Right now!"

Purge stood up, very concerned. "Oh shit, dude! Is it the horizon? Is it moving faster?"

Turducken waved the panty rag at Purge angrily, as if the question he had asked was insane.

"When has it ever done that? When? No, we have to get back. We have to leave now, goddamn it! Where the hell is Batshit?"

"Dude! Why? What's the rush?"

"The firehouse is on fire!" Turducken yelled. "Where is Batshit?"

They all began to yell as loud as they could for Batshit. A locked door near them started to make noises. Then the lock unlatched, and the door opened. It was Batshit.

"'Sup?" he said.

Turducken seemed flabbergasted. "How did you get in there?"

"Heh…I needed a wrench for the still…bolt was loose this morning."

"Lock that door! Make sure that door is locked."

"What's your problem?" Batshit said.

"The firehouse is on fire."

"Fuck!"

They could see the smoke rising off the firehouse from a mile away. Not only was this their home burning down, it was also highly embarrassing that a fire was burning down the firehouse. Echo viewed the fire through binoculars as they drove. He wondered what they would do. Would they so casually blow up their own home as they had done with the bakery? He considered his many things that were once again threatened by disaster. What did his things really mean to him? They were just things, weren't they? He could replace the entire pile with a quick trip to one of the many abandoned outlet malls. The engine of commerce had left a legacy so vast that even the needs of hoarders had been satisfied. He hoped the Audi would survive the demolition, but, on the other hand, if it did not, he would be free to leave. How could he lose?

As they got closer, Purge had an idea of exactly how the fire had started. He pointed Echo to the top corner of the firehouse.

"They keep the still up there. You know, when you brew alcohol, it evaporates into steam inside the still, and it can be, like, highly flammable. It could even explode! Dude, I've never been allowed up there. Who knows what's in that room, right? We call that shit beer, but it's more like rocket fuel, dude!"

When they arrived, the flames seemed to be more contained than they originally observed. The fire appeared to have just gotten started. It was possible that time dilation had affected their point of view, and what they had seen had been a view of what would have happened if they had not returned to fight the fire. Not an alternate present, but one that had not yet been affected by their being there. The Stryker screeched to a stop next to the garage entrance.

Turducken jumped out the top hatch with a fire extinguisher. "Get the other extinguishers. Quick!"

Batshit grabbed a small brown bag and ran after him. Turducken ran inside the building; Batshit started to follow, then stopped suddenly and turned to Purge.

"Stay out here." Sweat beads appeared on Batshit's forehead, and his jaw clenched. "We...make the bombs up there." He pushed Purge back and ran inside.

Purge stood frozen with indecision. For all the muscles he had worked so hard to enlarge, he had failed to nurture any sense of duty or bravery. The fire suddenly erupted in intensity. Purge paced with his hands on his head, not knowing what to do. He stopped abruptly, pulled some pills out of his pocket and tossed them in his mouth. He breathed a sigh of relief.

Echo rubbed his face, dismayed. "You know how this is going t—"

Kablam! The entire upper corner of the building detonated and blew out all the windows. Broken glass rained down everywhere. Purge and Echo hid under the Stryker. A brick bounced off the hood. *Boom!* Another explosion. Hundreds of thousands of pills fell from the sky. Meds of every color started to clog the street in unfathomable amounts. Echo envisioned Batshit shoveling them out the window by the bagful. *Bawhoosh!* One last explosion erupted. It was smaller, less of a boom and more of a fiery swoosh. Then it was over. For a moment the only sound was the soft landing of gelatin capsules falling from the sky. The firehouse door creaked open, its frame warped from the explosions.

Purge took the slowly opening door as a sign to run inside with a first aid kit. It was a futile gesture, but the only one he could make. Echo knew the men were dead. He leisurely walked inside to check on the condition of his things. The bottom-floor garage was relatively undamaged. However, the building was unsound; its thousand-year-old structure had been shattered by the sudden stress of the explosions. Support beams creaked as they adjusted to their new positions. Echo waited to see if anyone had survived. He knew they had not, but he waited anyway. He could have simply walked up the broken stairs to see for himself, but somehow seeing human bodies busted up into chunks of meat—especially meat he knew—would just upset his stomach. He was afraid of creating more memories he would have to forget.

After a while, he began to wonder what Purge was doing. He had not heard him for some time, and there had been no call for help. He knew what was up there, and he did not want to see it, but as he waited, he began to feel increasingly curious. He stepped toward the stairs.

Purge threw a duffle bag down. "Don't come up here, dude. It's a total disaster," he yelled.

Echo nudged the duffle bag with his foot, unsure of what was inside. "Is this them?"

Purge stumbled down the stairs sliding across half of them on his ass.

"Nah, dude, they are dead. I mean, like, totally dead. I wish I could tell you I saw something cool, like Turducken's nuts hanging on a doorknob, or Batshit's head ending up in a toilet. Truth is, I couldn't tell, like, who was who, and what was what. I just saw a big mess. I did find the keys."

"To the cars?"

"Hell yeah, dude!" He held up several key chains covered in something that had burned. "Let me just wash them off."

Echo watched as Purge ran over to the garage sink to wash the keys clean. He watched how vigorously Purge scrubbed. "You all right?" he asked.

"This is all fucked up, dude. I just want to get out of here."

"Wait, we can't just leave. What about those people that are coming back in a few days?"

Purge threw the keys to the Audi at Echo. They landed on the floor and slid across the garage. He caught them under his foot. Purge let out a worrisome nervous laugh. "It's over, dude. Time to bug out. There is nothing left up there. Totally nothing."

"I thought you guys were friends?"

"Yeah? Yeah? So? Should we bury them or something? I didn't even really know them, dude. They were just people, you know? I just want to get out of here, okay?"

"So do I, I just thought——"

Purge pushed over some shelving, causing a loud crash. He erupted with anger.

"Dude! What? What the fuck do you want? An explanation to how or, like, why? There are no answers, Echo! That's life, dude! They did it to themselves. We had a good thing, but good things don't last. Remember that. Like, fucking remember that. When you find something good, you can't take it for granted, you have to enjoy it while it lasts. Nothing lasts forever, dude. It only seems like it will, then one day, it's gone, and all you have left are all the things you should have, like, said or done, that you never did. You've been out there; you tell me, have you ever found lasting happiness? Do you think you could even tell if you did? Could you, dude?"

"I don't know."

Purge ran over to his duffle bag and picked it up. "Think about that, dude. What matters? All this shit? All this world? Or is it you? Do you matter? Do I matter? That *I* am happy *is* what matters. It's totally not selfish to want to be happy. *I* want to be happy, and dude, I'm going to find happiness, and if it's the only thing I find, then——"

He abruptly stopped talking, kicked open the door to the back lot, and within moments was gone, taking the Mercedes with him.

Echo stood there thinking about what Purge had said. Some of it struck a chord, even if it was an incoherent one. He thought about the word "happiness" and wondered what it meant to him. He wondered when he had last been happy in the real world, and he realized he could not remember. He was not sure what it was anymore. It was less a feeling and more of an idea. A vague, undefined goal out there somewhere needing to be found. He felt numb and distant. The building creaked again, and he looked up at the ceiling knowing it was the final resting place of two criminals who probably deserved better than what was given to them. He knew he did not actually care. He picked up the keys to the Audi. He held them in his hand. This was what he wanted. He wanted to leave, and now he could. Was it worth it? He wasn't sure.

CHAPTER 7

SICK AND TIRED

*

Echo sat in his sprint-blue Audi S4 and waited. The car was parked with the windows down, but there was no breeze on the highway. He was stopped on a hill that provided a good view of the mountains. He watched the waves roll through the clouds above. It was quiet, desolate, a nice place to be waiting for it. He knew it was coming. His heart raced, and a cold sweat washed over his body, as if he were suddenly shocked to realize what was about to occur. Then it died down; it was not ready yet. He was sick, and he was alone—the combination he feared the most. He never felt more alone than when he was sick. There was no one to soothe his pain and discomfort. No one to tell him it would be all right, even if it were not true. He had to trust that this was only food poisoning, and not the beginning of something more serious that would immobilize him.

His heart raced again. He exited the car faster than he had ever done before. He could feel it coming up now, and his only thought was to stand far enough away from the car so as not to cover it with the filth that exploded from his mouth. He heaved the entire meal out of his body into an undigested pile, an unrecognizable mess. His head pounded from the effort, and his body was cold. It came up again. Then again. Until finally there was nothing left. He tried to take a deep breath, but his inhale brought with it a rot that caused him to shudder. He coughed hard and shivered. He hacked poisoned saliva, and spat. He hacked again, a leftover chunk dislodged from a molar, nearly causing him to throw up again. He spat it out, wiping the tears from his eyes.

"Gross. Why does it have to be so gross?" he asked the Audi. He held his head. It was pounding hard. He could barely stand, but managed to get back in the car. He slowly drove down the road. He felt so weak. He faded in and out of consciousness, accidentally drifting across several lanes. Each time he came out of the blackness, he slowed down, worried he would run off the road. He was lucky the highway was empty, or he would have caused an accident. *I am so lucky!* he thought as he started to fade away again. He realized that he was in no condition to drive. He pulled over, reclined the seat all the way back, rolled the windows up, and turned the heater on. He felt so cold.

His mind drifted into a fevered sleep. He remembered the words of the hostess at the restaurant: "Gee, I really should wipe those tables clean, but that's one of the of the perks of a barbeque restaurant; nobody expects it to be clean, since the food is so messy!" He lashed out at this woman with profanity. It was colorful, and the best combinations of curse words he had ever come up with. *Why can't I curse like this all the time?* he wondered. He wanted to be angry at this woman for poisoning him. It was not her fault, though—it was his. Turducken's zoo massacre story had put him in the mood for barbeque. He ate at the first place he found: "Damn Good Dead Meat." The name alone should have warned him. Why had he eaten so much of it? Had it even been actual meat? He reached in the backseat for a towel to put over his face, and allowed himself to completely fade away.

When he slowly awakened, the world was distant, and his mind had not yet polluted his perception with thoughts. The car was too hot. The radio was crackling and picking up strange sounds that were almost like voices. Were there voices? His mind was still dim. Radio stations were hard to find outside of large cities. There was something about the atmosphere that prevented transmission over long distances. He always left the radio on just in case he ran across a station during his travels. Most of the time all he heard was the gentle waterfall of soft static. He heard the voices again. He sat up quickly. The radio was silent. He looked at the clock to see how long he had slept, but he couldn't remember the time it said when he'd begun, and it did not matter anyway.

He got out of the car to stretch. He felt better, except for the taste in his mouth and some burning in one nostril. He blew his nose, briefly reliving the sickness again. His body reacted to the grotesque experience with a shudder. He looked through the trunk to find some mouthwash. Then he noticed it. In his delirium he had parked in front of a large chain-link fence. Beyond the fence was a long grassy field. At the end of the field was a complex of large white windowless buildings nestled at the foot of the mountains. It was a government Think Tank.

Echo gargled the mouthwash. He wanted to dig out his binoculars to get a closer look, but he felt certain he was being watched. He could not see any movement between the buildings—no people, lights, or machinery. The brightest scientific minds had been imprisoned there. Collected from every company and university in the nation to work on a solution to an unsolvable problem: how to stop the world from ending. It was the final act of man's arrogant belief that destiny was somehow his to control. Everyone who had tried to enter a Think Tank had never been heard from again. No one knew what really went on inside Think Tanks. They just knew to stay away from them. The longer he stared at the complex the more uneasy he felt. He spit on the side of the road and drove away.

The highway was a long unending path dotted with exits that led to ghost towns. Not every place had emptied out—some areas thrived—but finding them was difficult. It seemed each region was emptier than it should be. The world felt like it should be fuller. The great structures no longer had a purpose. A six-lane highway made sense when there were enough people to fill it. Now it felt like driving down a river of asphalt, or the runway at an airport. Miles passed by uneventfully. The sun shined down at a steady pace, but it had no effect on the environment. The road retained an even warmth, never cracking, and the paint used to mark the division between lanes never faded. Nothing changed, ever. Everything felt as if it had been abandoned yesterday.

The sight of the endless highway eventually irritated Echo enough that he took the next exit he saw. It really did not matter what exit he took, since he had no destination anyway. He was wandering aimlessly, and he knew it. He was looking for happiness. He had no idea what that could be, what it would be, or what it should be. He was afraid he would not recognize it if he found it. He chuckled at his own thoughts. Happiness may not even exist. It was just a word that was made up to express an ideal that can never be achieved. Like the word "love." It was likely he would never be happy or feel love. He felt okay with that, but not completely.

His stomach growled.

"Am I hungry?" he asked himself, surprised. "Can I eat again?" He was not sure how much time had passed while he slept. He could have been asleep for days and never known it.

He passed by numerous stores—some that were boarded up and some that were left open, but abandoned. Boarded up stores were mostly corporate chains with heavily advertised names that promoted loyalty to their brand. Looters pillaged the brands they trusted first, trying to find comfort in familiar names, an apocalyptic fulfillment of their lifelong consumer programming. The open stores were new names, built after the end began, that had failed to find an audience in the dwindling, reclusive population. Preserved exactly as they were left, fully stocked and prepared for the day ahead, as if spontaneously deserted.

He felt he wanted a restaurant. He knew it was crazy to want to eat somewhere else so soon after his bad experience. He also knew that as much as he wanted to be alone—told people he liked to be alone—that he really wanted some company. Sometimes the need was so great he would feel a kind of attack where he wanted desperately to be around people, any people, just to alleviate the emptiness of his world. Eventually, the buildings thinned out again until all he could see were the rolling hills of Colorado, and behind them the wall of mountains, greenish and without snow. *How kind of the world to end on a mild summer day,* he thought.

Driving became increasingly tedious along the uneventful road. He tried to stay focused on the path ahead, watching for litter by the side of the road, looking for animals, anything that would demand his attention. The monotony of it caused his mind to drift away into thoughts and daydreams. People had always called it "going somewhere else" when a person would start thinking while he drove, and suddenly realize he could not remember the last few minutes he had driven. Sometimes a mind could drift away for an entire commute. A person could arrive at his destination without remembering how he had gotten there. It was easy to become lost in thought. There was simply too much time to think. He suddenly looked up and realized he was no longer driving. He was not even in his car. He was sitting at the counter of a diner, and he had no idea how he had gotten there.

CHAPTER 8

THE IMPOSSIBURGER

The man behind the counter passed by with a fresh pot of coffee. Echo leaned forward on the stool he was sitting on; it wobbled unexpectedly. He looked down at it, disoriented and frustrated, then looked up again at the man.

"Have I been here long?"

The man, a gray-haired balding fellow with astonishingly long mutton chops and mirrored sunglasses, walked back over, looked at Echo, then turned to polish the soap residue off a tall glass with a towel. He wore a Hawaiian shirt with a bright-pink artificial lei around this neck. He grumbled, then tossed the towel over his shoulder and turned around.

"Look, buddy, I don't have all day. Are you going to order something, or what?"

Echo glanced around the empty diner. The only other customer was a mannequin slumped in the far corner that looked a lot like an obese Elvis wearing oversized Vegas-style sunglasses and a white sequin-studded jumpsuit. It seemed to be relaxing to the Hawaiian music that quietly played throughout the diner. Echo nodded a "howdy" to Elvis. Then he noticed his car parked outside. He turned to the man again.

"Exactly how did I get here?"

"Same as anybody else, buddy. Through that door." The man's voice was as clean as the counter—crisp, yet high-pitched, quick, and impatient.

"When did I get here?"

"Well…" the man thought for a moment. "Buddy, I'm not sure. I just looked up, and, well, there you were. Sometimes I get so busy, I just don't notice things."

"Busy doing what?"

"In case you haven't noticed, I'm the cook, and the janitor, and sometimes a counselor, too. There is always something that needs doing. Buddy, are you ready to order, or what?"

"Order?"

"Order some food. Come on, you do eat, right?"

Echo's stomach growled on cue. He was famished. "It's kind of hard to order without a menu."

"Ashley!" the man called, loudly. "Why didn't you get Buddy a menu?"

Echo wanted to know what the deal was with the word "buddy." He sat at the counter trying to figure the man out. He was immediately distracted by a cheerful female voice from the kitchen.

"Sorry, just a sec!"

"Ashley?" Echo said as if the name were from a foreign language.

"And don't forget to tell Buddy about the specials." The man giggled. "They're for a limited time! Get it, Buddy? Time?" He laughed sarcastically.

Ashley burst out of the kitchen. She was vibrant and full of energy. Her hair was pulled back, half falling out of place, in a lazy ponytail that said she had been taking a nap. Her jeans appeared to be airbrushed onto her body, causing Echo to pause for a moment to wonder how she even put them on. She was not tall, not too young, at least four years of college, but in something useless, like poetry or aromatherapy. She looked across the room at him with a glance, then a longer glance, as if she liked what she was seeing. She smiled, and it broke through his cynical antisocial barriers with ease, and he felt a warm tickle. She bounded over to him, her ponytail bouncing behind her, excitedly.

He leaned over the counter to her. "By any chance, do you know how I got here?"

She looked at him confused, but she appeared to think the question was cute. "Wow, why are you asking me that?"

She had an unapologetic valley girl tone in her voice that took Echo by surprise. He found its purity charming.

"Because, I don't know…I don't remember."

"So?" she said with a smile. "So what?"

"Well, is this real? Am I here? Are you for real?"

"Oh my God, is this some kind of lame come-on?" She frowned.

"What?" Echo panicked. "No. I didn't mean it that way. I never meant to overstep our relationship with you as the proprietor of this establishment and me as the customer."

"Wow, our relationship? As if! Holy shit, stranger, are *we* jumping to conclusions!"

She tossed a menu his way and stormed off to the other end of the diner. She glanced over at him again as if realizing her overreaction. Then she noticed he was looking at her, so she sneered at him.

Echo folded his hands around his head trying to make himself smaller. He felt somebody standing over him and looked up to see the man. He thought for sure he would soon be asked to leave. The man held out his giant beefy palm. Echo did not know how to react. The man grabbed Echo's hand and shook it hard with a powerful grip that made him flinch. He jerked Echo across the counter with a big friendly grin.

"I think the girl likes you, Buddy. Good luck with that."

"I, I didn't mean to accost your daughter."

"Daughter? I don't think so. Look, Buddy, let me be straight with you. I'm gay." He took a step back to present himself. "Ta-dah!"

Echo's eyebrows scrunched up, confused as to how he was even supposed to reply. "How does that matter? Why do you keep calling me *buddy?*"

"Call me Palomino."

"Like a horse?"

"You got it. Because, you know, I'm——" He made some gestures with his hands as if he were trying to balance two grapefruits. "——like a horse."

"Like…a horse?"

Palomino grinned. "You got it, Buddy!"

"And she's just Ashley? Nothing special?" Echo said, trying to speed through the awkwardness.

"She can be special when the mood strikes her. She's one of those people who decided to stick with her real name instead of some made-up nickname." He leaned uncomfortably close to Echo, his breath smelling distinctly of pepperoni. "Nice girl. Got a big kind heart, and a nice round a——"

"Like a horse! Of course!" Echo said, appalled about where Palomino was steering the conversation. "I think I'm ready to order something."

"Sure thing, Buddy."

"Echo Gain, that's my name."

"Yeah, that's clever, Buddy. Rhymes. A lot of neat-o-ness to that, too. But I like *Buddy*. Don't you? Look, I can plainly see you haven't even looked at the menu yet. Everything we make here is good—very good—and I'm not just telling you that because I own the place. I'm telling you because it is good. Everything is made to order, and fresh." He paused to smell his pink lei of flowers. "Buddy, I usually recommend the soup and sandwich, but you strike me as a guy who would enjoy our signature specialty: the Impossiburger. It's impossibly delicious. Made from the perfect beef patty, the perfect seasonings, the perfect size, and it's a one of a kind. Just like you, Buddy!"

"I'll think about it," Echo said glancing at the menu, unimpressed with the hard sell on the burger. "How about the Mobius Melt?"

"Well, Buddy, that's a grilled cheese sandwich. Three yummy cheeses brought together: Havarti, extra sharp cheddar, and hickory smoked Gouda. Stuffed in between thick slices of white bread, grilled on top of creamy butter, with a dash of Dijon mustard. Comes with a cup of honey for dipping. You like dipping into honey, don't ya, Buddy?"

Echo wanted to hide, but Palomino kept plowing on.

"I can add avocado, tomatoes, even a wiener, but you don't strike me as the type that likes wieners. Right, Buddy? I should warn you, it's a big sandwich. Some customers find it difficult to finish a Mobius Melt. Once you begin eating, the cheese never seems to end. It's all about commitment. You can handle commitment, can't you, Buddy?"

Echo tossed the menu down on the counter. "I don't even remember walking through that door!" The stool wobbled again. He stood up. "What is wrong with this thing?"

"A tall guy must have sat there, Buddy. Just spin the top cushion around to lower it. That should screw it in place. You know how to screw in place, don't you?"

Echo spun the stool cushion around. It started to wobble more and then fell off the stand with a loud metal clang. The racket spooked Ashley on the other side of the diner. She looked at him, grinning, while biting her lip and squinting her eyes. It was a look that said, "I like this guy, but God is he stupid, or what?"

Palomino groaned. "Next time, try spinning it in the other direction."

Echo moved over to the next stool at the counter and sat down. His face was red with embarrassment.

"Can you just cook me something normal? I had a bout with sickness two, no, six…hell, it was at some point in time that was pretty recent; I just can't remember when." He took a deep breath. "Why can't I just have something normal, you know, without the craziness?"

Palomino threw back his head and laughed at him. "Normal? Buddy, tell me what is normal anymore? Tell me anything that has been normal in the last hundred years. The last thousand. Can you? Sure, things are weird, but there is a lot of fun in weird. I can make you a BLT. Or how 'bout a cheese steak sandwich? I can do that if you want, Buddy. After all, you are the customer, right?" He smelled his flowers again as if drawing strength from them. "Live a little, take a risk, experience something completely new. You strike me as the type that hears that advice a lot, but never actually listens to it. Am I right?" He started playing with his flowers a little. "You know what, Buddy? There can't ever be a normal because there never was a normal. The whole idea of normality is, when you think about it, completely abnormal."

Echo held his head in his hands. He wanted to stuff Palomino's towel down his throat the next time he said "Buddy." He glanced at Ashley, and she smiled at him. He felt his patience return.

"Okay, so what do you recommend then?"

Palomino's voice sang. "The Impossiburger."

"I'm just not getting what is so impossible about this burger."

Palomino walked over to the fridge and opened the door.

"See that patty in there, Buddy? That fresh, pink, juicy, meat patty? It looks like I made it yesterday, right? Wrong. It's the only Impossiburger ever made, and it is the only one that ever will be made. See, Buddy, no matter how many times I cook it, no matter how many times I serve it, and no matter how many people eat it, there will always be a fresh, pink patty in the fridge. I can serve the same burger over and over. I can even serve it to you twice. But every time I open that door—" He snapped his fingers once at each shoulder. "That same burger will be right there waiting for me to cook it again."

"Yeah, right." Echo said cynically. "That's impossible."

Palomino giggled enthusiastically. "I like to call that patty a parallel patty. My theory—and keep in mind, I was only a mild-mannered CPA—is that I'm not serving duplicates of the same burger. I am, in fact, serving burgers from parallel universes, or maybe even nearby dimensions." He smiled, waiting for Echo to be impressed, but he frowned when Echo looked confused.

"Don't worry, Buddy. It's hard to understand without seeing it."

Palomino put the plastic-wrapped Impossiburger on the counter. He closed the fridge, then opened it again and placed another Impossiburger on the counter. He kept doing this until there were forty more burgers piled up on the counter. Each burger was exactly the same, and every time the fridge was opened, there was exactly one patty in the same spot. Echo could not believe it. Palomino encouraged him to come behind the counter and try it for himself. Echo opened the fridge faster and faster, and each time a burger appeared, even if the door had been closed for only a split second. He shook his head.

"This is crazy."

Palomino giggled again. "Buddy, you want to see crazy? Watch this."

He opened the fridge and stuffed all the burgers in until every space was filled with beef. He shut the door, then opened it, and all the burgers were gone. Only the single Impossiburger patty was there, waiting. Echo checked the back of the fridge for a trap door, a trick wall, anything. Palomino watched him with a smug grin.

"I know what you're thinking, Buddy: Where did they go? Probably back to where they came from. Every time I open that fridge, I wonder if I'm stealing a burger from some other dimension. I figure somewhere out there is a fridge that's always empty, just like how mine's always full. You know, because things tend to balance out like that. Well, Buddy, are you hungry, or what?"

Echo stepped away from the fridge. "I guess, I mean, shit, man, I don't know what to think. Does it taste good? Is it safe to eat something like that?"

"It's a damn good burger, Buddy."

"Great. I guess I'll take one."

"You got it. Any Fries? I don't think you'd like an onion ring. But I can whip up some sweet-potato chips; you'll have to wait for them. That okay with you, Buddy?"

"Yeah, the chips, those sound good. Besides, I'm in no rush. I can hang out here for a while." He glanced at Ashley.

Palomino was pleased as he watched the two of them make eye contact. "Go get 'er, Buddy!"

Echo's face turned red again. Palomino wrote the order down, then lowered his voice a little.

"I'll try to extend the cooking time…don't you let a good opportunity pass you by. She's a very nice girl."

He started humming a happy tune as he took a fresh patty from the fridge. He walked slowly toward the kitchen door dancing a little two-step that made Ashley laugh. When he was beside her, he suddenly stopped and gently pushed her in Echo's direction. Then he resumed his singing, all the way into the kitchen.

Ashley straightened her hair out, fidgeted a little, then let out a confident huff. She marched over to Echo, trying not to be too excited, but as they got nearer to each other, the butterflies grew.

"So, what would you like to drink?" she asked.

"What do you have?"

"Sodas, stuff like that," she said, indifferently. Then her face lit up, "I made some sweet tea. Would you like to try some?"

"Of course," he said.

She put a glass before him and poured in the tea. She watched him anxiously as he took a sip. The tea was sweet, so sweet he had to cough to prevent his pancreas from seizing. He tried to pretend he enjoyed it, but it was obvious to Ashley he had not. She looked mortified. He had no idea what to say.

"It's a little sweet." His eyes watered.

"Just like her, right, Buddy?" Palomino said from the kitchen, obviously eavesdropping.

Ashley fidgeted nervously. "I'm so sorry. Can I get you anything else?"

Echo liked something about her he couldn't place.

"Maybe you and I can just sit together and talk. Like two norm...I mean, talk like two people."

"Okay." She smiled at him, took the tea away, and fetched him some water.

"You sure you have time? I don't want to get in the way of your job if business picks up."

Palomino let out a high-pitched, "Ha!" from the kitchen.

Ashley smirked a little. "This is about as busy as it gets."

It wasn't funny to her; it was a little sad, and her desire to speak with him seemed to originate from an unspeakable loneliness.

"Sometimes we get people in, sort of. It used to be so busy, but that was a long time ago. Or I suppose, a short time ago—is two hundred years a long time?"

"Depends." Echo had no idea what the right answer was for her.

She was quiet, then walked around the counter to sit down on a stool next to him. He watched her cross her legs and swing around to rest her elbow on the countertop. He could not tell if she was flirting with him or if she was just being friendly.

"Cute boots," he said, trying to find out.

"Aren't they so cool?" she said, excitedly. "I picked them up at an outlet mall a couple miles from here. They were buried in a store-room. I guess nobody took them, because they are so small. I have really small feet. So I figured, whatever! Their loss, my gain, right? I think these are so cool because of all the buckles on them. They also make me a little taller." Her posture slouched after she finished speaking. She seemed unsure of herself. Was her smile forced? Echo wondered.

"No, they do look really cool. Like something from a video game."

The reference failed to register any response from her. He had left the door open for her to jump in and say something about video games, but instead she kept looking at her boots as if she had not heard him. He changed the subject.

"Well, what kind of car do you drive?"

"Oh, I don't own a car."

"How did you get to the shoe store then?"

"I have this scooter. It's a purple Vespa. It's always sunny, and no one is ever around anymore. So I just ride my little Vespa everywhere. I have so much fun. Some days I take it out just to ride around."

"That does sound like fun."

"I just like how the wind feels in my hair." She pulled back her hair and redid her ponytail. "So, what kind of car do you drive?"

"It's that blue Audi parked by the door." He pointed at it and felt a strange sense of déjà vu.

Ashley sat up on the stool to glance out the window. "Oh my God, that's an awesome looking car!"

He took a sip of water, watching her fiddle with her hair once again, apparently waiting for him to say something else.

"So...?" she said.

"So..." he said.

The conversation had suddenly gone flat. She sat on the stool swinging her legs and waiting for him to say something. No words came to mind. He had the distinct feeling that she was faking her friendliness toward him. Her actual thoughts were hidden away, deep inside, behind that cheerful gaze. He felt like he could not trust what she said, as if she were only telling him what he wanted to hear. He wondered if Ashley was as lonely as he was. He wanted to be with another person very badly, but he feared making a connection. Isolation was the safest course, yet, he knew he could no longer stand being alone.

He swiveled toward her. "So. Do you want to check out my cool car?"

Her mouth dropped open into a smile. "Oh, my God! That would be so awesome!"

"Let's go then."

As they walked out to the Audi, he saw his things piled in the back-seat. He felt uncomfortable that they were there. The backseat was packed full. He had placed a black blanket over the pile to make it less noticeable against the black leather interior of the car. Ashley didn't seem to mind the pile. She commented on how new the car smelled and how she could not remember the last time she had smelled that scent. He showed her the stereo that could not pick up any radio stations, and the built-in navigation system that did not work because all the satellites in space were gone. She seemed fascinated with everything, though she was probably exaggerating her reactions. Did she like him or was she just desperate to speak with someone? Anyone. He just could not tell.

"It's pretty quick; dual intercoolers and a supercharger."

He had no idea what he was talking about. He had just regurgitated a bunch of words that sounded cool in the manual. She seemed to care less about what he was saying than the fact that he was explaining some-thing to her. She folded her hands, excitedly.

"So do you think we can we take it for a spin?"

"Yeah, I think so. Put your seat belt on."

He started the car. Static filled all the stereo speakers. He quickly turned the radio off, feeling a little embarrassed.

The diner was built in the middle of a traffic circle where four roads met. Echo was surprised no one had joked about all roads lead-ing to the diner. The sign that was supposed to display the name of the diner was mysteriously half smashed. A bright-green homemade infinity symbol had been painted on a white bed sheet and hung from the top of the damaged sign. This, Echo assumed, was supposed to be the name of the diner. He took the Audi around the traffic circle a few times, as fast as he dared to go. It seemed fast enough to Ashley, who laughed every time the engine growled. It took him a minute to understand that he was alone with this girl. He remembered that Palomino had advised him not to let an opportunity pass him by. He had no idea what to say to her.

"Ashley…Ashley…Ashley." He just started talking as he sped around the diner. "I like your name. I, uh, don't hear regular names that often anymore."

"Oh my God, I thought it was so lame when everyone started using their made-up names from *Conundrum*. How can anyone call himself Torpedodog215? Lame."

"Yeah, I know, right?" he said, trying not to take her comment personally.

"So, it's like they don't want to be real people anymore, like they are in total denial. Before the end, you had your online life, and you had your real life. You could turn off everything and be a real person. Now, oh my God, everyone is so lame. It's like all the real people disappeared. Like, all the basements of the world let the lame-os out."

She seemed hostile. Maybe he struck a sore subject with her. Made-up names could be a trigger of some bitter feelings for her, just as the word "Cayenne" was to him. He drove the car down one of the roads to show off its performance to her. He pressed the gas pedal harder, causing the engine to release a satisfactory rev. As he drove, she seemed to relax more. She began to twirl her hair happily. This made him feel more comfortable, too. He rambled the first thought he had as he watched the road.

"It's nice out here. I always did like how I can see the mountains from anywhere in the state. Helps me to remember what direction west is, because, you know, compasses just spin now."

"So, when I first saw that happen, I was like, this is so real, it's so not a joke."

"That's nothing, you should see the crazy stuff that happens near the border."

She looked at him sharply. "Wow, you've been there? Have you been to the edge?"

He was happy to find something she seemed interested in.

"I've been very close. I made it as far as the army perimeter. They said I could go to the edge, but they advised strongly against it. Something about there being no means of return."

She acted impressed. "So what was it like being that close?"

"A lot of strange things happened; they are hard to describe."

"So, like what?"

"It was hard to tell how much time was passing, and sometimes I was not sure what was real. There was this noise, too. A high-pitched whine of absolute silence that was everywhere. The army guys played music all the time to keep themselves sane. Most of all, there was this feeling…"

He paused. He could tell her, but it was personal, and telling her might make her think something that he was not actually thinking. He wanted to be honest. He breathed a deep sigh and decided to risk it.

"It was this overwhelming feeling. Like you did something that you can never take back. This feeling of permanence, forever…and loneliness."

She suddenly seemed scared that they were alone, speeding away from the diner. He could tell she felt trapped as she curled against the door, moving as far away from him as she could. He realized he had no idea what she had been through, and any number of terrible things could have happened to a pretty girl like her. Maybe something had happened that drove her to hide out at the diner. He thought it was odd how Palomino pushed them to be together, and that maybe it was something she had not actually wanted. He regretted saying anything at all. He glanced at the clock. He quickly decided it would be his way out of this mess.

"Shit! That can't be right," he said, trying his best to sound surprised.

"Oh my God! What's wrong?"

"According to this, we've been gone forty minutes!" His lie was obvious: far less time than that had passed.

"Forty minutes? Are you serious?" She played along. She had needed an out. "I need to so get back. I have…I'm so sorry about this. I have a ton of work." She cringed at not even being able to fabricate a good excuse.

Echo played along, too. "Don't worry, I told you this car is quick, right?"

It was a disaster. He hated himself. He hated her. He hated everything. He slowed the Audi down just enough to make a sharp U-turn. In his mind, he thought, "Fuck it," and pushed his foot down hard on the accelerator. The car took off far faster than he had ever gone before. He was so mad. He wanted it to be over. He wished he had not cornered her in the car. He wished he understood what she was feeling. He watched the tachometer redline. He let off the gas, worried that he would ruin the car. The diner was in sight now. She opened the door as soon as they pulled into the parking lot. She bolted from the car before he even parked. He sat in the car for a few minutes hating anything he could think of. Then he decided to just leave. He was no longer hungry. There was nothing there for him, and there never was. Whatever it could have been, it would never be. Never. Never. Never.

CHAPTER 9

HELP YOURSELF

———

Echo woke in a hotel room. He lay in bed, not moving, warm under the sheets, safe and cozy in the cold air-conditioned room. He had slept for a long while, but he was still tired. He was always tired. The depression was constant. The room was dark. A thunderstorm pounded the window with rain. It was not real. It no longer rained. It was a feature of the hotel—one of the many upscale chains built long after the end began. The Doomsday boom, they called it, or the Judgment Day economy. Construction kept people busy; it kept people working and gave them purpose. An entire industry grew around the problems brought on by time dilation. It worked for a while, but eventually despair won out. The hotel was largely self-service. The few remaining staff that still worked there did their jobs through a haze of pills. He wondered if he was the only guest. He had seen no one else.

Time passed by. Nothing decayed. Nothing was made new. Everything had stopped. Echo got dressed and made his way down to the lobby. It was large and impressive. A beautiful starlit sky was outside, and the moon was just entering a new phase. He missed the moon. Looking at the artificial sky touched him in the same way as seeing a photo of an old dear friend he had long forgotten. The hotel manager presented him with a bill. It recorded his being there for the equivalent of three days. Had it really been that long? When had he ordered so much porn? He looked at the list of titles trying to remember any of them. He could not even remember masturbating. He felt so alone. He wondered what the point of living was anymore. He signed the bill, but paid nothing; the room was free, courtesy of the federal government's positive well-being initiative.

He walked outside into the never-ending, never-changing, bright sunlight. It had been a long time since he had traveled this far south. He thought he might be in New Mexico now, but was not sure. It could have been Arizona. It really did not matter. He was lost no matter where he went. He drove for a while. Through a town, across streets and various roads. The map he had was inaccurate. Some places had been demolished in order to reuse their materials somewhere farther away from the ever-encroaching edge of the abyss. Most everywhere else had been deserted. Everything felt as if it had been abandoned yesterday, and in some sense, it had.

It was always so quiet. The sounds of life used to surround him. There had always been so much happening. Planes passing over in the sky, the distant congestion of traffic, and the occasional dog barking. Pets of all kinds were rare anymore. Most had been eaten. Food had always been a concern. There had never been any danger of it going bad or molding away, only the dread that it would one day run out. Food production had been maintained for as long as possible, but eventually fresh resources dwindled to near nothing. Luckily, mass suicides, individual despair, and enforcement of the death penalty for all violent crimes led to a rapid decline in population. It had practically crashed, leaving vast amounts of land and goods for those few who remained.

Echo yawned as he drove. For some reason he slept worse in hotels. He wanted to believe that staying in a room that mimicked the past would somehow soothe his pain. Instead it only reminded him of what he no longer had and, in the case of women, never had. He had once agonized over whether he should hire an escort during a stay in Reno. He remembered driving to the place, walking inside, and finding out the young woman in the ad he had seen had killed herself the week before. He had sought pleasure from a stranger in more pain than himself. He never forgot how guilty he had felt, or how selfish.

He pulled the Audi into the empty lot of a convenience store. The electronic doorbell dinged as he walked inside. The air was cool and brought with it the smell of candy and beef jerky. The refrigerators hummed gently, evoking in him a kind of comfort that usually came from watching the sky. The store was spotless and fully stocked. He slowly walked up and down the small aisles considering what he wanted to take. There was even fresh bread—only a few hundred years old. He could see someone else had been there before him and had taken only what they needed. He would do the same. There was no reason to hoard. He saw a sign hanging on the door to the back room. It warned him that there had been a suicide in there and that all the stock had been put out already. He felt tired and left the door alone.

He walked around the store loading up a handbasket full of different snacks. He was in no hurry, and he had no concern of being interrupted. He felt safe in his isolation. He read the ingredients of everything he picked up. Much of the food was filled with pharmaceutical chemicals, leaving only a small selection for him to choose from that were free of meds. The pills were in everything. They even had their own aisle across from the magazine rack. He walked over to the magazines to browse through them. The men's magazines had long been cleaned out, but a science journal caught his eye. Its cover was of the last photograph ever received from an orbiting satellite. It showed a quarter of the Earth consumed by a shadow, as if a bite had been taken out of the planet like an apple.

The photo was famous, not because of what it showed, but because of what it triggered. In the wake of the image, a wave of panic swept the planet, and after it, despair. He chuckled as he flipped through the pages rereading the articles. The graphs and charts inside it, explaining what was thought to be happening, were so simple a child could understand them. As more of the planet was consumed, it was estimated the time dilation would increase. Seconds would stretch to months, months into millennia, and so on. It all sounded so figured out, so understood, so confident. Then the math was proven wrong, then proven right, then wrong again, and no one knew whom to believe. Religious leaders declared it was the rapture and called their followers home. Faith had always had a simple kind of credibility to the masses. There was nothing to understand; you just had to believe. He shook his head in disgust. He kept the magazine. He thought it might make good toilet paper.

CHAPTER 10

MASHED POTATOES

———

Every street was empty, and every street looked the same. Carbon copy houses lined the sidewalks like rows of unmarked cardboard boxes in a warehouse. The suburbs were a labyrinth of abject monotony. Cars were few and far between. Most were taken with the residents when they evacuated to somewhere else. The houses stood locked, waiting for their return. Echo sped through the desolate streets looking for something. Looking for nothing.

He considered breaking into one of the nicer homes to see what was inside. He came across one house with the lights still on and children's toys in the yard. He could see from the road that bodies were floating in the pool. He gritted his teeth and drove on. He feared what he might find inside the homes he passed. He was not sure why he was driving through the suburbs. He had not done it in so long; maybe he was curious if anything had changed. Nothing had.

He turned a corner at full speed while fiddling with the radio. When he looked up, he saw that a mail truck was blocking the street. He slammed on the breaks, screeching the Audi to a stop. A man was pacing behind the mail truck. He stared at Echo, not the least bit surprised. Echo rolled down the window.

"Are you fucking crazy? You can't park that thing in the middle of the street!"

The man stopped pacing. He was a mailman, or at least he wore the uniform. He faked confusion. "Well shoot. I did put these here blinkers on, clear as day. Maybe you shouldn't have been speeding." The man paused, then emphasized both syllables in the word "asshole," and gave Echo the finger, accompanied by a generous smile.

Echo gripped the steering wheel tightly, wrenching it as if it were the man's neck. He was pissed. He considered running the man over with the Audi. No one would ever know. He shook his head and fought the appeal of murder. He shuddered that he had actually considered it. He let out a deep breath and then parked the car. He put a pocketknife in his jeans, just in case the man was nuts. He got out with his arms open in a friendly manner. He smiled and walked over to the pacing man.

"I think we got off on the wrong foot. My name is Echo Gain."

"On the good foot, then…" The man grinned. He seemed friendly, with a bit of a gut, a bit of a beard, and a bit of a limp to his walk. He had a distinctive southern accent that made it sound as if his mouth could not quite wrap around the words he was saying. He acted like Echo was not there, then suddenly stopped and pretended to notice him for the first time.

"Howdy, didn't see you there. Name's Tuber...you know, like a potato."

"What are you doing in the middle of the street, Tuber?"

"Why, I'm a crop-dusting."

"Crop-dusting?"

"Fella, it's crop-dusting. I've got me some gas, and I don't want to pass it in my truck, so I got to walk around to work it out. It's like crop-dusting."

Echo slowly nodded. "Okay, well, I guess that's not too weird."

Tuber chuckled. "You want to see weird? Heck, you should try working at the post office. Weird every doggone day."

"I thought they stopped delivering mail a long time ago?"

"Now, I reckon that might be true officially, but I swear, if we don't get this stuff moved on out of the station, we'll be buried up to our elbows in it."

"There is no way there can be that much mail anymore."

"Well shoot, you don't need to take my word for it. Just come on back to the station and see for yourself. We got a mean poker game on tonight, could always use another player." He stopped pacing, then walked over with his hand extended. "Name's Tuber by the way...like a potato."

Echo shook his hand amused by the reintroduction. "Nice to meet you, Tuber."

"You too, you too. Yep, you too."

"I don't know about that card game, though. I mean, I just met you, and you don't even know me. I could be some kind of OCD, homicidal maniac, with a fetish for stomping."

"Oh, come on now, Echo. Shoot, don't give me that ol' hemming and hawing. Now, you ain't no psycho, are you? You're just some poor fella who had a run of bad experiences with bad folks, and now you go and think all folks are that same way. I reckon you just drive around angry about everything, lonely as a lost prairie dog, wanting that thing you can't even understand and wishing you had it right this minute."

Echo folded his arms defensively. "I see we don't actually have to meet, because we already have met. Do I know you somehow?"

"Know you? Heck, everybody is just like you." Tuber snickered. "By golly, do you really think it's just you out there a wandering around? I must a met a dozen fellas just like you—guys and gals that, for one reason or another, feel like they are all alone in this world. You folks spend all this time thinking, or saying that you're thinking, but you're really just daydreaming. Wishing that something or another went your way when it didn't. And it won't, 'cus it can't. You're not out there exploring—you're just feeling guilty about the past. A guilt trip. I have a pretty fair idea that's what you're on. Now, you can go get in your fancy blue car there and roam somewhere else, or, and I say or, 'cus this is the offer now, or, you can take a chance. Heck, what have you got to lose?"

Echo's lips curled, remembering a few recent experiences. "Well…"

"Now, you must have heard the old phrase: We're all in this together. Haven't ya? Out here we're all strangers in some ways, and family in other ways. 'Cus we only got each other anymore. They ain't no more babies coming. All there is, is us, together till the end. Now, my friends at the post office would surely like to meet a brand-new face. I'm sure you have some stories to tell, too. Heck, we could tell you a story or two. The deal is, you trust us, we trust you. Shoot, we don't even care if you bring a gun."

"I don't have a gun."

Tuber slapped his hand to his forehead dismayed. "Fella, you have to say you have a gun, even if you don't. Now, you remember when the president announced that it was the end of the world? He spoke clear and confident, like a good father. He told everyone not to panic. What's the first thing folks do? They panic. Most of those crazies were shot dead, but not all of them. By golly, they're out there, waiting like coyotes in hills. You should always carry a piece."

Tuber reached in his jacket and pulled out the largest pistol Echo had ever seen.

"Smith & Wesson Model 500. It's like a doggone cannon. I'm a good shot, too, but most of the time I just need to whip it out. Then coyotes get all quiet, afraid I'll lay down the law. I can get you one if you want one, but you have to have strong wrists to fire it. Bucks like an angry wife. A skinny fella like you may not be able to handle it."

Echo had never needed a gun. Isolation had always been his best defense, but lately he was pushing his luck by meeting strangers.

"Look, I don't know about a card game, and hanging out. I mean, that's a big gun. A really big gun, and no offense or anything, but I seem to remember that postal workers and firearms are not a good combination. Isn't that where the term 'going postal' came from?"

Tuber was shocked. He put the gun away and rubbed his beard, almost beside himself.

"Echo, it pains me to hear you say that, it truly does. That just stabs me in the heart and in the ass, at the same darn time. Shoot, we ain't all like that. Heck, I'll let you hold my gun. When we get to the station, we can give you all our guns. If that is what it will take to prove we ain't bandit coyotes."

"I don't know, look at what you're telling me here. Playing poker in a room full of strangers armed with guns. It just screams 'bad idea.' I got to wonder just how many graves are in back of that post office. Are you really delivering mail or are you just spreading body parts around so nobody can figure out your crimes?"

"That don't make a lick of sense. Now, why would you say such a thing? You do remember that all federal employees were deputized, don't ya? I want to say you have trust issues, but I don't think that will even begin to cover it. Delusions is more like it. Heck, there are bad folks in the world, really bad folks, but that's not the whole of the world. There are good folks too, and gosh darn it, a postal worker is some of the best folks you will ever have the privilege of meeting."

Tuber climbed back into the mail truck to continue making deliveries. He leaned out the door.

"Now, just so you know, we play for Girl Scout cookies. Now, that's cookies." He shooed Echo away, disgusted. "I ain't ever heard of anyone going postal over some darn cookies. Shoot."

The mail truck geared up, the tires squealed, then it sped halfway down the street and abruptly stopped. Tuber got out again and began delivering mail. Echo hated himself for being so paranoid. He walked down to Tuber. He noticed that the mailbox Tuber was about to stuff mail into was already jammed full of letters. Tuber began pounding more letters into the mailbox by the fistful. The sound of paper ripping filled the air. Tuber watched Echo as he approached.

"…And did you get enough time to gird up your loins? I swear, you folks like to overthink things. I bet you don't date that often either, do ya?"

"Hey, you don't know me. Yeah, you are right about a few things, but you don't know me."

"Well, shoot, I don't pretend I do. I've known all kinds of folks like you, but *like* you don't mean they *are* you, now does it?"

"I'm in."

"In what?"

"I'll play poker with you guys."

"Oh, geez…" Tuber forced the mailbox closed, breaking the hinge. "Now, it ain't like that at all. All we want is good company, and that's all we provide in return. It'll be good for you to meet honest folks for once. Every experience doesn't have to be bad."

"But they all seem to end that way."

"Now, I beg to differ, yes I do. It's always been your life; you control it. No matter how out of control it may seem to be, in the end, it's what you decide it should be, and that's how it is. You make the choices, you do." He smiled. "Don't you worry—I won't remind you of that after we clean you out of cookies tonight."

"I'd appreciate that."

"Well, I have to finish my deliveries."

"Why? I mean, just look around; nobody lives here. This place is totally abandoned."

Tuber put his hands on his hips and looked around at all the houses.

"Well, shoot, I guess it is. Thing is, that mail keeps a coming—" He seemed confused for a moment. "—From somewhere. Now, I only need to do this block and the next; then we can head to the station. You can wait in your Volvo, and I can come get ya, or you can scoot along behind me."

"It's an Audi, not a Volvo."

"What's the difference?"

"Audi is German, and Volvo is Swedish. That's a big difference."

Tuber thought about it. "Well, I'll be. Learn something new every day, every single day! Whew. Sure miss them Swedes—they the ones that made that hot chocolate, right?"

"More like pickled herring. The Swiss were the ones with the chocolate."

"Well, I miss the Swiss too, then. Heck, I guess all of Europe for that matter…kinda strange when you think about it." Tuber's mind drifted.

He suddenly shifted his mood to something more positive.

"Oh well, it is what it is. Now, just follow along with that Audi, and tonight we'll have ourselves a good time with some good folks. Heck, tonight is only two blocks away."

It took Tuber about fifteen minutes to make deliveries to the rest of the homes. His mail truck was still packed full of mail when he announced to Echo that it was the end of the day. Echo had trailed behind the deliveries, picking up dropped envelopes that had spilled out of the truck and placing them in what he thought was their corresponding mailbox. He noticed that the mail Tuber was stuffing into the mailboxes seemed to be random assortments not belonging to the street. Some of the mail appeared to be addressed to entirely different states—many that no longer existed. He decided not to ask Tuber about it. He guessed there could be any number of reasons as to why he would be doing that, ranging from giving himself purpose—finding a meaningful way to pass the time—to a complete mental breakdown. Tuber seemed sane enough. Unfortunately, Echo was not sure he was a good judge of sanity anymore.

CHAPTER 11

JUNK MAIL

———

The post office was located on a corner where two streets met, wedged between the fenced borders of several preplanned neighborhoods. It was a triangular building composed of chiseled gray stone bricks and bunker-like glass windows. Modern in design, but with a medieval flare. The only thing it lacked was a moat.

Tuber causally drove through a busted chain link fence gateway. It led behind the post office to the motor pool, where the mail trucks were kept. Echo crept along behind him, cautiously. There were two other trucks parked in the back, and one of them looked as if it had been set on fire months ago. Black skid marks across the pavement told the story of some sort of conflict involving another vehicle. Echo followed the trail with his eyes. The marks led to a bullet-ridden ice cream truck crashed at the far end of the lot. It was not a good sign. He found a parking space near the gateway and backed the Audi in. He aligned it as best he could with the exit, so that if he needed to leave in a hurry he would be able to do so.

After he parked, Echo walked over to the crashed ice cream truck. He noticed that the driver's seat had been torn apart by gunfire, but he saw no blood. Tuber shouted at him from across the lot, "He weren't selling ice cream, I can tell you that much for sure."

"What was he selling then?"

"Several flavors of misery."

The area was dead silent. Echo could hear the muffled jingle-jangle of Tuber's holster swinging under his jacket with each limp he made. It unnerved him to be reminded of the gun. They walked across the lot to a giant metal door. It looked like the opening to a dungeon, and it appeared to have been damaged by several rounds of buckshot. Tuber knocked on the door twice. A series of locks were heard unlatching behind it. Then it abruptly opened a bit. The kind face of a short woman peeked out, warily. She looked at Echo with disdain and immediately set to lecturing Tuber for bringing a stranger back to the station.

"I've only come to play poker, ma'am," Echo tried to reassure the woman.

"Mmm-hmm, that's what that asshole that drove that ice cream truck said, too. He was no ice cream man, neither. I don't mean to let no psychos into our home. Nuh-uh." Her tone softened, seemingly in spite of herself. "I don't mean to pigeonhole you like that...as just some hoodlum. I don't know you, and I don't need to know you. And you don't need to know us, neither."

"Now just a darn toot'n minute, woman! This here's a friend," said Tuber.

"Don't you 'woman' me, potato head!"

"Doggone it, woman! Will you just let us in? He's not a psycho. Heck, he doesn't even own a gun. He doesn't look like the type that's any good with knives, either, except maybe to butter bread." Tuber winked at Echo. "Now, you know it's not like how it used to be out here. The military swept the whole area for strange folks years ago after everyone moved to Salt Lake. That's why it's so quiet. Everybody's gone, remember? Remember?"

The woman looked puzzled, as if she had tried to remember, but could not. Then her anger suddenly fizzled as if she had completely forgotten why she was mad in the first place.

"Did I cause a fuss? Mmm-hmm, I don't know what about. You're a fine young man, just fine."

She opened a bottle of pills and tossed several colors in her mouth. She smiled, her eyes serene and distant.

"Well, come on in! Don't just stand there letting all the cool air out. I'm gonna fix you up a real nice guest pass. Mmm-hmm!"

"Guest pass?" Echo asked.

"Uh-huh! We can't let you non-federal employees just walk around like you own the place now, can we?"

She suddenly smiled at him, as if she had just seen him for the first time. "I'm Karat, by the way. Like gold, not like what you eat."

"You can call me Echo."

"Come on in, Eco."

"Echo."

"Huh? Echo? Honey, my voice ain't that loud, is it?"

Echo couldn't tell if she was joking. Tuber patted his back apologetically. He couldn't tell either.

The interior of the post office was one large room reminiscent of a warehouse. Sunlight poured in through skylights on the vaulted ceiling, illuminating everything with a soft natural glow. The space had been divided into sections using shelving as walls. Mail was everywhere. Piles and piles of mail. Plastic tubs filled with envelopes were stacked shoulder high around the walls. Packages were piled haphazardly in every direction, forming small mountains with narrow pathways cut into them. Grease-stained envelopes that had gotten caught in the wheels of large movable pallets lay crumpled on the floor. Echo could see the silhouettes of two other people sorting through gigantic heaps of mail. The daunting size of the piles made their efforts appear utterly futile. It was a task that could never be completed, even with an eternity to do it.

Tuber scooted through a narrow passage lined with stacks of boxes. Echo followed him. Every step he took brought with it the sound of something tearing beneath his feet. The passage was so tight he could not bend down to see what he was stepping on. They passed by a window to the lobby. Without customers it had been shuttered and put to use as a dumping area for the excessive amounts of mail. It had been filled waist high end-to-end. All the doors into it were hopelessly obstructed by the weight of the fill. They came out of the passageway into an open area—a vast field of envelope piles that had become its own separate landscape. Echo glanced at a phone bill lying on top of a plastic tub near him.

"Hey! This is from Florida."

Tuber nodded. "Yep. Undeliverable. We usually toss those in the lobby."

"But the lobby is filled."

"Not yet, it ain't."

"I've never seen so much mail."

"Let me show you something."

He led Echo to the other side of the building, where there was a loading dock. Two trailers were parked at the dock, both of them filled with unsorted mail on large, wheeled pallets. Tuber pulled out several pallets to empty one of the trailers. Once it was empty, he closed the trailer door and then reopened it. The trailer was filled with mail again. It was not more of the same mail; it was new mail. Echo explained that he had seen this phenomenon before on a small scale with a hamburger, but the burger was always the same burger. This was similar, except that what was arriving was new.

Tuber nodded again. "Now, I bet that when you walked in, you thought we were crazy hoarders. That's not it at all. Not at all. That darn mail keeps a coming, and it keeps a coming. It never stops a coming. It comes from everywhere all over the doggone planet. Places that don't exist anymore. Shoot, maybe they do exist, and we were just told they don't exist, that's why it comes. The only real way to know if a place doesn't exist is to go there yourself."

"Trust me, they don't exist. Everything east of Wichita is gone."

The reality took a moment to sink in with Tuber. "Well, shoot. It has to come from somewhere. Heck, there must be a reason why it's sent here. We're just a local post office. Makes no doggone sense." He pushed two pallets out of the way to reveal a sign on the wall.

"You see this?"

Echo looked at the warning sign.

"It says *This location is unusually susceptible to weakened intersecting dimensional surface peripheries induced by entropic strain with a high probability of repeatable breach events.* Does that mean the mail is from some parallel universe—or universes?"

Tuber's head nodded fanatically. "Now, you know who put that there? The government. One day a bunch of lab coat-wearing varmints showed up with this here sign. According to some calculators, this was a focal point of a bunch of big words. I don't remember what them fellas said exactly. Brains not so good with things I can't touch with my own doggone hands. All I remember is they left this sign and a black box in the bathroom. Gave me a phone number to call if anything unusual goes on."

Just then Karat ran out onto the dock with a guest pass. She clipped it onto Echo's belt, then said she was pooped and needed to lie down for a while. She slowly walked back inside.

"Pills," Tuber said. "She takes too many of those darn pills. She used to be sharp as a desert cactus. The mail went and wore her down. It was plain impossible to keep up with. It just keeps a coming, and it makes no sense at all. When everyone moved to Salt Lake, she stayed 'cus we're the only friends she has left. Then that ice cream man pushed her over the edge. Never been the same since. Now, it's just pills."

"I hate those pills."

"So do I, so do I, but what else can you do? Got to do what you got to do to survive this. She's a strong sort. She'd never do herself in. I think she's just tired. Heck, I think we are all just plain tired." He rubbed his beard. "I reckon it ain't all bad. We do have a few perks. We are the highfalutin' nexus of all mail, after all. We get everything here. You name it, it's come out of that trailer at some point. Undeliverable. Time came we just decided to start keeping things."

"But isn't that dishonest?"

"Heck, I don't know. I don't think it is. Now, at least I don't think it is at all. When we decided to open that first box, there was a lot of hooey. We all felt guilty just thinking about it. It was addressed from Russia to some guy in Virginia. We knew those places didn't exist any-more. We let it sit for a week thinking about it, just to get used to the idea. Then we opened it and found three bottles of vodka. We put those to good use right away. Shoot, given the way things are, no, I don't think it's dishonest. It's salvage. Let me show ya."

They walked back inside past a man with headphones on listening to music. Tuber suddenly stopped to introduce the man.

"Oh, this here is Killahurtz, you know like a dial on the radio. Killa-hurtz, this is Echo. He's going to play poker with us tonight."

Killahurtz removed his headphones to say hello. His voice was star-tlingly deep.

"The Killahurtz spells his name k-i-l-l-a like a killa. With h-u-r-t-z on the end, because he hurts people. Got it?" He laughed like a superhero. "The full name of the Killahurtz is Killahurtz14-55-28. But nobody in their right mind uses numbers in a name. So it is just Killahurtz, or if you want to be proper, *The* Killahurtz. Do you seek to challenge Killahurtz in a game tonight?"

Tuber whispered something in Echo's ear about Killahurtz speaking the way he did because of some personal trauma. Echo found it embarrassing to be told such a thing right in front of the person. He pulled away from Tuber and smiled at Killahurtz.

"I'm going to give it a good shot."

"The Killahurtz accepts your challenge and passes a judgment on you, and that judgment is that the Echo is cool. The Killahurtz is down with conversing further this evening. The Killahurtz is planning to beat back reality with some mad card shuffling. The Echo is invited to enjoy the high-speed Internet of our lounge. Feel free to log on to our *Conundrum* server and connect with the great cloud. I invite you to institute a beat down on all the silly robo-troll-shark-zombies that dare cross your path."

"Thanks, but I gave that up a long time ago."

"The Killahurtz is envious of the strength of your soul. Fighting dragons in *Conundrum* is the center of Killahurtz's life. The Killahurtz feels like reality is just the time between epic gaming adventures across the universe. More real than real."

Echo cringed. Tuber hurried him along to meet the only other person left. He cautioned that the man was a perpetual drunk and a hater of tofu. The man was slumped over a chair sorting mail at a slow but steady pace with one hand. When they approached, he swiveled his chair around with a yellow toothy grin. His face was bright red; his nose and cheeks were redder still. Tuber introduced the man.

"Now, this is Hooch, 'cus he drinks—"

"Alcohol!" growled Hooch. His voice sounded like a slurring phlegm-filled blender trying to grind down nails. The sentences he spoke swayed in tone like a ship on high seas. He held a bottle of Tennessee whiskey in one hand, which he sipped from directly.

"Diiid you know," he growled, "that…the liver is the *most* resilient oooorgan in the body? You could *cut* it innnn half, and it will grow back to regular size innn twoooo *weeks!* Two weeks!" He took a sip from the bottle; then he looked at Echo angrily. "Arrre you a liberal?"

"I, I don't really have a preference, really," Echo stammered. "I guess I'm undecided, or independent."

"That's *bull*shit!" Hooch had another drink. "It's your God-given *right* toooo have an opinion, and toooo express that opinion."

He sipped the bottle again, almost falling over.

"Capitalismmm perpetuates an *attitude* of narcissismmm and, and entitlement. Marketing did thisss to us. How long could we market to the youth before *they* became…disenfranchised about their ownnnn future? They *never* understood what harrrrrd work was. They just click, click, click, click the computer to be rich. Instant gratification. *This* country used toooo be the envy of the world…*then* we allowed ourselves toooo become spoiled. We got *old,* and we got *stale.* We ran *out* of good ideas. The world ended because Ammmerica gave up. We could have stopped thissss…We were *great* once, we were…great." His eyes filled with tears.

Tuber patted Hooch on the back. "You still up for a game tonight, partner?"

Hooch took another drink and wiped his eyes. His voice was wet and unstable. "I'll *be* there." He stumbled backward a step.

Tuber motioned to Echo that this was a good time to move on before Hooch caught a second wind. Tuber took Echo to the bathroom and showed him the mysterious black box installed on the wall. It had a single red light that was always on.

"I hate this darn thing. I don't know what the heck it is. Shoot, I got hemorrhoids from pushing on my ass harder than I should, just so I could get out of here faster. Thing's not plugged into anything, it never blinks or beeps, it just sits there. I wonder if the doggone thing is even real, like the lab coats just put it here to make us feel better about taxes."

They continued down a hallway to a couple of storage rooms that had been created out of unused office space. One was filled with foodstuff they had found in various boxes. Tuber pointed at a pile of candy canes.

"Whole lot of it is holiday themed. I reckon the rest is giant orders of freeze-dried survival rations that never reached the folks who ordered it. Heck, when the bottom dropped out, folks went nuts, ordered all kinds of things thinking it would save their lives…darn fools." Tuber let the thoughts drift away. "Anyhow, we have this stockpile here. If you want anything, just yell. Now, you can have anything except the alcohol, 'cus that all belongs to Hooch."

Tuber opened the door of the next storeroom. It was filled with electronics, movies, music, clothes, jewelry, and just about anything else that could be ordered off the Internet. They had a surprising amount of pornography stacked in the corner. They were using it for toilet paper. Tuber chuckled.

"It's funny; I reckon the first thing we ran out of, and the hardest thing to find, was toilet paper. Now, we do have some, just a little, but it's reserved for Karat. It being the end of the world, we figured it best to keep her comfortable. Shoot, she's the only lady we got. Not many opportunities to be polite anymore."

At the end of the hall was the employee lounge. It had been converted into a game room dedicated entirely to *Conundrum*. There were several desks, each covered with large dilapidated computer monitors, achievement-based pill dispensers, and biofeedback headsets. Thick cables ran across the floor connecting a stack of dust-covered *Conundrum*-branded game consoles to a cloud micro-server. The micro-server was how *Conundrum* bypassed the effects of time dilation over distance. It used a mysterious patented process that linked clouds together to form something called the "agile atmosphere system." Few people ever concerned themselves with exactly how it worked. The only thing that mattered was that it did. The room was jam-packed with refill cartridges for the pill dispensers, empty snack packages, guidebooks, spreadsheets, and overused computer tablets that had burned out long ago.

"Yep," Tuber said. "This is where we live our other life."

"The better life?"

"Now, don't go telling me you got something against *Conundrum*. Do you know how many lives it saved? It gave people a reason to live again."

Echo walked around the room remembering all the time he had spent playing the game. He missed playing it in the same way he missed the moon. He patted one of the computers affectionately. He sighed.

"It was a lot of fun."

"Darn toot'n! Still is, too. Would be a heck of a lot more fun if they could keep it updated. Heck, we love the game anyway. All of us do. By golly, we play together at least three times a week. I don't know how you left it."

"It wasn't easy. Sometimes I still miss it, and all the friends I made."

"What did you specialize in?"

"I was a rock star for a while. I had a great band. We released two hit singles. The money I got helped fund my research efforts into building a battle tank with a sonic guitar cannon."

"I think I read about that on the forums."

"Too bad it got destroyed during the war."

"Which one?"

"The invasion of Ganymede. I did a bunch of other stuff, too, but rock star was my favorite, and it's why my name is Echo Gain."

Echo thought about it bitterly. How fake it was. The concocted lies and cheap thrills of the game had led him to believe he had actually accomplished something in life. When in fact, he had achieved nothing at all. He couldn't even sing. The computer did all the work for him, and he pretended it was real.

"Yeah, hundreds of years in isolation in order to be a rock star, fight fascist goblins, resurrect alien dinosaurs, explore the ruins of Camelot, drive cattle on the planet Mars, and become the leading diplomat for a nonexistent country formed after the end of World War XVIII, and founded by the four horsemen of the apocalypse."

"Those fellas were some good players."

"Were they? I don't know what that means anymore. The game becomes your life, and you live it. You know?"

"I do. There ain't much left in this world for me but this game and the mail. I can respect that you left. Heck, I don't reckon that's something I could do myself. I ain't afraid to tell ya it makes me happy to live that other life online and leave this stinking reality behind me for a while. I feel like I can be who I always wanted to be."

"I used to feel the same way, but one day I lost interest. It's hard to explain. I think it was my first rubber band. I woke up in this white room. It was weird. Funny how people you don't know, and never met before, can say a few words and turn your whole world upside down."

"Yep. Them things can do that. Women especially. That's where the game comes in. Helps to smooth out life's rough parts, makes it easier to forget all the bad things…Never did make friends with those dog-gone cat people. Finicky bunch, them."

They both laughed at the absurdity of making friends with virtual cat people. In many ways, they felt sorry for each other, but for different reasons. The laughter faded.

"Yep. It's like comfort food, my favorite TV show, and a hot girl-friend all wrapped up in one."

Tuber watched as Echo thumbed through an old game guide. He rubbed his beard and conceded.

"Heck, we know it's a fantasy world, but the real world is pretty much dead already. I log in, and I just feel more alive. There's always something to do. I suppose it's easy to poke fun at it when you think about it. Maybe I'm not being productive. That I ain't living life to the fullest, but doggone it, what does that even mean?"

"Sometimes I wonder if I should have tried learning every martial art or reading every book. I do have the time, right?"

"That ain't all it's cracked up to be. Now, I knew this fella once, he took to buying books and learning like nobody's business. One day, he says to me, he ran out of books to read. That he read everything there is, and that was all there ever will be. Next day he killed himself, right in the front yard, just like that. Imagine running out of things to do and knowing there would never be any more."

"Nobody runs out of things to do; you just find new things to do. I mean, you just keep going. That's what I do, at least. Maybe that guy just got tired."

Tuber nodded. "Shoot. When you live this long, you get worn down, like an old pair of shoes. I reckon we appreciated life more when we only had so much time on this earth. It's so easy for folks to waste time now. I guess it's 'cus we have so much of it."

It was quiet for a few minutes. Tuber sat down at his computer to check his e-mail and update his status, with a few embellished details about his day. Echo looked around the room as Tuber pecked at the keyboard. He noticed another warning sign left by the scientists hanging on the wall buried behind some papers about game strategy. A phone number was printed on the sign.

"Hey, Tuber, is this the phone number they gave you to call?"

"Hold your horses," Tuber said, finishing up some typing. He looked up. "Yep. That's it. They told me to call that if anything strange started happening."

"Did you try it?"

"Many times. Why, the first time mail appeared in that trailer, we called. It's just a darn busy signal. I'd just speak into the phone anyway;

I figure maybe they were listening, who knows? Hooch thinks that black box is connected to a Think Tank somewhere."

"What do you think?"

"I don't give a hoot'n hell. Nothing I can do about any of it. Can't change the world. It is what it is."

Tuber returned to reading posts on the forums of *Conundrum*. Echo decided to rummage through the storage rooms to see if he could find any treasures that would make his journey easier, or at least more entertaining. Walking into the second storeroom, he saw something that caught his eye. He picked up an unopened laptop box. He yelled out the door into the lounge.

"Hey Tuber, can I take one of these laptops?"

"Which one? Is it out of that there stack of ten? The gaming ones?" Tuber yelled back.

"Yeah, can I have one of those? It's much better than what I have now."

"Help yourself. That there thing is the last laptop ever made. Heck, I heard they were building them right up until the factory was destroyed. Best damn graphics you ever seen, too. Supposedly they toughened it against the effects of the abyss somehow."

"Sounds kind of vague, don't you think?"

"I reckon it's just marketing hooey. Shoot, nothing drives folks to buy something new more than fear, and folks sure are afraid these days."

Echo examined the box, impressed with the specifications. He opened the box and was shocked by how advanced the machine looked. It had the thickness of a dime and came with various mandated government crisis manuals preinstalled. Strangely, the machine did not have a copy of *Conundrum* included. Echo searched through a stack of software in a plastic bin. He quickly found one of the many free copies mailed out en masse to the public shortly after the fall of Europe. *Conundrum* was by then completely funded by the federal government as part of its depression amelioration program. The free copy came with samples of the latest antidepressant pills, each one cleverly named after a hero in the game. He took these things, along with a hard drive filled with nearly all the music ever recorded, out to his car. As he opened the trunk, he accidentally dropped the free copy of *Conundrum*. He noticed the game company's address on it and realized for the first time he had never been there before.

An intercom speaker crackled. "The game is on!" Killahurtz announced like a DJ. "Players to your table. Players to your table."

Echo put everything in the trunk and closed it. He tossed the free copy of *Conundrum* into the passenger seat of the Audi and went back inside.

CHAPTER 12

RETURN TO CINDER

———

Echo stepped inside the post office. The cool air of the interior surrounded his body with a soft caress. He wanted to walk back out, warm up, and step inside, just to experience the sensation all over again. He could hear Hooch grouching about something from somewhere behind the stacks of boxes. He looked forward to sitting down for a game of poker with these fellow misfits and outcasts.

He carefully made his way toward the voices through several box-lined corridors. A clearing opened up before him revealing the concrete floor of the post office. It was the first time he had seen the floor since he'd arrived. Piles of mail surrounded the clearing like termite mounds surrounding a pond. Hooch was hand-vacuuming cookie crumbs off of a well-worn poker table that stood in the middle. Killahurtz wheeled a pallet full of Girl Scout cookies over, and parked it next to his seat. He handed Echo a folding chair with a cushion made of packing foam duct-taped to it.

"The Killahurtz asks you to check yer guns," he sang. "Check yer guns, Check yer guns."

Echo held open his hands. "Nada."

Killahurtz chuckled. "You are hereby under the protection of Killahurtz. May your enemies flee at the very sound of his name."

Hooch pulled out a sawed-off shotgun from somewhere on his person and set it behind him. Killahurtz sat down at the table leaning an AR-15 assault rifle against a box behind him.

"Let's go!" he sang. "Let's go! Game time!"

Karat stumbled out of a pathway looking like she had just woken up. Hooch asked if she had her gun. She told him she didn't need it. Hooch snarled.

"You neverrr, everrrr, know when *it* might happen…*again*."

She swatted the air to rid it of Hooch's nasty breath.

"Mmm-hmm. You know, you really redefine 'shitfaced,' you know that? I don't need you to remind me about nothing. I'm sick of thinking about it. If it happens again, it just happens, and I'll just live with it."

"If *it* happens again, is that a bad thing?" asked Echo.

"Don't you worry none, Echo. We just talking shop here."

Killahurtz and Hooch looked at each other with concern. Killahurtz broke out the deck of playing cards and started shuffling. Hooch put a heap of Girl Scout cookie boxes on the table and sat down. Echo pulled his seat up and sat next to Killahurtz. The foam cushion hissed a foul odor out as he sat. Killahurtz coughed. A card jumped out of the deck he was shuffling. Hooch handed it back to him. They politely ignored the stench.

Tuber walked in last and set his gun on the floor behind his chair. He started to sift through the Girl Scout cookies and pass out boxes to each of them.

"Whew," he sighed, detecting something in the air. "Folks all here? Good. We're darn tired of eating these things—we've got so many of them. That doesn't mean you can't. If you want to eat some, just speak up, and we'll get you a fresh box to chew on. But don't go eating your game chips. That makes Hooch real mad."

Hooch frowned angrily at Echo, then smiled and took a long sip from his bottle.

Echo gave a halfhearted nod that he understood. "Should I have a gun here? Every time Tuber says 'shoot,' I want to duck, you know? I feel kind of left out. I mean what if *it* happens again?"

Hooch snarled. "Karat don't have aaaa gun, either."

Tuber grinned. "Aw heck, Echo, you don't even know how to use one, right? By golly, it's just a little poker game; nobody gets shot over cookies."

Killahurtz cleared his throat. "BobsyourUncle! Remember...*that* guy?"

"Oh geez. Well, shoot, he did get shot, didn't he? What an asshole." Tuber chuckled, a little embarrassed in front of Echo. "Heck, we didn't kill poor Bob. I just shot near him, you know, to scare him real good."

Hooch sipped his bottle. "That guy shhhhhit his pants. We threw that chair *away*...I think." He looked under the table at Echo's chair, suspiciously.

"Heck, that's why we don't drink absinthe at the darn table no more. All that horsing around, somebody was bound to get themselves hurt."

Killahurtz sighed. He turned to Echo. "The Killahurtz assures the Echo he will have a good time. A good time will be had by all. The Killahurtz approves the telling of many stories, jokes, and the friendly teasing about the cards dealt. This the Killahurtz approves. Fun for the whole Killahurtz family. Good friends, good times, together. Can you feel the love?"

Hooch snorted cynically and learned toward Tuber. "I love you, man."

Tuber paused what he was doing. "Oh geez, I love you, too, Hooch, ya rascal."

"Be rrrright *back*, gotta pissss quick!" Hooch ran off to the bathroom with his bottle still in hand.

Karat yelled after him. "Try lifting the seat up this time, you drunk fool."

He screamed at her something so garbled no one could understand what he said; then he slammed the door. She made a wry face. "I don't know how that man gets on with himself."

Tuber sat down and pulled his chair up to the table.

"Here, take this." He handed Echo a black Sharpie. "Use that there to mark your boxes so you remember the value of your cookies. Now, are you ready? 'Cus here we go. The Trefoils—the shortbread cookies—they are worth one dollar. The Thin Mints are worth five dollars. You with me? Okay, good. Now, the Do-Si-Dos—those are the peanut butter sandwich cookies—they are worth ten dollars. The Tagalongs—the chocolate-covered, peanut-butter-filled ones—those are worth twenty-five dollars. The Samoas—the coconut ring ones—those are worth fifty big ones. It's important not to get the two peanut butter varieties mixed up, got all that?"

Echo marked all his cookie boxes with the corresponding values. "I can understand the Samoas being worth the most because there are so few in a box, and they taste good. But I thought Thin Mints were more popular than the peanut butter cookies; aren't they undervalued?"

Killahurtz rolled his eyes. "Oh, here we go again…"

Tuber shook his head. "I reckon they are more popular, but that's how we ordered them."

Echo thought about it, but it didn't make sense. "Do you really need that many lower denomination chips?"

Tuber erupted. "Doggone it, Echo! Who cares? It's just a game. It's an argument over nothing. It doesn't matter if we played with cookies or cow chips; these are the rules we play by. Just relax, try not to think so much. Shoot."

Echo felt stupid. "I'm sorry, you're right. I was making something out of nothing…" He sighed. "Any chance I can get an extra box of Thin Mints to snack on while we play?"

Killahurtz reached into a nearby carton and handed some Thin Mints to Echo. "The Killahurtz gives the Echo the good stuff. Killahurtz pro-

131

vides cookies from the secret stash that predates the takeover of medicinal chemical flavorings. They don't make them like this anymore."

Echo thanked him. "They don't make a lot of things anymore."

Killahurtz laughed. "The Killahurtz agrees."

Karat opened all her boxes and organized her cookies.

"Where the hell is Hooch? I bet that fool is hosing down the whole stall with piss again. I swear I will tie his rope in a knot!"

Tuber looked down, embarrassed for a second time.

"If he is, he's a going to clean the whole doggone mess up. He made us a promise after…that thing he did."

Echo dared to find out. "What did he do?"

Karat looked disgusted. "He took a *shit* and *missed* the bowl."

Killahurtz laughed hard. Karat threw a pill at him. He dodged it. "The Killahurtz offers his most sincere apologies for being so thoroughly entertained."

Their camaraderie made Echo feel welcome. "It's almost as though you two were married," he joked.

Killahurtz looked away, and Karat squinted her eyes at Echo. "No reason for marriage when you can't have kids."

Echo had forgotten that though lives had been extended to near immortality, women could no longer have children. Some may get pregnant, but nothing would ever grow. Men often forgot about this, but women never did. He hated himself for not remembering.

"I didn't—I mean, the two of you get along, and I thought, people marry each other for lots of reasons. I didn't mean to upset you."

Karat smiled. "It's fine, Echo, it's fine. Some things still get to me."

The bathroom door opened to the deafening sound of a toilet flush and patriotic singing. Hooch ran back to the table.

"Ah...What'd I missss?"

Karat frowned at him. "Did you wash your hands this time?"

Hooch's face glowed red. "My *handsss* are cleaner than those envelopesss I've been touching all day. *Yes,* I did wash them, with *soap* this time." He was desperate to change the subject. "Hey, Echo, I tell you about my movie idea yet?"

Karat closed her eyes. "Glory, not again."

Echo acted intrigued. "What is it, Hooch?"

Hooch perked up. "You know the oooold book *Charlie and the Chocolate Factory*, right? *And* you know how back in the *Vietnam War,* they called theee enemy Vietcong *Charlie,* right? Ssso...my idea issss that there is this chocolate factory *run* by the United *States* during the war, and...and it gets invaded during the Tet *Off*ensive. I call it...Charlie *in* the Chocolate Factory. Get it?"

Echo forced a small grin on his face. "That's great, Hooch, brilliant."

Killahurtz shook his head with a low chuckle, and began dealing cards. "The Killahurtz decrees that the small blind is a dollar, big blind is five, dealer button moves clockwise as normal, and—"

Hooch dropped his cards. "*What?*"

Killahurtz groaned. "The Hooch's hand was revealed to the Killahurtz. All cards must be returned for a do-over. So commands the Killahurtz."

Hooch stood up, his head cocked strangely, with his ear to the ceiling. "W-w-what?"

Karat tugged on Hooch's shirt. "Sit down, fool. Just what the hell are you doing?"

Tuber got mad. "Did you put pills in his drink again, Karat?"

She was irate with the accusation. "Sit down, Hooch. We all know you crazy already."

Hooch wouldn't sit. "Do you hearrrr...*that?* Is it him?"

Everyone at the table froze. Echo was confused. "Him, who?"

Then they heard the distinct melody of an ice cream truck, and it was speeding toward them. The sound of a crash came from the parking lot. Echo dropped his cards. A cold sweat spread through his body. Killahurtz and Hooch stood up with their guns in hand.

Karat seemed to lose her mind. "Not again! Not again! No! Oh, Lord! Not again!"

Tuber grabbed Karat and Echo by the arm, pulling them away from the table. He dragged them through a narrow corridor, knocking over a shelf.

"We're going to the fort. Quick! It's made of books. Lots of thick books."

Echo was surprised by the strength Tuber possessed. He thought about his car and his things. His heart raced. "What the hell is going on?"

Hooch started yelling. " Rig*marole*! Rigmarole! *Rig*marole!"

Another crash came from the parking lot. Echo was suddenly filled with anger knowing that his car had just been destroyed. His things would be strewn across the lot. He had no desire to take a mail truck as his next car. He could be trapped there for days now until he could find something else to travel in. A crash erupted on the other side of the station now. It was as if the truck were circling around it. Tuber moved a pallet revealing a small fortress of tightly packed boxes that had been hidden in the far corner of the station. The fortress of boxes was very much like what a group of small children might build.

Tuber handed Echo a tub full of books. "Use these here scraps to fill any gaps you see." He pointed at Karat. "Now, don't let her go get hysterical on us."

Echo heard another crash outside. "What's going on? It sounds there's like another ice cream truck out there."

The loud grind of a parking brake was heard, followed by heavy footsteps running toward the back door. Tuber looked nervous. "All you need to know is he's crazy. Keep your head down no matter what. Hear?"

Tuber pushed the boxes closed, sealing Echo and Karat into the small fort. Echo could hear Killahurtz and Hooch shouting. He heard a metal banging sound as if someone was trying to kick the door in. He turned to Karat, who seemed petrified. Echo tried to speak with her. There was no response. He shook her a little and tried again.

"Karat! Karat! Do you know what's happening? Who was Tuber talking about?"

She took a pill and relaxed. "Uh-huh. It's Rigmarole. Some guy named Rigmarole. He was just some fool we played with in the game, you know?"

"Wait, you mean in *Conundrum?*"

"He got a big crush on me. He turned out to be a stalker. He got mad one night and come to kill us, but we were ready and killed him first. Now he's haunting us like a ghost. He's a ghost that can't die. He keeps coming back all over again. We can't shoot him enough. It's a living hell. I can't take it no more."

She poured pills into her mouth and swallowed. Her face went blank. She stared at Echo as if seeing him for the first time.

"Huh. Do I know you? Is this real?"

"No, it's not real. It's a dream. Just lie back and relax," he said.

She lay down behind the boxes and curled up. Echo ran his hands through his hair. The metal banging sound was growing louder. He was mad at himself for trusting strangers. He should have known it was too good to be true. Something always went wrong. He shook his head to clear his mind. He could not allow himself to drift. He was in deep trouble. *What if I'm shot?* he thought. *What if everyone else is shot?* He had to remember not to panic. He had to be prepared. He needed to find a way to escape. The mountains of clutter around him filled him with claustrophobia. There had to be another way out. He turned to Karat.

"Is there another way out of here?"

She almost answered, then rolled over with a vacant smile and giggled.

There was a loud metal slam followed by a crash. People began shouting at each other. Echo heard the voice of a stranger yelling back. Threats were made. A gun was fired. *Pop! Pop! Pop!* More firing. A stack of boxes fell somewhere. A shotgun went off. The stranger shouted. *Pop! Pop!* Hooch screamed out in pain. *Boom! Boom!* More shouting and cursing. The stranger let out a yelp. *Ka-pow!* The stranger groaned. Then came an avalanche of envelopes. *Pop! Pop!* Voices told someone to stop. Then it was silent.

"We got him. It's over…again," Killahurtz shouted in a normal voice, abandoning the heroic personality. "So proclaims the Killahurtz…" he tried, but it just wasn't in him anymore.

Tuber moved some boxes out of the way, opening up the fort. "It's okay to come on out. We fixed his wagon but good this time."

Echo climbed out of the fort. Nothing looked any different. There was a thin layer of smoke in the air, and the smell of gunpowder. Hooch was casually wheeling a mop and bucket over to an area near the back door. His hand was wrapped up in gauze. Tuber led Echo over to where the dead man lay. They passed the card table; it was untouched. Everything seemed the same. Echo had expected there to be a lot of destruction given the noise. He guessed his expectations had been unrealistically skewed from playing video games. The body had been partially buried by a pile of envelopes. Blood was soaking through them. It was a grisly mess, and Echo was glad he could not see the stranger's face. Tuber motioned for Hooch to mop up the blood before it spread too far. He looked at Echo.

"Now, I reckon you're thinking about how I said we were good folks, that just because we have guns doesn't mean we go *postal*. I'm sorry as all get out to disappoint you, Echo. I really am."

Echo couldn't stop staring at the bloody corpse. "Great, another dead body. I hate seeing these. I don't think it bothers me anymore, but every time I see one, I just know I'm getting more fucked up inside."

Killahurtz pushed an empty cart over to remove the body.

"This guy don't stay dead. He's a psycho gamer. It's like we are being punished for playing that game so much. This guy has got infinite lives." He felt Echo staring at him puzzled over the absence of his deep voice. He looked away.

Tuber waved off the nonsense. "I reckon its 'cus we keep killing him wrong somehow."

Hooch mopped up some blood. "It's like tying your shhhoes with… spaghetti…it's *bull*shit."

Echo wanted to escape. Then he remembered his car. He rushed outside to the parking lot to see how bad the damage was. To his surprise he saw no damage at all. Nothing had changed. He ran to the side of the station where he knew he had heard a crash. The derelict ice cream truck was there, unmoved, just as he had seen it before. Everything was fine. Tuber walked up behind him, looking not the least bit confused.

"Expecting to find something?"

"What was going on out here? Did that really happen?"

Tuber grit his teeth. "Yes. And yes and no. Now all that noise was like a big replay from the first attack. He drove around and around ramming our trucks. Heck, Killahurtz shot up his windshield just to get him to stop. So this guy, Rigmarole, thought he'd storm the building instead. So we shot him. Every time right before he comes back, we hear the noises again. Like an…echo." He smiled. "Shoot. I wish I could tell you he was regular as clockwork, but he ain't. Sometimes he comes two days in a row, sometimes not for months, but we know he's a coming. He's always a coming. Hooch says we all have the post-traumatic stress 'cus of it, too. Oh, and no, we don't know why he drove a doggone ice cream truck. I figure it's 'cus he was a psycho, and that's what psychos do."

"Just how long has this been going on?"

"Long enough to complain about, I guess."

"And you knew this could happen when you invited me?"

"Oh, don't go getting in a huff now, shoot. Heck, he visited us a week ago, and I figured the odds of this happening while you were here for just one day were pretty doggone slim. Shoot, we could all use meeting a new person to break the tension around here. This fella was a bad experience…let me rephrase that, he was a *very* bad experience, like meeting a rabid coyote face-to-face. Don't mean all folks are the same, right?"

Echo did not feel like answering. Tuber, like so many people, was not interested in being someone's friend as much as having a friend. Echo held the bridge of his nose.

"So, what do you plan on doing with the body?"

"Oh, we toss it in the back of the trailer the mail comes out of. It just disappears. Easy peasey."

Echo's head rattled with shock. "You need to stop doing that."

"Why's that?"

"Are you really that dense? I'm willing to bet that the only way that guy is coming back from the dead is because you're throwing his body into that trailer. I mean, when you close that door, who knows what happens? You're dealing with forces nobody understands. Do you really think that body is just being absorbed back into the universe? Anybody ever tell you how impossible it is for us to even be living through all this? There is something about the human mind and time that there could be a weird connection. Maybe this guy wants to come back here."

"Now you know I think that's just a load of manure. This fella made a choice, it went bad, and now he's trapped, living it over and over again. Just like that. It's his fault."

"You can believe that it's all his fault, or you can consider that maybe it was the choice that you made *for him* that's causing all your problems."

"Doggone it, what should we do with the feller's body then? It's got to go somewhere."

"Burn it in a Dumpster."

They heard the dock door lift. Tuber started walking backward.

"Echo, just you wait here a second, I need to go stop them. Just you wait, and we can talk this out…everybody together."

Echo watched Tuber run off to stop the body from being loaded into the trailer. He had no idea if what he said was really the answer to what was happening there. He looked at his car; it was in great shape. He looked back at the post office. He could hear loud voices, an argument over something. Echo could feel his anxiety climbing. Why was he listening to this guy? Why was he waiting for him? Waiting for what? He just watched them gun down a total stranger. He was told a story. It made sense, in a strange way, but did he believe them? Did he trust them? The answer was no. He jumped in the Audi and sped away. In the back of his mind, they were chasing after him, yet when he thought about it, he knew they couldn't leave, even if they wanted to. They were stuck.

CHAPTER 13

PILLAR OF CLOUD

———

There it was. The nameless game studio that had created *Conundrum*. A barren concrete campus of eight giant, equally spaced, rectangular glass buildings arranged in an octagon. The game studio had a name once, but it had long been forgotten. Swept away by a government that no longer saw any value in remembering the past, lest it remind people of better times. The game *Conundrum* and the private company that had developed it were now one and the same.

"Indivisible, under God, with liberty and justice for all," Echo said as he watched from a distance on a hill, through a pair of binoculars.

It had taken nearly a month to find this place, using the cryptic address on the free copy of *Conundrum* he had taken from the post office. It was a secluded facility nestled deep in the Mojave Desert, far from civilization. Secretive, but also obvious once found. He noticed several dozen cars parked in an expansive parking lot that could hold thousands. He could see people coming and going. He assumed these were employees, but there seemed to be surprisingly few. The guard towers were empty. The place felt like it had peaked long ago and was now slowly winding down.

He wondered if his arrival here was inevitable. Through his travels he had never completely escaped the game. It saturated society. Hidden away behind closed doors and quiet streets, the game lived in the shadows. Despite being playable anywhere and anytime, most people preferred the comfort of their own homes, where they could forget what real life was and the difficulty of living through it. He considered those who played the game in such rapt isolation to be the living dead. It was an opinion he felt he had earned since he had once considered himself one of them. He remembered a time when coming up with clever ways to shortcut biological needs was something he bragged about on the forums of *Conundrum*. He promoted self-starvation as a lifestyle that maximized game time. He would have died at his desk had he not woken up from the game's hold. It had taken him years to regain his full health, and he regretted letting himself waste away like that. And yet, even now, he missed playing it.

"A finite life demands action to achieve goals. Without the milestones of age we are lost in time, unable to define our lives, choking on our own pointless dreams." It was something he once heard in the white room. He missed being there. He felt the weight of depression returning. He set the binoculars down.

He used to fear getting old. He knew now that it was not aging he feared. It was that he would one day realize how much he could have done with the time he had, but had chosen not to. There was no way to avoid regret. Living too hard and reckless created just as much guilt as playing it safe. There was never a right way.

"I want to be happy," he said, with determination.

The last time he thought he had felt happiness had been in the game. He had come here to meet the architects of that happiness. It made him angry that it was not real. He hated them for building such a clever lie, but he admired them for giving the world something to live for. Who were they? What could they tell him? What did they know? Did they care? He wanted to meet the individuals who had led the free world into an eternity of virtual indentured servitude under the guise of escapism.

It was time for answers. The game had led him into the desert, and now it would lead him out of it.

CHAPTER 14

CONUNDRUM

The Audi passed through an unmanned checkpoint and several open gates. It cruised onto the game studio property without incident. The campus was a shadow of its original glory. Neglect had taken over the landscaping, leaving parched brown grass, uncared for brittle trees, and an encroaching desert that had eaten away most of the massive parking lot. Decay such as this no longer occurred naturally, and sure enough, as Echo drove closer, the evidence of human meddling was everywhere. Countless tire tracks from the desert had brought in the sand, the trees were scarred with writing carved into their trunks, and several centuries' worth of spilled alcoholic beverages smothered the grass with a poisonous glaze.

"Life without the responsibility of a tomorrow," Echo said quietly, observing the mess.

He drove through the giant lot toward the building that most appeared to be the main office. It had a dusty cracked fountain out front in the shape of a popular hero character from the game. The hero stood triumphantly on top of a pill with sword in one hand and a biofeedback headband in the other.

Echo marveled at the pompous fountain blatantly flaunting the fact that pill addiction was the secret to the game's lasting success. He cruised by it, curious about the type of people that would commission such a thing. He parked in a spot reserved for visitors just outside what looked like a lobby door. He stepped out of his car and heard the distant thumping of a deep bass speeding toward him. He turned in time to see a black SUV skid to a stop in front of him. The windows vibrated from the pounding of the bass. The passenger-side window rolled down, and the door opened.

A man with a shaved head, pierced eyebrows, and ears that stuck out like the pectoral fins on a fish, jumped out of the SUV. The man wore a metal chain for a belt that was clasped together by a padlock. He leaned his head side to side, cracking his neck. He waved for the driver to turn the music down and clumped toward Echo in unlaced work boots that were several sizes too large. As he approached Echo, he kept his fists clenched and his arms tense so that the veins stood out. He looked Echo up and down, suspiciously sizing him up.

"What the fuck are you doing here?" the man asked in a harsh raspy voice layered with attitude.

Echo stood his ground hiding his cowardice behind an immediate hatred of this intimidating stranger. He knew the worst thing he could do was show fear to a person such as this.

"I came here to meet the people who made *Conundrum*," he announced boldly. "I really liked playing the game, so I decided to come meet the people who made it."

The man nodded, then smiled, revealing a mouth full of gold-capped teeth.

"Fuck, yeah! We love our fans. What the hell is your name?"

"You first. Just who are you?"

"Apeshit."

"Great. You know, I knew a guy named Batshit once."

"Yeah? Was he queer?"

"Excuse me?"

"I said was he a queer? We're not big on the fucking gays here. We only allow men to enter the studio. Not faggots. Men only. Real men. Got that? Are you a real man?"

Echo tried to remain cool. "Yeah, of course I'm a man."

"Do you like chicks?"

"Yes. But what does it prove if I say so? I can tell you anything because you don't know me, just like I don't know you. How do I know this badass homophobic attitude isn't just a front to hide your own latent desires to be with men? Maybe you're the one who's gay. Have you ever kissed a guy? Have you?"

Some catcalls and hoots erupted from unseen people inside the SUV. Apeshit looked infuriated. It seemed he'd never had anyone turn the tables on him before. Apeshit's lower lip trembled a bit, and for a second Echo thought he might cry or throw a fit. Echo knew if he made enemies he'd have no chance of getting inside the studio. He extended his hand to Apeshit.

"My name's Echo Gain."

Apeshit frowned and toughened up again. He gave Echo a high five instead of shaking his hand.

"Fuck, man. You got some nerve. I ought to bust your ass for speaking to me like that. Fuck. You're lucky I'm such a cool guy."

"Yeah, you seem like a cool guy, all right. I bet you do some cool things, don't you?"

"Fuck, yeah! I'm the fucking studio art director. I got the Midas touch, yo. Everything in that game looks so fucking good because of my eye for epic greatness."

Echo nodded, feigning that he was impressed. Since nearly the entire game was created by the minds of the players, the position of art director was probably the most useless one imaginable. The doors of the SUV popped open, and two more people got out. Apeshit introduced them as Badword, the lead programmer, and Grody, the senior game play designer. Echo noticed that Grody's right hand was pinching deeply into his own ass. To play with hemorrhoids, he assumed. They approached him to shake hands, and Echo quickly waved hello to avoid doing so. The SUV sped away to park at another building.

Grody's comb-over fell into his face. He pushed it back into place without ever removing his right hand from his ass.

"Hi! Man, it's good to see a fan drop by. It's nice to know you guys are still out there!"

Badword folded his arms over his enlarged, food-stained belly. His voice squawked like a crow.

"I assume that you are here for some kind of tour?"

Apeshit answered for Echo.

"Fuck yeah, he is! He's come to pay his respects to the Gods, yo. We love our fucking fans, and we take care of them like family. Fuck, yeah! You're a lucky dude. Everybody is in town this week for planning. I'm gonna hook you up with the man!"

Grody smelled his fingers.

"Man, you are so lucky. Most fans don't get to meet the boss. He's too busy. Man, this is a guy who is so busy, he threw his phone away because he didn't have time to answer it."

"Fuck, yeah! I'm gonna hook you up, yo!"

Badword groaned. "Echo, right? Come on, let's get you inside. You can wait in the lobby. We don't have a receptionist anymore."

"That fucking lawsuit is still pending, too!" Apeshit snapped. "Women can be such cunts, yo. Know what I mean?"

Echo forced himself to smile. He had always envisioned *Conundrum* being spun out of a lab by scientists. He wondered why he had ever thought that. These people seemed to be part of the upper echelon of management, but they acted like immature frat boys. He walked with them, occasionally nodding or laughing at the garbage they spewed. It was possible they had all gone mad over the years. Though he suspected he was witnessing their true character. The front door to the lobby was made of thick ballistic glass with a reflective mirror coating. Echo's companions had some trouble remembering their passwords to open it. Badword admitted they had taken an excessive amount of pills at lunch, even by their standards. After a few minutes of fumbling about, Badword typed in some numbers, the lock disengaged, and the door opened, releasing a sudden gust of cool air from the lobby.

Apeshit pointed at a large glass desk where the receptionist used to sit and laughed. "Fuck. That's where I asked if I could smell her panties."

Badword shook his head at Apeshit. "Echo doesn't want to hear about that. He's a fan. He wants to hear about the game."

"It's a great story! It's so fucking funny, too."

Even Grody looked uncomfortable. "Man, Apeshit. Will you let it go? It's gross."

Apeshit clenched his fists. "Fuck it! Nobody around here has a sense of humor. I'm the fucking art director! Nobody appreciates anything I do. I made this game what it is. Fuck all of you, yo…except you, Echo. I un-fuck you. You're fucking all right in my book, but the rest of you can go fuck yourselves."

He clumped down the hallway. An armored door buzzed open. He stepped inside and was gone.

Badword shook his head again. "I'm sorry about that, Echo. He's moody. Look, you need to wait out here. We're not allowed to let anyone onto the production floor, for security reasons. There's some refreshments over by the awards case, and that orange chair still has some lumbar support if you want to sit down. I'll go speak to the boss. I'm sure he will be happy to spend some time with you."

He and Grody walked up to a different armored door. It buzzed. "It was nice to meet you, Echo. Have fun!"

Whatever was beyond the thick armored door was dark and cavernous. The door buzzed again and retracted. It closed shut with a loud clank. Echo was alone in the lobby. He meandered around inspecting the various things on display. Most of the lobby was filled with awards for *Conundrum*. In the largest awards case was a Nobel Peace Prize and an Emmy. He wondered how the game had gotten an Emmy. The refreshment stand next to it was loaded with pills and not much else. He picked up some *Conundrum*-branded bottled water, but when he read the label he saw it had been fortified with antidepressants meant to remind the drinker of the game's all-natural manna springs. He set it down and folded his arms, waiting.

A steel door next to the empty receptionist desk buzzed and clanked open. Echo turned to meet whomever would be walking out. No one came. He waited. Then suddenly, an unshaven stout man with badly dyed bleach-blond hair jogged out. He wore a dull shirt, an obnoxiously bright necktie, and faded stonewashed designer jeans.

"Sorry to keep you waiting, amigo! I'm Cuentista, the creative director of *Conundrum*. Welcome, welcome, welcome. What brings you here?"

The man spoke as if his words were an endless freight train barreling out of his mouth at full speed. Each sentence ran over the end of the previous one, crushing it under the weight of the next thought. He had a peculiar accent as if he had once come from somewhere else, but it was hard to place because his tone was so Americanized. He spoke so quickly, he barely had time to breathe his next breath. Echo offered to shake his hand. Cuentista threw up his arms suddenly.

"Hey there! Hold on! You know how many germs are passed through a handshake? I don't know about you, but I don't want to be sick for the next decade!"

Echo put his hand behind him. "My name is Echo, Echo Gain."

"A game name. I love it! What can I do you for?"

"I guess I was just interested in learning more about the game. I mean, I spent so much time playing."

"Came to see your enabler?"

"Enabler?"

"Your drug dealer! There is no sense in denying it anymore, right? We gave the world something to do…and the world gave us a Nobel Peace Prize. Too bad about Europe! Ha!"

"I never expected you to be so open about it."

"I have nothing to hide. What's there to hide anyway? The game is going to die like the rest of the world. We're just the sugar that helps the medicine go down."

He led Echo through the steel door to a flight of steps. As they climbed, Cuentista walked at an angle so that he could continue speaking while watching where he was going.

"There's a conference room up here. We used to use it when heads of state came to visit with a localization request. Did you know the Chinese wanted all their pills to be red? Ha! I'm kidding!"

Echo listened as the man steamrolled over his own words, not caring if what he said was understood.

"The room overlooks the whole studio. I'd take you inside, but the guys are working. I know you didn't come here to see pasty pale people chained to rows of cubicles in a dark room, right? You came for answers! You're not the first. I don't think you will be the last, either. I have answers…and I'm going to be blunt with you: To lie anymore is just a waste of your time, and of my time. Who knows how much time we actually have anymore? Ha! And it doesn't matter! Nothing matters anymore! Nothing at all!"

At the top of the stairs was a short hall lined with closed metal doors. At the end was a double-wide door made of polished wild tambran. Cuentista picked a plastic dongle off his belt. He swiped it over a metal square on the double-wide door, where the handle would ordinarily be. The door buzzed, clicked twice, and swung open automatically.

Cuentista watched it with a smile. "You should have seen this place a hundred years ago. Armed dogs with guards patrolled the parking lot…or was it the other way around? You had to get frisked by two different guys every time you entered the building. Turn your head and cough…hello there, doctor! Ha! All in the name of national security. Government couldn't afford to build spaceships, but they could waste money making sure a building full of pasty geeks was well protected! God bless America!"

Cuentista walked into the conference room. He suddenly turned and blocked Echo from entering.

"You know they wanted to build spaceships, like for real. They told me once—I think it was the secretary of defense, or somebody—they couldn't build them. Our technology was too primitive. Guess we should have been developing better rockets instead of faster graphics cards. Ha! But then…I don't know…we did send people to the moon once using our primitive technology. Personally, I think it's an aversion to hard work that kept us grounded. Who likes math, right?"

He gestured to a chair. "Here! Sit down. Have a seat. Relax. Take a load off!"

The conference room was large and smelled strongly of uncapped markers. An unusually thick glossy black conference table dominated the room. On one side of the room the entire wall was a whiteboard, and on the other side were windows overlooking the whole studio. Very few people were working on the floor below. Rows upon rows of countless small cubicles filled the space packed together like cells in a beehive. It was dark except for a few dim lights and glowing computer monitors. A few desks had Christmas lights blinking on them. Most desks were covered with assorted amounts of clutter ranging from toys to pornography to empty soda cans. A line of waste bins in the corner overflowed with discarded junk food. On the far end was a group of well-used cots lined up against a blue-violet tinted window. It reminded Echo of a homeless shelter.

"Do people live here?"

"Well, the game doesn't run itself, right?" Cuentista smiled. "Have a seat. For God's sake man, sit! These are Hermann Miller chairs…the best…great for your back…and your ass, for that matter!"

Echo sat down in one of the chairs at the table. Cuentista opened a panel in the wall and took out a tray full of refreshments. He set it down on the table in front of Echo and enthusiastically motioned for him to enjoy himself.

Cuentista gathered a group of colored markers from the lip of the whiteboard and began to draw as he spoke. At first it appeared as though he was creating a diagram; however, it quickly became clear that whatever he was drawing was completely incomprehensible.

"America is a culture that worships the ideal and idea of celebrity. Wait, let me back up!" He erased the whiteboard and started over. "Our lives—I don't mean yours and mine—or yours in particular, okay? Our lives are, by default, mundane experiences. Most people are born into situations they have no control over. Born into poverty, disease, poor education, etcetera. Of course there are other people who are born into great opportunity who waste it. Life is what you make of it, and most people don't make much of it. But many people want to; that is the key—they *want* to. As long as they *want* to, you can work with that. You can turn that intangible 'want' into motivation to do things, buy things. You can tell people that such-and-such car will give them the luxury they deserve and make *them* feel like such-and-such celebrity of the moment."

Cuentista poured himself some water in a glass, spilling most of it on the floor. He tried to rub the spill away with his foot. He continued.

"Where was I? America is a culture that worships the ideal and the idea of being a celebrity. Here are these people who can do those things you always wanted to do, or maybe even things you can never do… like a three-way with a donkey and not get arrested! Ha! I don't know, right?"

He paused for a moment to sip some water. He looked over the mess of lines and shapes he had drawn and began to color them in.

"One day I had this idea: What if there was a video game that allowed everyone to be famous? On paper it sounded crazy, but it was a start.

It took years, and what we basically built was a social echo chamber that amplified multimedia network connections to ear-bleeding levels of insanity! Okay, you have games, right? Then you have social networks. Then you have both in a big cloud. But what they did not have was everything else. It used to be that social connections fed into a virtual lifestyle experience. On this website you see this funny video, so you're going to share it with friends. If enough people share it, and it becomes popular, we call it viral. Ha! Up until our game came along, socializing through the Internet meant people popularizing their own interests through connections. And with that, they promoted themselves. They felt important. Their identity was made up of the sum total of all that stuff. So, what we did was, we took all of that—not to become another part of your life—no—we engineered the game to be your *entire* life. Your whole life. We surgically implanted the game into the center of everything you thought you knew. Instead of supporting fringe interests that grew into more popular interests—or sharing them—we became the source. We made ourselves the beginning and end of popular discourse. We became the structure of society itself!"

Cuentista stepped back from the whiteboard to observe what he had made. None of it made sense. Then he drew a single line through all the shapes and objects connecting them together. The mess suddenly resembled a small village. He began filling the village with little stick people.

"Anybody can be anybody. But if you want to be *somebody,* you need to play *Conundrum*. Ha! We can't take all the credit. We were popular when we launched, but it was the government and the drug companies that made us epic. Apparently they had pitched their idea to a couple of game companies and were rejected on various 'moral' reasons. Ha! Morality! They came to us and said, 'We can make pills that will make the game more real than anything life has to offer.' We were greedy fucks back then. Hell, we are greedy fucks right now! Ha! We took the money, we took the pills, we took over the whole goddamn world. I know, I know, only an asshole would brag about getting hundreds of millions of people addicted to a video game. But let's look at it from the perspective of a player. It's like waiting in line. Nobody wants to wait in line. Everyone wants to be first. Better yet, they want to be treated special. A register is going to open just for them! Again, like a celebrity—important self-importance! Me, me, me, me. It's all about me. Don't kid yourself that people are not selfish. Being selfish is how you make money. How many rich, honest men do you know? Ha! None! Only the best liars date the pretty girls! It's a *me* society, and we catered to that. The only reason to talk to somebody is to tell them something. And the only reason to tell anyone anything is if you benefit from the interaction!"

He began to draw hearts and happy faces floating in the sky above the village.

"You can have it all in *Conundrum*. You can be beautiful. You can be unique. You can be pampered. Hell, you can even have sex! I had to ban those sex pills from the studio. Good God, you wouldn't believe the mess. Ha! Where was I?"

Echo was baffled. "I just don't know if I entirely get what you're saying. I mean, I understand it, but I guess it just sounds nuts."

"Why? You enjoyed the game. Don't tell me you didn't."

"Yeah, I played it all the time."

"You even changed your name to be the name of the avatar you played, right?"

"Everybody did that, even people who never played."

"It was the thing to do, wasn't it? We started that trend. I remember reading books about secret governments and conspiracies. I remember thinking, Damn! I wish I could be one of those guys. Maybe I need to be more direct and simple so you can comprehend what we did here. *Conundrum* was not designed to just be a game or a social networking cloud. It was designed to be your best friend and God. God was our greatest competition. Religion was at the center of people's lives. It wasn't easy to get that kind of fanatical trust…but we did. We became the center of hearts, minds, and culture. We were everywhere, like God was supposed to be…only we really existed! Imagine what people would do if God spoke to them?"

Echo sighed. "Anything?"

"That's right! Ha! We were never that direct. But the social engineering we performed was on an unprecedented scale. We had the army psyops in here plotting out future social trends. As long as people thought it was their own idea, we could make anything popular. Through simple psychotropic viral messaging we could suggest things…convince people to do things…introduce new ideas. Even an idea like…suicide."

Echo scoffed. "I bet you think I'll just sit here and believe whatever you tell me, don't you?"

"Ha! I like you. You think for yourself. It's good to be smart when the herd charges toward a cliff. It might just save your life to think differently!"

He took another sip of water.

"We collect tons of data from every player. One day we noticed we had a group of players that popped a lot of pills, whose activities were simple, predictable…and communicated through truncated catch phrases. We told these players we were recruiting them for…something or other. Ha! I can't even remember anymore. But we told them they would be given an exclusive new pill to try. Exclusive equals celebrity equals self-specialness importance. Basically, we gave them a pill that killed them dead. Two or three seconds flat. About as much pain as pooping. And they took it willingly! Then it was simply a matter of running an algorithm that duplicated their personas. Ha! Over half the game is full of fake people now. And business is better than ever! If I was philosophical, I'd have to wonder what that means. But I'm not, so who cares?"

Echo shook his head in disgust, not believing any of it. "You're crazy."

"Everyone is crazy. Anyone who claims to be sane is lying!"

"I meant you're out of you mind—you're out of your fucking mind."

Cuentista looked a little irritated.

"You ever wonder why there are so few people near the event horizon? The government said they were migrating the population toward the West Coast, but if you think about it, there should be millions and millions of people crammed together. There should be refugee camps. There should be food shortages, water shortages, sky-high piles of shit. But there aren't. There are two things nobody ever seems to think much about. One, that there is not logistically enough stuff left to live on for thousands of years. Two, that guy I used to know online is not that talkative anymore! Ha! We had so many people playing the game that we were actually able to control a substantial portion of this country's population. You could say we cared enough to not let people die by whatever horrible fate awaited in the abyss. Or you could say we killed these people in order to maintain a realistic balance of the population."

"That's sick. I mean, you're saying the whole game is about population control."

"Better to let people die happy than starve to death under a rule of anarchy in overcrowded ghettos. We all have to make hard choices."

"How can you talk about choice? You tricked people into killing themselves. They had no choice; you made it for them."

"Ha! That's why you have a government...to make these choices for you. If we left it up to individuals, they would always choose themselves first, at the expense of everyone around them. The generation of self-sacrifice is long past. The generation of today truly believes that they are individuals of significant special importance. When they are not. We are all sheep...every last one of us. So, anyway, that's how I was able to buy three houses and a yacht."

Cuentista set the markers down and picked up the tray full of refreshments.

"Danish? They are fresh. Or as fresh as things get anymore! Ha!"

Echo could not think of anything to say. His mind was overloaded. "I can't believe this. I feel, I feel disturbed."

"Just stop it. Stop thinking that way. This is old hat to us now. We had all the liberal idealistic debates ages ago. The real fantasy is that we could crowd an entire nation into California under a rainbow and sing songs together...cataclysmic bullshit. This is how it is. The world is ending. Besides, we don't make anyone take the pills. We just make it popular to take the pills, and the people do the rest. Drugs have never been hard to push. People seek pleasure, fame, and money...and we offered all of that…artificially. But it's close enough to the real thing. Closer than the average person will ever experience."

Echo let out a deep breath. "I was never into the pills."

"Interesting…" Cuentista walked over to the window overlooking the studio. "So you liked the game by itself? Just vanilla?"

"I guess I always thought it was fun because of the other people who played."

"The game was good, but never that good. The pills and unlimited government funding were our tipping point. We had the resources to duplicate, rip off, and outproduce our rivals. But it was really the exclusivity of the pills that allowed us to dominate the market. It's just interesting that you liked the actual game." Cuentista smirked thinking about it. "Did I tell you I used to be a school teacher? Ha!"

Echo sat in his chair, exhausted and traumatized from the alleged purpose of the game. In the end, he realized that he had spent centuries in an empty room, alone, engaged in a fantasy built to control him. He was more disgusted with himself than ever. Even if people knew of the murderous intent of the game, it would never stop them from playing. Not now, not when there was so little else to live for. He felt empty. Far emptier than he had before. The world was sick, and it deserved to die.

Just then there was a knock at the door. Two large security guards dressed in gray uniforms and sunglasses were standing at the entrance of the conference room.

"Sir?" barked one of them. "We heard yelling. Is everything all right, sir?"

Cuentista laughed.

"Fine. Fine! Ha! Sometimes I just get too excited! Gentlemen, this is today's tourist, Echo. Echo, Security…Security, Echo."

"Sir, we've been looking for you because you missed that conference call to Seattle."

Cuentista's face soured.

"Hard to believe they are planning to launch a new operating system in this market. Ha! I'm pretty sure it's ego driven. I need to call them back. As soon I can get this wrapped up, I can move to Santa Monica and set sail on my new yacht. Have to hurry, too. The ocean is draining a foot a year!"

Echo shook off his melancholy. "Draining? How can that be?"

Cuentista jumped excitedly.

"It's draining into that big hole that's eating the world! Not much time left. Ha! Time! Better buy yourself a good jacket! Speaking of which—"

He turned to the security guards at the door.

"Gentlemen, take Echo down to the showroom, and let him have anything he wants. Even the washing machine! It's a treasure vault, Echo! Filled with riches. Feast, my friend! Feast!"

Echo could not believe Cuentista could so casually offer him the spoils of mass murder. Everything in the building had been built off the deaths of millions. Even if there was an insane logic to why the game existed, it did not mean Echo had to like it. He hated the self-righteous attitude. He hated Cuentista's speedy neurotic way of talking. He hated how this monster had justified what he had done. He hated how the world had bought into it. He hated himself for joining in. He stood up, angry at this asshole. At this murderer.

"How could I possibly take anything from this place? You profited off the deaths of innocent people! Have you no conscience?"

Cuentista's smile immediately faded. "I don't like the tone of your voice. I don't think you fully appreciate what we did for this country. Or for humanity! We're heroes!"

Echo kicked the chair aside and yelled, "You goddamn fucking asshole shit douche bag motherfucker!"

The two security guards were on him in an instant. They were very strong, and Echo knew he had no chance. They swept him up off his feet and rushed him out the door. Echo continued to yell as he fought them.

"I believed in this game! I gave my life up for this game!"

Cuentista grinned as he followed the group down to the lobby. "I really wish we could have been friends. I thought you were cool. But now you get nothing. You get to be thrown out on your ass like a fool. And for what? For a few curse words? Ha! I built a kingdom; what did you do? Nothing! Just like everyone else! Another pathetic morsel who thinks that just because he can think a thought different from the rest, *that* makes him somebody. But you're not…you're nothing…a big fat zero!"

Cuentista watched as they sped Echo through the lobby. He laughed. "You know, sometimes that front door sticks. Just remember to push real hard!"

Echo barely felt it when he hit the ground.

CHAPTER 15

FLYOVER COUNTRY

Echo had driven aimlessly for weeks, disillusioned and bitter. He was somewhere close to Colorado again. At least he thought he was. He crawled through overgrown sun-baked grass up a hill carrying his binoculars and wearing a camouflaged boonie hat. He pulled the hat down low over his eyes and peeked through the grass to get a better look at the fortress below him. It was a Costco, and it sat in the middle of a parking lot like an island citadel surrounded by a paved lagoon. Echo made sure to keep a low profile. He held a piece of cardboard over the side of the binoculars facing the sun to prevent creating any reflection that would draw unwanted attention to himself. The Audi was hidden in the service garage of a gas station behind him. No one used gas stations anymore, so he figured it was safe. He focused the binoculars.

The megastore had been fortified as if to guard from an invasion. Overturned cars were positioned around it to form a wall, and upended truck trailers had been converted into guard towers at each corner. Piles of tires formed a secondary wall around the main building. Behind them were several tool sheds with smoke pouring out of them. He could smell hickory and guessed they might be smokehouses. It was not unusual to see people overindulging in things that brought them comfort. He could see a posse of overweight men patrolling the perimeter on riding lawnmowers armed with what appeared to be sharpened golf clubs and hunting rifles. The whole scene might have been comical if it were not for the real danger these kinds of people represented.

"When you think of the phrase 'post-apocalyptic,' this is exactly what comes to mind," Echo said to himself. He said this to comfort his own nerves. The worst-case scenario was always running into human beings who preyed on other human beings for no other reason than to feel in control of something amid all the chaos.

This was not the first time Echo had seen a megastore fortress. He usually ran across them near small towns a couple of miles away from the highway, where the absence of police had created a vacuum of authority. They were uncommon enough that Echo would stop to observe them when he had the chance. Watching them felt exciting; it was the same kind of excitement that he felt watching wild animals from a distance. It was dangerous, but profoundly interesting.

People had all the time in the world to build elaborate fortresses, but few had the audacity to do so. Some forts had declared themselves sovereign nations. In the past he had even seen goofy homemade flags with bizarre country names usually based off some popular space fantasy or obscure religion. He could understand why they built these things. It was to feel secure and empowered. He could understand them, but he could never be one of them. These were people who had gone off the deep end. They ran their own segregated societies that were cult-like and fanatically xenophobic. He never ventured too close to a fortress because of the stories he had heard about them. If he were to approach the fort, he knew he would risk his car, along with the rest of his things, being stolen. He could be interrogated for no reason other than hateful paranoia, and be told to convert or be kicked out into the wilderness, naked.

It was easy to say that such criminal acts would never happen, but they did. The world was ending, and people were scared. Although, by world-ending standards, people were living through it in general comfort. They had food, electricity, water, plenty of pills, and even periodic garbage pick-up, courtesy of the National Guard. Why were there forts? What reason had they to build such things? Were they that afraid? He had heard the weak argument that many of them built fortresses out of self-defense. To defend against what, though? Monsters? Zombies? Aliens? Pagans? Liberals? Hollywood had perpetuated the myth that human beings would always rally together for grand causes…that when the chips were down everyone would put aside differences to help one another. It was a lie.

Echo set the binoculars down, thinking, "We are, by nature, opportunists. We celebrate the agony of others if it means we can avoid such misery ourselves."

He rolled over onto his back. The sun was hot. He wondered if the moon was still up there. Had it been affected by whatever was happening? Was it the cause? He thought he had seen the moon once, between the waves in the sky. He never saw it again. He wondered what the planet must look like from outer space at this point. He wondered why the aliens had not come to save them. Maybe there were no aliens. Maybe it was because Earthlings were not worth saving. It would be like saving ants off a sidewalk. Why bother? He could hear the sound of the riding lawnmowers drawing close to the hill. They were such animals, just like a pack of dogs. He crawled down the safe side of the hill, grinning at the thought that he too was no better than an animal. He remembered the turtle. He wondered where it had been going.

He stumbled for a moment. He felt something on his forehead. It was pressure, like a thumb between his eyes, pressing hard. He could feel the sudden pull of it on his body, and at once he knew what it was.

"No, it can't be. It's too soon for another one," he said out loud.

He complained, knowing the rules of the world were broken. He felt it again, as if he were being pulled into another room by unseen hands. It was a rubber band. He could not allow himself to snap back while out in the open. He had no idea how long he would be gone and risked being found by the lawnmower militia. The last thing he wanted was to wake up surrounded by those men.

He felt immediately tired and struggled to keep walking. He had to get inside. He had to hide. He could feel his mind going; things were very far away now. The darkness crept in around his eyes like a swarm of gnats clouding his vision. It felt as if he were being drawn away, as if he were being siphoned from the world. He had no choice. He had to hurry.

He fell and caught himself. It felt as if he had stopped himself from falling *through* the ground. The sensation was overwhelming. With each step, he fell, and with each step after that, he fell farther. He dragged himself to the garage entrance, stood up, and closed the garage door. He could not feel anything now. It was as if the ground were no longer there. He stumbled into his car. His body wanted to lie still and sleep. He told his arm to yank the car door closed. *Clump!* It slammed shut. He slumped over the center console and fell into another time and place.

CHAPTER 16

THE WHITE ROOM

———

Echo found himself in a white room about the size of a two-car garage. Bright white light glowed out of recessed slivers on an otherwise unbroken ivory ceiling. There were no windows. A sizable Persian rug lay in the middle of the room, bordered by an indigo leather couch, a wooden park bench, and two steel folding chairs. A tall black door stood in one corner of the room. It lacked a handle and had a glowing red light embedded into it, suggesting it was locked. He could not remember ever trying to open it.

He sat on the park bench in the room, holding his head in his hands, waiting for his mind to fully arrive. His mouth had the familiar nine-volt battery flavor he had never gotten used to. The room carried a slight hint of artificial lemon in the air, as if it had been cleaned not long ago. He knew where he was because he had been in the white room many times before. But he had no idea when it was or how he had gotten into the room in the first place. It was the same for the three other people who always shared the room with him. He had only ever met them in the room, and as far as he knew, he had never known any of them in person. After spending so much time with each other in the room over the years, they had become friends, more or less.

As his head cleared, he glanced around, feeling a sudden positive energy at the sight of these three again. There was a man in his later years with tight curly gray hair, a pronounced nose, and a scowl that he had used so often, it had become permanently etched into his face. He went by the name Cogito. Across from him was an obese man whose true face had become almost entirely lost in fat. He was Friskybiscuit, and he clapped his hands together as he plopped down on the couch like an excited child dropping into a pool. Finally, there was Cayenne, a pale young woman with dark-rimmed glasses and messy jet-black hair. She looked at Echo and smirked. All he had ever been able to do was return a sheepish grin. That was the extent of his relationship with her, and it was the most successful one he had ever had with a woman.

"Oh, that's just great." Cayenne pouted looking at the white hospital scrubs she was now dressed in. "I can't stand these awful clothes!"

Her voice was small, intelligently quick, with a hint of nervousness, like a rabbit. Her complaints were valid, but they were all stuck wearing the same thing.

Cayenne seemed to always be the one who started the conversations they had here. The room was immediately filled with the same old comments they always made about their predicament. Why was there a park bench? Has anybody looked under the rug to see if anything was there? Why are we all dressed like doctors? Are we patients? Why are these slippers I'm wearing so small? Why are they suede? And on it went until everyone had a say. They never said hello to one another. There was something about the place that felt impersonal. Even though they all knew each other, they were still strangers. It had become the only place Echo felt he could let his guard down.

Friskybiscuit vigorously rubbed his bald head. "Well, I'm dead. *Doot.* Just like that. Just thought you guys should know."

Everyone was shocked. His usual easygoing onomatopoeia-flavored childlike tone had delivered the news with the same dauntless grin he always seemed to have.

"Yeah, heart attack. *Beep beep—eeeee.* But it was quick."

Cayenne put her thumb to her mouth and chewed on her nail.

"That's morbid!" Then she asked a little more quietly, "Did it hurt much?"

Friskybiscuit shrugged, smiling again. "Nope. Nothing. Like a light turned off, *click.* Then I'm here, *click*, light turned on."

He struggled as he thought about it more. "I'm not sure how long ago it happened. I guess I know that time has passed. But I don't know how I know that."

Cayenne sat down on the far side of the couch across from Friskybiscuit. She folded her legs up, compacting herself into a tight ball.

"This has to be a rubber band, right? I mean, if time is linear and all that, the only way to see a dead person again is to go back in the past. Or do you think it's something else? Something we haven't ever thought of?"

Cogito stood against the wall with his back toward them. "Hey, who gives a fuck what it is!" he shouted suddenly.

His voice was sharp as a knife. He used his wit to cut his way through anything he believed was nonsense, and he was the type who believed everything was nonsense.

As usual, Echo mediated. "That's a little hostile, don't you think?"

"Hey, I don't." Cogito spun around pointing his finger. "You can't take this…this whatever the fuck it is, for granted any longer. There is no guarantee we will meet again after this one."

"What makes you say that?" Echo asked.

"Hey, maybe because I'm dead, and we already know he's dead, too."

Friskybiscuit was stunned. "You're dead? *Dum-dum-dum-dum!*" he hummed dramatically. "When did that happen?"

Cogito coughed, reached in his shirt pocket, and pulled out a cigarette.

"Hey, it was cancer…lung cancer." He looked at the cigarette wondering how it had ended up in his pocket. "It was the cigarettes. The cancer killed me in three hours. Goddamn time bullshit. Doctor gave me some pills and told me I had at least six hundred years!"

Cogito discovered a lighter in his pants pocket and used it to light the cigarette.

"It hit me hard. But, hey, I knew I had killed myself…" He looked at Cayenne. "At least it was me who decided I should die. Still a hell of a lot better than being in the military, where they tell you to die, and you die. Hey, a fuck's luck, right? People's lives come at wholesale prices, isn't that right, darling?"

Cayenne thinned her eyes. "Oh, why do you always have to be such an asshole?"

Cogito blew smoke out his nostrils. "What kind of doctoress paints her nails black and chews them? Huh? Hey, I never believed for an instant you were what you said you were. You're a pretty little liar. Completely full of shit."

Cayenne rolled her eyes and pouted furiously.

Echo held his hand up as if stopping traffic. "Just settle down. There's no need for that."

"Hey, here we go. You always jump to her defense. You always do. She never told us her real name. She's never told us much of anything about herself. She always just sits there listening. Goddamn it, Echo, you don't even know who she is."

"I don't really know who any of you actually are."

"Bullshit! Hey, if you added up all the times we've been here together over the last hundred years or so, it would amount to...to..." Cogito felt the wind leaving his sails as he struggled to figure out how much time they had spent together. He sighed and let his anger subside.

"Goddamn it, I've spent more time here than any fishing trip I've ever been on. At least I think I have."

"That's just it though, isn't it? Did we ever figure out when this is? This is the only rubber band that I snap back to over and over again, but it's never the same. Each time I'm here, it's new and different, like I'm experiencing it for the first time."

Echo eyed Cayenne. She noticed, and her mood lightened.

Friskybiscuit grinned. "*Presto chango!* Maybe it's just magic?"

Cogito snorted. "Hey, if you believe in that shit, you may as well break out the tarot cards and burn some sage, for fuck's sake."

Cayenne stopped chewing her nail and tucked her arms inside her shirt. "I really hate to admit this, but I think Cogito is right this time."

"I am? Well, hey, how about that! About what exactly? About before when I called you a pretty liar? Hey, guess what? You still are!"

"You are so impossible! I meant about us not wasting the time we have. Sheesh! Oh, which, by the way, is exactly what we are doing right now…blabbing."

"Huh…" Cogito relaxed his shoulders a little and sat down on a folding chair far from the others, near a sliver in the wall that drew the smoke out of the room.

Cayenne turned to Echo. "So…how's the depression been?"

Echo always felt uncomfortable when she asked him that. "Not good. I sleep a lot. I'm tired all the time anymore. I, I know I'm depressed. I can feel it constantly."

Cogito had no sympathy. "Take some of those pills. Hey, I hear you can see colors you never thought possible. Why, you could be the first to name some of them!"

Cayenne scoffed at the suggestion. "Oh, come on! For real? Advice from a man who killed himself with a chronic addiction? Oh, please!"

"Hey! Hey! Hey! That wasn't advice, pretty girl, that was fact. You take pills to get better. If you don't take them, you die." He violently sucked on the cigarette. "And, hey! Let me tell you something about advice. Advice is so often given by those who have no intention of doing what they recommend. Advice is formulated from a perspective, filtered through an opinion that is upheld through arbitrary ideals, which proliferate the core of the advisor. Therein, any advice is merely the projection of what the advisor thinks is correct and not necessarily what is best for the advisee. All advice is bad advice, and the only response that can be made to any advice is: "Go to hell," and sometimes, "Fuck off."

"Really? *Really?* I mean, who talks that way anyway? Who?"

"I talk that way, girl. But, hey, why don't you tell me to my face what you truly think? Huh? But you won't, will you?"

Cogito growled and turned toward Echo.

"All women talk shit behind your back; it's what they do. Hey, it's really no different from men talking about what a great ass a girl has behind her back, or how fat her ass is, and how it looks like a bag full of potatoes you want to punch," Cogito said as he looked at the cigarette he had been smoking with disgust. He bent it in half and pushed it into his mouth. He started to chew angrily. He winced from the chemicals leeching into his gums.

"Sex. You don't need to fear that, either. It's a biological need; that's why you want it, because the body wants it. There is no love. That's just a word that describes dopamine released in your brain. Love is just a lie perpetuated by fucking advertising agencies intent on selling you a fantasy that can only be achieved through buying diamonds, birthday cards, and cars."

"You're a horrid man!" Cayenne shouted, hiding her head in her arms.

"Enough!" Echo yelled. "Everyone, just chill out."

But Cogito had just begun. "Hey! Hey! Hey! You don't get what I'm trying to say at all, do you? Everything has changed. Women are harder to figure out than ever. They used to have a gut feeling for what they wanted, and that was driven by the latent desire to have a baby. But they can't do that anymore, can they? Hey, they are just as lost as the rest of us. I guess what I'm trying to say is…" He let out a deep breath. "All that's left anymore is companionship, and that's never perfect, but it's something, and that's what you should look for—somebody to talk to, especially when all of us are gone." He licked flakes of tobacco off his teeth. "Hey, it's always easier to be alone, but it's no way to live. That's how I died. Alone. Don't be me, Echo. I made a lot of bad choices."

Echo put his head in his hands again remembering what a fool he had been with Ashley. How could he even begin to trust anyone? People had always let him down. They betrayed him. He glanced up at Cayenne. Her head was tucked down in her arms. She was still angry at Cogito. He hated how looking at her evoked a strange warmth within him. He knew nothing about her, and he knew he projected what he wished she was on the blank slate she provided. He hated himself for that, and in some ways he hated her.

The room was quiet, as if the life had been drained out of it. Friskybiscuit looked around at everyone. He could see they were all unhappy, but he had run out of good jokes to tell. The longer everyone was quiet, the more anxious he felt. He took a deep breath, held it long enough to feel his anxiety, then let it out. He did it once more. Echo turned his head and grinned.

"Breathing exercises?" he asked.

"*Doot!* The same thing I taught you. Helps with stress, anger, sadness, and anxiety. You just breathe in the sunny ions, *tra-la-la!* Then breathe out the tar, *blah!* Breathe in the sunny ions, breathe out the tar. Everyone should try it. It's calming. Puts things in perspective. *Whoosh.* Clears the head so you're open to positive thoughts. It's something Cogito should try. He seems to spew out tar every time he talks."

"Well…" Echo grinned again. "He *is* a smoker."

"*Boo-hoo.* That's no excuse." The pun had flown right over Friskybiscuit's head.

Cogito listened as he chewed his cigarette.

"Hey, it's hard to be positive when I'm fucking dead. Think about it. Breathing deeply is only going to make me more depressed than I already am. It just reminds me too much of how I died."

Friskybiscuit tried to put a positive spin on things. "Maybe you're not dead; maybe it's something else. Something *lah-de-dah* magical."

"Hey, trust me, I died. I remember every minute of dying and every regret that crossed my goddamn mind during it. Rest assured, I'm dead."

"But here you are. *Doot.* See? You and me. Somehow we still exist, right?"

"Existence is overrated," Cogito growled, growing angry again. "Existence is a never-ending trauma of the unexplained. Things happen. Hey, you don't know why, and nobody can explain it. Fate. Destiny. Horseshit. You can run with the excuses of religion: '*It's what God intended…It's all part of God's plan.*' Again, horseshit. If I told you life was just a series of random events without logical order, that's a fucking scary idea. If you knew you only lived once, one time only, would you live life differently? How strange it would be not to have the crutch of everlasting life or reincarnation to fall back on when you faced the possibility of dying. People, Americans specifically, treat each other bad, without respect, because of a culture of forgiveness by God, and a, quote, *better* life after death. It's why goddamn assholes sit at home watching TV or play video games instead of planting gardens, raising children, and finding ways to enjoy doing math…" He paused, his brow raised. "Hey, does anybody here even remember what I'm talking about? I am so far off the fucking track, I don't even remember what my point was."

Cayenne's head snapped up out of her ball. "Your whole point is that there is no point to life or anything at all. You just live."

Echo rubbed his forehead, desperate to change the subject. "I met a guy once who called everyone he met 'asshole.' It wasn't because he didn't like people; it was because it was easier than learning everyone's name."

Cogito chewed voraciously. "Hey! That's me, isn't it? I used to do that."

"Oh, for heaven's sake!" Cayenne blurted out. "This is about entropy! I mean, you do realize that, right?"

Cogito threw up his hands. "Let's hear it, science girl. Hey, don't hold back those pretty thoughts. Just go head and put it all out there again, so we can pretend we are learning something new."

"Grrr! Can't you just listen for once? Think about it. We are supposed to be moving toward entropy. I don't mean the abyss, I mean universal entropy. See, as we age, we go from being in an orderly state to a more chaotic state. Our cells become more disorderly with each division. They lose parts of their genetic programming, causing mutations and stuff. That's why I can see hairs growing out of Cogito's old-man ears. Those things don't belong there! It's chaos."

Cogito chewed. "Is chaos making gray hairs grow on my nuts, too?"

Echo shot a look at Cogito. "You've had plenty of time to speak. Go ahead, Cayenne."

She looked irritated. "Thanks." She paused to make sure she was not going to be interrupted.

"I guess, when I think about it, it's not about time; it's about us. See, the natural order of things is to progress from order to chaos. The progression from start to finish, from young to old—from orderly to chaotic—is how we measure time. In our universe things only move from order to chaos, they don't move from chaos to order. It's always one direction, so it's called 'the arrow of time.' Okay? But, with the abyss, the arrow is broken. It's like the momentum of time has stopped. Like time has more than one direction now. Or maybe even no direction at all. That's why we can live, but not grow old, get sick and die in just a few hours, and relive moments of our lives we should have only lived through once. We should all be moving forward in time, except we're not." She thought about it some more. "I feel like we are caught in the middle between order and chaos, and all there is, is…chaos. I think that's become some kind of advantage for us. Somehow we are surviving something we shouldn't even be able to perceive. All this should be totally beyond our ability to understand. But somehow we are living through it. I mean, it's like, we've been set free, and anything is possible now."

Echo half-laughed. "That's a pretty crazy theory, Cayenne, even for you."

Cayenne seemed unsure of herself. "Was it? I really didn't mean to sound crazy." She sighed. "Oh, I don't know, I really don't. I just wonder if there is more to all this. I mean with what's happening. I keep wondering if there is something more I could do, or should be doing, instead of just passively riding along until the end."

Friskybiscuit clasped his hands together. "It's judgment day. That's what people have been saying since the beginning. That's why this day never ends. Science has always tried to beat down religion. But, *ka-pow,* religion fought back. Observation, that's what science is based on. *Doot.* Seeing is believing. *Doot.* Facts. *Doot.* Papers. *Doot.* All flushed away now. *Whoosh.* Let's face it, nothing makes sense anymore, no matter how much you want it to. The only thing left is faith. Think about it. All this time we have, just waiting. It's purgatory. It has to be. You need to use this time to reflect on your person and make amends."

Cogito sneered. "Hey, I wish I had gone to your church sometimes. Wow, goddamn. Hey, then other times I don't give a flying shit! You know there was a guy who painted a wall to see how long the paint would take to dry. Turned out that sometimes the wall was wet, sometimes the wall was dry, but it was never only one or the other for more than an hour. There are two ways to handle that. You can go nuts and drink the paint, or you can accept it, even though you can't explain it."

Friskybiscuit smiled. "*Doot!* That sounds like an argument for God."

Cogito growled. "Hey, it ain't! See, Echo, you're a creative person, and that means you think with an open mind. New things don't bother you so much. You're open to new ideas, open to adjusting your perception of reality. Most people have closed minds." He glared at Friskybiscuit. "Their door is shut. They see the world one way and only one way. Nothing can change that. When something disrupts their perception of reality, they get scared. That's why all those holy religious types went mad early on and killed themselves. Hey, no offense, Friskybiscuit, but people like you worry me."

"*Doot-dah-doo!* I think that's the nicest thing you've ever said about Echo."

Cogito was disgusted. He chewed his cigarette, lost in his own thought process. "It strikes me that people tend to affix beliefs and labels to themselves in order to create an identity. They want to be somebody, so they either create some fantasy or adopt one created by someone else, and that becomes who they are. Hey, I am a such-and-such because I define my life around so-and-so. Total ignorance. But we conditioned ourselves to these ideas. Then this whole end-of-the-world deal happened. It robbed people of their identity. It over-whelmed our culture, fractured the herd, and people drove them-selves crazy with fear and hysteria that they brought on themselves. Hey, there is nothing to fear but fear itself, right? But it's true. Hey, Echo, every time I've met you, you said you were afraid of something. It was always something this, something that, but the sum of all that fear is driven by one thing. It's always one root thing. Did you ever figure that one thing out?"

Echo hated being put on the spot. "I think there is no fucking point to anything anymore! Everywhere I go things are falling apart. Every person I meet is fraught with despair. I just drive around aimlessly look-ing for anything and always finding nothing. I keep asking myself how I can escape this. And I know that I can't. I don't even know why I bother."

Cogito handed Echo a cigarette. "Hey, so, kill yourself. You just want to fucking give up? Why? Over what? Huh?"

They waited to see if Echo would take the cigarette from Cogito. He turned his head away from the offer, slumping his shoulders.

"Awww," said Cayenne. "You always project tons of existential emptiness. I think it's kinda cute."

Echo felt his heart skip a beat the moment she said he was cute. He wanted to believe no one could see his feelings, but he knew his thoughts were easily read on his face. He quickly hid his reaction behind a wall of resentment.

"Cayenne," he sighed, "I don't get why you say things like that to me."

"Oh, come on!" she teased. "You need to cheer up. Don't be that way. Things are messed up, but it's an exciting time to live. Just think about what you are living through! How can you be so bitter when so many cool things are happening around you?" Then she realized something. "You're not dwelling over unrequited love, are you?"

"Look, I don't want to talk about it. It doesn't matter anyway," he said, feeling embarrassed in front of her.

"Sheesh. You just can't run away from your problems like that, Echo. Eventually they catch up to you. Trust me, I've been there."

"It's worked out fine so far," he told her curtly.

"All I said was that I thought you were cute, and you crawled right back into your shell. You're such a nice guy, too. You never ever seem happy when I see you, and that makes me sad."

Sometimes Cayenne really touched a nerve inside him.

"Let's think about that for a second. Every time you've seen me, we've been right here. That amounts to what? A day of my life? Two days? Three at the most? You don't know me at all. You don't. You don't even know when or where 'here' is. I've never been here before. I know I'm not here now, so this has to be some inevitable future."

"Oh, come on. Nobody snaps into the future, and you know that. It's impossible," Cayenne said as if convincing herself.

Echo was frustrated by the way she answered. "You just gave us this whole spiel about how anything is possible now. So I ask you, why not?"

"Because you just can't snap to a memory before you can even remember it."

"Hey! Hey! Hey!" Cogito jumped in. "So what the hell is this?"

"Here is now," she said.

Echo felt tired and rubbed his face. "Can't 'now' be defined as the amount of time it takes to think a thought in the present? That's like a couple seconds. That would mean each second after 'now' is the past. Here can't be 'now' because I'm somewhere else other than the present. It doesn't make sense."

"Chaos." Cogito nodded.

Friskybiscuit laughed. "*Doot*. It's a rubber band."

"Of chaos."

Echo doubted any simple explanation.

"There has to be some connection between time and the mind. It always seems like people snap back to traumatic events, like violent death or something."

Cogito coughed noisily. "Hey, it's me, right? I'm the traumatic event here. I say things, and your mind gets traumatized with mind-blowing goddamn truth. Holy shit, goddamn it!"

Echo ignored Cogito. "I really think that's the key. There has to be some connection between time and the mind."

Cayenne looked restless. "What about the soul? What is this, right here, right now? Is this the past? Or is it something else? A shared memory? And if you guys are dead, how can we be remembering anything at all? Are we having a meeting in some kind of alternate universe? Or could it be like what Frisky said, that, you know, this is some kind of afterlife?"

Cogito squinted his eyes. "Yeah, if most of us are dead, where the hell are we? Hey, where the hell *am I*? How do we know? How do *I know*? Maybe this is all bullshit, like a delusion in your goddamn brain."

He pointed at Echo. Echo felt his head hurt at the exact moment Cogito pointed.

"Why does it have to be my brain?"

"Because Cayenne doesn't have much of an imagination," he snapped.

She ignored the insult. "Come on, Echo, if this really is the end, whether or not we ever meet again, just try and remember that only you can be happy. It's not something you can simply find and suddenly there it is. Take some risks, not dumb ones…I mean, be careful, but live your life, okay?"

This stung Echo. *Live my life?* he thought, *Do you know how hard it is for me to do that? My life is just this thing that I keep doing, and I don't know why. If I stop coming here, I'm afraid I'll have nothing left. I've lost everything else. I don't want to lose you too.*

"Cayenne, I…"

They stared at each other. His face flushed with the warmth of feelings he couldn't hide. He sat at the edge of his seat wanting to do something. But he knew if he said anything he would hurt worse than he already did. His mouth clamped, holding his thoughts inside, hoping she understood why.

"It's okay," she said.

"Is it?."

"I understand; really, it's okay."

"No, no it's not." He clenched his hands.

"Don't do that, Echo. Don't punish yourself. Don't regret the time we had. I know it can hurt to remember, but it doesn't have to. Don't remember that I'm gone: remember that we were together. Don't let grief eat you up inside. You have to let yourself live."

Friskybiscuit agreed with her. "*Doot-dah-doo!* And keep looking for some answers!"

Echo could feel time was growing short; his anger turned to worry. "Maybe there are no answers. Maybe this is it, and there is nothing else."

Cayenne uncurled from her ball; she stood up and stretched. "Look, if you really want answers, I think you know exactly where to find them."

Echo knew what she meant, and he didn't like it. "The Think Tank? I don't know about that…I've heard things about those places. Besides, every time I take your advice, my life gets turned upside down."

"But always for the better, right?" she said.

"I don't know anymore…"

Cogito groaned. "Hey, why the fuck do you care? You heard the girl, it's chaos. Order is out of fashion. Hey, answers won't come to you if you sit on your goddamn ass. Don't let chaos revolve around you. Damn it, man, be the center of it! Be the cause! Everyone is the architect of their own reality, but they always seem to fail to take advantage of the goddamn possibilities."

"Wait, is this real?" Echo said, suddenly feeling odd.

Cogito coughed on his cigarette. "What is real? Hey, what I see as red may actually look blue to you. If perception was universal, everyone would enjoy the same goddamn things."

Echo watched as Cogito put the lighter in his mouth. He heard it light and watched as Cogito began smoking out of his mouth without a cigarette. Echo felt the pit of his stomach drop out. He looked directly at Cogito.

"Are *you* real?"

Cogito grinned. "Sometimes." He blew smoke out of his nose.

Echo stood up. Suddenly, his head felt strange, like he was spinning. He reached behind him for the park bench. He tried to sit back down, but as he sat, he fell through the bench, then the floor, and finally into darkness. He opened his eyes with a start, or had he had them open the whole time? He was in the garage now. He could smell a faint lemony scent on his hands. The garage was quiet. He could hear nothing except his own movement. The garage felt big and empty. It smelled stale, musty, and damp, with a hint of ancient gasoline and long discarded motor oil. He sat up slowly expecting to feel faint, but there was none of that. Then he thought he heard a noise. He looked outside, but there was nothing. He was alone.

CHAPTER 17

IPSO FACTO

———

Echo felt cold. He turned the Audi's air-conditioner down, then off. He was still too cold. He rolled all the windows down, but the thought of getting out never crossed his mind. He was in a staring contest with a Think Tank. It was the largest one he had ever found. It was hidden deep within the mountains inside a natural valley. Several dozen massive white squares of various shapes and sizes formed a strange windowless city before him. He picked up his binoculars again. He fumbled for the control knob to the headlights with one hand and flashed the high beams at the complex, blinking them on and off a few times. He knew he was being watched, and he wanted to make sure he had their undivided attention.

It had taken him a long time to find this Think Tank. He had wanted to find a big one. He thought his chances of meeting a higher ranking whoever would be better with a larger one. This was an assumption based on nothing, though. He also had a feeling about this one. This one felt right. He felt excited about it, an excitement that came from the

191

anticipation of finally meeting his fate. To go to a Think Tank was to ask to die, and he had spent enough time considering this outcome to know that he was ready. He had had enough. He no longer cared, and from that came a kind of reckless courage he had not experienced before. Instead of running away from what he feared, he would run toward it and discover for himself what he was so afraid of. He was tired of wandering around, of searching for nothing, and finding even less.

"Cayenne…" he said. He set the binoculars down, balled his hands into fists, and beat on his thighs. He suddenly stopped—realizing the stupidity of his actions. He hated her, even though he knew that was not true. She was the embodiment of something he could never have, and he worried that she was just a delusion. He tried to compose himself, but there was no escape from his despair. He could no longer find solace in the world around him.

"Nobody cares."

A solitary road led to the gate of the Think Tank. Beyond it was an unmanned security booth with a raised metal barrier arm. It was wide open as if daring intruders to enter. Echo could see no lights, no guard towers, no features of any kind protruding from the white buildings. A wave of goose bumps caused his neck hairs to stand on end. He could feel hidden eyes watching him. He knew they were waiting for him. He looked over at the passenger seat where his trusty red sledgehammer was sitting. Even after searching several dozen hardware stores, he could find nothing better. He hoped it would be enough to break into one of the buildings. He had no other plan if the sledgehammer could not breech a building, but he felt confident that time was on his side to figure out another way in.

He put his foot on the brake and shifted the Audi into drive. He gripped the steering wheel tightly, rhythmically tapping his fingers across it. His anger was aimless and without reason. His depression felt deep and hot, as it mixed with the anger into a strange fury. He wanted out. He wanted out of the monotony that was his life, and this was the only option left. It was drastic and dangerous, but at the same time, exhilarating. He was ready to find out what would happen to him. What was really going to happen to him, not just another daydream about what *could* happen. He was going to find out once and for all, and no matter what happened, he promised himself he would not be afraid.

"But I am afraid," he said, feeling his patience evaporate into disgust.

He took his foot off the brake and slammed the accelerator down. The Audi lurched forward roaring at full throttle. He immediately regretted not taking more time to think before committing. He wanted to believe that if he thought about it long enough, he would eventually become comfortable with the idea. He knew this was a lie. There would always be 'what ifs.' He would never be comfortable. No, what awaited him were answers. Soon he would know, one way or another, what went on inside one of these places.

"And if I die, I hope I don't see her in a rubber band. I hope that's it. Because I am done with all this shit."

He felt an inferno of rage boil up inside him as he drove. He had to let it out. He began to scream at the top of his lungs. A tirade of curse words filled the car. He leaned on the car horn. It wailed over his screams and reverberated throughout the valley for miles. He wanted to wake them up. He wanted them to know he was there to meet them.

"Oh yes!" he yelled. "I'm coming, fuckers! I'm coming for you!"

The Audi blasted past the open gate, through the security booth entrance, and into the complex. Echo weaved between the white buildings, hollering out the window like a madman as he drove. He dared them to come out and meet him. He told snipers to aim true. He told them about all the candies he missed eating, and then blasphemed Jesus, hoping it would fire up someone enough to do something about him. But there was nothing. He drove around the complex screaming until he had run out of things to say. Frustrated, he slowed the car down and started looking for a door.

The giant white buildings were made of corrugated metal walls that were rooted directly into the smooth pavement. There were no external pipes, air ducts, or electrical wires. He could barely see panel lines on the metal walls where the corrugated sections had been fitted together. They were arranged in an irregular pattern that cast overlapping shadows between them, choking off the sunlight in a manner that reminded Echo of being in the middle of a forest full of tightly packed sequoias. He circled each square looking carefully for any weakness or detail he could attack. Then he spotted a rectangular indentation that was about the size of a door, conveniently hidden under a shadow. He pulled over in front of it and turned the engine off. He scanned his field of vision and listened. It was silent.

He got out of the car with the red sledgehammer in hand. He heard only the sound of his own footsteps as he walked. He took a closer look at the indent in the wall. It was in the shape of a door, but had no other indications that it was a door. He guessed the hinges were inside and that the door swung inward. He ran his hand across the edges. He thought for a moment that the truth he was discovering was that Think Tanks were elaborate lies constructed by the government. Empty structures surrounded by rumors and propaganda in an effort to give people a sense of hope in a hopeless situation. The only way to be certain was to break in and see for himself.

He stepped back from the door and lifted the sledgehammer up. He hesitated for a moment. He realized that if nothing was inside, if these giant square buildings were just a hoax, then he would have to figure out something else to do with himself. That prospect made him cringe. He pulled the sledgehammer back and swung. *Bam! Clang!* The space behind the door echoed as if it were hollow. He struck the door again. He took a couple of steps back in order to get a short running start. He struck the door once more and then kneeled down to examine his progress. The red paint of the sledgehammer had marked up the door with pink streaks. The metal was not dented or harmed in any way. This made him angrier. A stronger man would be able to damage it. He cursed at himself for being so weak. He picked up the sledgehammer and swung again. *Bam! Clang!* Then came the sound of a hundred combat boots rushing toward him. This made him smile.

CHAPTER 18

INTO THE FRYING PAN

Echo stood still staring at the white metal door in front of him. He could hear the sounds of countless soldiers surrounding him in a thunderous commotion of boot stomping and weapon-safety-removal clicks. Nervous sweat soaked his shirt. He took a deep breath, reminded himself that this was what he wanted, and then let his breath out. He tried to remain calm.

"Drop your weapon! Drop your weapon! Drop your weapon!" shouted a chorus of well-trained professional voices.

Echo tossed the sledgehammer aside and held his hands up. A soldier grabbed his hand. Abrasive tactical gloves looped a plastic tie around his wrist, then his other wrist, zipping them together tightly. Already the hood, trunk, and all the doors of his car were open. The soldiers waved strange instruments all over the vehicle. The instruments beeped or whooped as they passed over his things. In the sky were floating bright white spotlights that illuminated the shadows cast

197

by the giant buildings. The lights appeared to be beaming out of a pair of cube-shaped UAVs that hovered silently without sound or any perceivable means of propulsion.

"Weird," Echo whispered, watching the cubes float.

One at a time, the soldiers searching his car began yelling, "Clear!" They all shouted toward a person hidden just beyond the glare of the spotlights. It was hard for Echo to see very far. He could tell there were hundreds of men running around between the buildings securing the area. He could hear a single loud curt voice barking at the men. This voice was passionate and stern, like an angry father. The huge man who it belonged to emerged from the glare of the spotlights and walked briskly toward Echo with the momentum of an avalanche.

"Mister, my personal policy is to shoot crazy bastards on sight. Have you anything to say that could possibly cause me to consider otherwise?"

Echo's mind froze. All he could think about was that he had never seen a chevron mustache as perfectly thick and as large as the one covering the face of this man who had just threatened his life.

"How do you groom that caterpillar?" he asked.

The man had no reaction. He turned to a soldier by his side and asked him to bring up one of the limited edition *Conundrum* gift boxes for platinum achievers. The man explained to Echo that inside it was a specially formulated suicide pill. The pill delivered a lethal command to the brain, releasing a lifetime of dopamine in just a few seconds while slowly shutting down the lungs. The asphyxiation supposedly enhanced the euphoric pleasure of the dying brain, easing the victim through the gateway of death in a manner considered enviable given the alternatives. No one had ever turned down the opportunity to die in this way.

"You know, I'm not big on the pills," Echo joked nervously. "In fact, I don't think I've had anything more than an aspirin in years."

He watched the soldier run beyond the glare of the spotlights to retrieve the box. He started to sweat profusely.

"Look, I don't know what I have to say here. I really don't want to die. I mean, I get how that pill works and what it does, but I don't want it. I want to live. I came to find all of you so we could talk."

The angry man's mustache twitched. "Talk?"

Echo could see the soldier now returning with something silver in hand. He breathed urgently.

"Yes! I came here to find answers. Nobody out there knows what's going on. They've all gone crazy. I've been almost everywhere, and all I've seen are things I wish I hadn't. There is nothing left out there for me! Nothing! That's why I came here, because I figured you guys are the only ones left that haven't gone completely insane!"

He hoped that they had not gone insane. If they had, he was in deep shit.

The soldier peeled off the protective wrapping and opened the silver collector's box. The catchy musical theme of *Conundrum* played. Inside the box, the pill was suspended over a mirrored platform lit by golden lights. The angry man looked at Echo with a frown. His hand began to stroke the burly mustache. The man paced back and forth in front of Echo as the soldier stood with the box open. The theme of *Conundrum* played from the tiny box amid the surrounding silence of the hundred men with trained weapons and floating spotlights. Suddenly the man's radio squawked, which spooked Echo. A garbled voice sounded. The man grabbed the radio and put it to his ear.

He listened, nodded, and turned toward his men.

"Right. The doctor wants to take this one in for an interview." He gestured toward the men standing around Echo's car holding the strange scanning devices. "Scan this man for sanity."

Several soldiers ran over with the same devices that had been used on the car. They ran them up and down Echo's body. They frisked him; took off his belt, his shoes; and turned out everything in his pockets. Through the commotion, Echo could hear the angry voice growing much calmer as he conversed over the radio with another voice that had benefited from a higher education. The scanning continued with probes being stuck into his nose and armpits, lights being shown into his eyes, and various needles being pressed against his head. All the devices made pleasant noises that seemed to affirm his sanity. Finally, the last device showed a green light. Bewildered, the men took a step back. They turned toward the angry man and confirmed Echo had checked out as sane.

"You guys put a lot of faith in green lights," Echo cracked.

The mustache twitched again. He ordered another soldier with a computer tablet to his side. The angry man stepped in front of Echo and looked him right in the eye.

"Mister, I want your name," he snarled. "And don't give me that video game bullshit, either. I want your real name. The one you were born with, and I want it now."

Echo thought hard as he hadn't used his real name in at least a millennia, but he managed to remember it and even spelled it out for them. It was easier for him to remember his social security number since he had often used the numbers for lotto tickets in *Conundrum*. The information was entered into the tablet. The man with the mustache frowned.

"We show you played *Conundrum* for nearly three centuries. Then you stopped? According to this you should have achieved death just before eastern quadrant twenty passed beyond the event horizon. Right. Something tells me you weren't even there, were you?"

"The pills were never my thing. One day I just gave up playing and started driving around."

The mustache twitched. "Gave up? Mister, nobody gives up the game."

Another man, a scientist, walked over, looked at the tablet briefly, and approached Echo. He was thin, almost underfed, wearing unkempt clothing and a lab coat covered in coffee stains. His eyes darted about seemingly perplexed by what he was seeing. His body moved constantly as if he lacked the patience to stand still for even a moment. He spoke in a brisk, sophisticated manner, like an anxious prodigy who wanted to avoid having his brilliant thoughts interrupted.

"Um, hello! Very nice to meet you and those other pleasantries. Um, you've been out there all this time, on your own, without any pills? None at all?"

"Yeah."

"Do you drink?"

"No"

"Smoke stuff?"

"No way!"

"Um, compulsively masturbate?"

"What? No! Look how clean my car is!" Echo held up his palms. "No hair, either!"

"Um, you are depressed though, correct?"

Echo sighed. "Yes."

The scientist turned to the angry mustached man. Their voices were hushed, but Echo heard enough to understand what was going on a little better. They seemed to be interested in the fact that he had survived so long without pills. They also appeared to be baffled by his health, given the "deteriorating conditions." Eventually the soldier with the collector's box was dismissed. The two men continued to discuss something that seemed to be growing in importance.

Echo interrupted. "Guys, if you don't mind, could you tell me what the hell is going on?"

The angry man grinned. "Mister, I'm guessing you want to be called Echo Gain?"

"Echo is fine."

"Right. Mister Echo, you drove onto our base like a maniac and you proceeded to willfully destroy government property."

The scientist cut off the mustached man. "Um, Echo, how long have you been out there? How many years do you think have passed?"

Echo thought this was a strange question. "Since the end? I don't know. About a thousand or so. At least that is what the calendars said last time I looked."

The scientist introduced himself. "You may call me Sonnet."

The man with the mustache groaned. Sonnet continued. "That is not my real name, of course. My, um, angry friend here is known colloquially as Bombast. That is not his real name, either. In the interest of, um, of better facilitating encounters such as the one you and I are having now, we have adopted these game code names. Though I'm afraid they are not as clever in meaning as those among civilians. Um, I do not want you to be alarmed by what I am about to tell you, and, um, you must understand that we will keep you restrained for now while I speak to you. For your own protection, of course. The calendars you have seen are incorrect. We purposely created them to be incorrect so that, the, um, the general population would not know how much time has actually passed."

Echo started to feel good about getting answers, any answers. "Just how much time *has* passed?"

"Um, by our calculations? Nearly six thousand years."

"No fucking way. That's crazy. That's completely crazy."

Sonnet observed Echo's reaction. "Um, well, yes, crazy, I suppose. You see, Echo, as the phenomenon increases, so does the amount of time dilation. As the remaining surface area on this planet is consumed, the dilation grows, and time is stretched longer. Um, this inevitably leaves us with absolutely tremendous logistical problems. Necessities such as food and water will not endure indefinitely."

"I know."

"Um, you do?"

"Obviously. That's why you guys kill people using the game."

Sonnet licked his lips. "Hmm, um, yes, I suppose that part is somewhat obvious. It's certainly cheaper to make pills than bullets. Pills are more effectual than prisons, and death is its own form of incarceration. We keep a constant rate of death to maintain an artificial equilibrium."

"Right," snarled Bombast. "Bullets are reserved for the on-site criminal prosecution of the most violent offenders. Crazy bastards that deserve to be shot."

Sonnet rolled his eyes. "Yes, um, unfortunate, but necessary to maintain the presence of authority. If we did not take such measures, anarchy would spread throughout the remaining population. It's, um, a, um, a shame that the general population must be treated like a herd of animals, but such are the times we live in."

"Right." Bombast agreed. "It's like culling the herd…not enough grass for everyone when the grass never grows."

Echo nodded. "It's good to hear an answer. That's what I came here for, some good answers."

Bombast looked at Sonnet, then at Echo, with suspicion. "Mister, you keep saying you came here for answers. That has to be the worst lie I've ever heard."

Echo laughed. "No worse than your lies."

Sonnet rubbed his chin. "Um, what have you heard?"

Echo took a shot in the dark. "Like the ocean. It's not actually draining, is it?"

Sonnet frowned. "Um, that is somewhat correct. The ocean is drain-ing, but not because of the phenomenon; it's because of us. We have been using desalination to convert the ocean's water into drinking water, and, um, a type of electrolysis to replenish oxygen into the atmosphere. It is a process that we have been using for, um, at least several thousand years. Even the ocean is finite. It's interesting that this is known, given the exceedingly slow rate of conversion."

"You can't hide the truth from people. Eventually it will get out."

Bombast's mustache twitched. "Right. I suppose you came here to get answers so you can tell everyone what's really going on."

"No. I came for myself."

"For answers?"

"Yes."

"Right." Bombast looked at Sonnet with a grave expression. "Mister, most intrusions are made by pill-crazed fiends or deluded maniacs who have lost their minds. We shoot those people. On occasion we get the lost loner who is looking for some existential bullshit meaning greater than himself. We give those pricks the pill."

Echo cringed. "I take it everyone who dares to enter a Think Tank dies?"

Sonnet snickered. "Um, I know it's not funny, but, um, it is in a way. The general population wants to desperately believe that some-how everything will turn out fine. Unfortunately, the human psyche was never meant to survive in this type of environment. We developed these, um, unique pills to protect our minds."

He held up a metal bottle with a radiation symbol on it. "Um, sadly we cannot produce enough of them for public consumption, and even if we could, the window of opportunity has passed."

Bombast jumped in. "Right. Normally we don't have friendly conversations with bastards like you, but in this case there may be an exception. Mister, Sonnet and I would like to offer you a deal."

Echo smiled like a fool, not understanding. "I don't get it, what kind of deal?"

Sonnet gestured wildly with excitement. "You are, um, well, you're somehow immune to what's been going on. Um, it could be a mutation, or gene combination, or anything, or everything. We don't know. The entire population takes some kind of pill to stay reasonably coherent, and you don't."

"I know I've met other people that don't take—"

"Um, they don't matter, Echo. They are not here. What matters is that you are here now. You decided to come here for whatever inane reason you had, and now, um, we can make a deal. Yes?"

Sonnet nodded. Echo nodded in return, figuring he had no choice in the matter. Sonnet clasped his hands together and paced in a circle.

"Um, this is the deal. I will provide you with answers, or um, as many answers as I can supply. You will allow us to install an experimental device on your vehicle. Then with this device installed, you will drive to the very edge of the phenomenon and deposit it thusly."

Sonnet made a motion of setting something large down.

"And?" Echo asked skeptically.

"Um, that's it."

"I take it this is a suicide mission?"

"Um, not for you, you're immune."

"Okay, well, why?"

"Um, because even though we may never fix what is happening, we can learn from it and, um, possibly escape it."

"What if I say no?"

Bombast's mood lightened. "Then, mister, you have the honor of becoming a platinum achiever."

Echo could see he was not joking. "Great."

Sonnet couldn't understand why Echo was not more excited. "Um, it's a perfectly acceptable deal. I tell you the answers I know, and you, um, drive to the edge."

Echo knew there was a catch. "But...?"

Bombast folded his arms. "Any answer you learn, you can't share with the general population. Understand, mister?"

Echo thought this idea was laughable. "How are you going to enforce that? You going to put a mind-reading bomb inside my brain?"

Bombast smiled. "Something like that."

Sonnet arrogantly brushed some dust off Echo's shoulder. "Um, you didn't think that technology was stagnant all these years, did you? We have made some incredible advances, and we are actively working on many more. All our efforts have been focused on finding a method to counter entropy and its influence. Um, is it a deal?"

It was all happening so quickly. Echo had no time to think it through. "Sure, I mean, yes. I've only been to the border once; I can go again. I guess I can go beyond it, but I don't know if that's possible."

Sonnet seemed annoyed that Echo would have any doubt. "Um, we have technology that will protect you all the way to the edge. And, um, your natural immunity should provide the rest."

"I guess it's a deal." Echo regretted it immediately.

"Splendid!" Sonnet made a small hop of joy. "Um, I guess now we should take you down into the base. We *are* ready to go inside, right, Bombast?"

The two of them exchanged a look that made Echo feel like he was missing out on a conversation.

The floating spotlights went out suddenly. Bombast pointed at a glowing entrance that had risen out of the ground. It was a stairwell that had been pushed to the surface with large pneumatic actuators. Half the troops marched down. The rest appeared to be waiting behind to follow Echo. A group of white-coat-wearing scientists pushed the Audi into a separate, larger entrance, down a ramp, and out of sight. Bombast motioned for Echo to start walking. Sonnet led the way, humming as he went. Echo followed Sonnet down metal mesh stairs into a hallway that acted as a staging area. There, the soldiers stored their weapons, switching from rifles to what appeared to be cattle prods. Sonnet took Echo through a door into a plain office lobby filled with elevators and cheap plastic potted plants. He pressed the down button for an elevator, and they waited.

Sonnet reached in his pocket for a pack of gum. "Nicotine?" he asked.

Echo raised his eyebrows. "You smoke?"

Sonnet popped a piece in his mouth with a look of disappointment. "Um, no. We found a cache of gum a while back. I decided to try one, and now I can't stop. Human beings are prone to addictions. Um, actually I think our entire history can be defined by our addiction to one thing or another. *Conundrum* and the pills were just a natural extension of that."

Echo thought about the game, but another question came to mind. "So I take it, it was easier to build the game and pills than to build spaceships?"

Sonnet rolled his eyes as he chewed loudly. "Um, don't get me started on the spaceships!" He paused and looked closely at Echo. "How did you hear about the spaceships, anyway? Hmm, never mind how, I guess. It's hard to keep secrets for so long." He thrust his hands into his pockets to get comfortable for the tale he wanted to tell.

"Um, so, we had, um, if you can believe it, a planetary evacuation plan, um, at least for North America. Operation Emergency Exit, wasn't it?"

He looked for confirmation from Bombast. Bombast gave none. Sonnet continued.

"We were taking everything. Animals, art, historical relics, the secret formula for Coke, um, the important things. There was even an ingenious plan to launch into space using an exp—"

Bombast suddenly coughed. Sonnet censored himself and skipped around whatever he had almost said.

"Um, nobody knew if this device would work. It could have, theoretically, overcome the forces of the phenomenon."

"What happened?" Echo asked.

"Um, politics essentially killed the effort. Corporations attempted to gain influence through lobbyists. Funds were diverted by politicians to their home states for pet projects instead of using them to hire qualified manufacturers. Um, endless congressional investigations questioning the legitimacy of science they did not even understand. Closed-door hearings on the role of God in interstellar space travel. Inter-party bickering over details as mundane as carpet color. Gridlock in the face of certain doom. It was, um, incredibly ridiculous." Sonnet chewed his gum, quickly remembering. "Hmm, I had to testify fourteen times. Um, it was horrible. The best minds had come together with good solutions and plans…ideas that could have made a difference, only to watch them fall on the deaf ears of a selfish few. At the time, we thought there was enough, um, time, to waste. At the rate of expansion, we calculated an enormous lead time before us. While we were frustrated with the process, there was no sense of urgency."

"Did they ever approve it?"

"Um, eventually fear compelled them to approve a plan that nobody liked, but it was the only one everyone could agree on. Unfortunately, we overestimated our own ingenuity. Our technology was far, far too primitive for the task, and it never worked the way it was supposed to. Eventually, several crucial facilities fell into the phenomenon, and the plan had to be abandoned. Instead of researching a method of escaping, resources were devoted toward efforts that would allow the remaining population to, um, to meet the end comfortably. Hmm, the focus transitioned to what this country knew how to do best—um, namely, manufacture pharmaceuticals and video games. Not the most noble of ways to end existence, but, um, without Asia, we had run out of viable options."

An elevator dinged at the far end of the lobby. Metal doors slid open. The soldiers held the doors while Bombast pushed Echo into the elevator. Sonnet joined them. The soldiers stayed in the lobby, leaving the three of them alone. The doors clinked shut, and Bombast ran a card across an unmarked panel next to the door. The elevator began to move, and Echo's ears popped from the rapid descent. Bombast kept one hand on Echo's shoulder the entire time, carefully watching him.

Sonnet snapped his gum. "Um, the first fifty floors are dedicated to the manufacturing of pharmaceuticals."

"The first fifty?" Echo asked in disbelief.

Sonnet continued chewing his gum. "Um, video game production is handled at a facility off-site." He stopped chewing. "Echo, the doctors are going to need to examine you before we can allow you into the base."

"Examine me?" Echo felt Bombast's grip tighten.

Sonnet nodded, staring down at his feet. "Um, it's a standard procedure. Nothing to worry too much about. Um, correct?"

Sonnet looked at Bombast. Bombast nodded.

"Right. It's best you don't panic."

"Panic?" Echo suddenly realized he was trapped.

The elevator came to an abrupt stop. The doors glided open, revealing what looked like a hospital emergency room. About a dozen men dressed in orange level-A, fully encapsulated hazmat suits rushed inside and surrounded Echo. They grabbed him by the arms and legs and lifted him up onto a gurney. They quickly strapped him down with restraints. Echo was paralyzed with fear. He made eye contact with Bombast, who for the first time seemed sympathetic.

"Don't fight it," Bombast said calmly. "Mister, all we are asking of you is to trust us."

"Trust the government?" Echo yelled.

"Right."

There were so many men holding Echo down, he could not see below his neck. He felt the prick of a needle. And then, that was it.

CHAPTER 19

LIKE NO BUSINESS I KNOW

———

When Echo opened his eyes again, a certain amount of time had passed. How much time, he was not sure. He was alone with Sonnet in an office that had a retro feel to it. It contained metal filing cabinets, framed certificates on the wall, and a heavy oak desk that stood between them. A setting sun beamed through the slits of hanging blinds. The skyline silhouette of New York City haunted his view. The windows on the many buildings reflected the light like glittering stars. An air-conditioner kicked on, sending a gentle breeze behind the window and causing the skyline backdrop to sway out of position. It had seemed real for only a moment, but the moment was worth it.

Echo's head felt light. He took a deep breath and looked down. He noticed he was not wearing his normal clothes. He had, at some point, been dressed in a white jumpsuit with blocky orange markings on one side that resembled a giant bar code. He tried to remember what had happened after the elevator ride. His mind was blank, and his mouth felt tingly and tasted metallic.

"Crazy," he said, trying to lick out the taste.

Sonnet scrolled through a computer tablet, with a grin on his face. He knew Echo was awake but chose to ignore him. Sonnet's desk was covered with paper test results. Echo guessed the results were from his examination.

He tried to sit up. His head felt woozy. "Sonnet? Where am I?"

Sonnet haphazardly tossed the tablet onto a stack of papers. The papers slid off his desk, crashing to the floor. He ignored the mess he created. He folded his hands under his chin and stared at Echo, fascinated.

"Um, paper is hard to come by anymore due to the limited number of trees. Hmmm, but it still has permanence. If, um, a computer hard drive crashes, the data is in all likelihood irrevocably lost. Technology habitually fails at the least opportune time. Paper, um, paper does not fail. Um, it can burn, soak up water, dry out and turn yellow, but it can never fail. You were of such importance that I requested these printouts."

"Great. I mean, if I were any more important, my results would probably be printed on toilet paper."

Sonnet smirked. "A double-quilted four-ply at least!"

They laughed. Then they stopped.

Echo checked his body for anything out of the ordinary. "Just where am I? Where have I been? I can't remember anything."

Sonnet sat back in his leather chair. "Um, you won't. Ever. That's how the drug we gave you works. Um, the actual question is not where are you—you already know that—it's *when* are you?"

"When?"

"Correct."

"How long?"

"Um, about a month has passed."

"About a month?" Echo knew a person as precise as Sonnet had an exact date he was withholding.

"Correct." Sonnet slumped down in his chair. "It takes time to do a proper, um, thorough examination."

"I expected nothing less than for you to be thorough, and I hope you found everything you were looking for. You know, between you and me, I keep my best secrets up my ass."

Sonnet reached in his pocket for his gum. "Um, I can understand your hostility. I know it can be somewhat difficult to accept, but, um, we are the government, and we do know what is best for you."

"You do?"

"Um, we do," Sonnet said conceitedly.

"Didn't Bombast call you a doctor?"

"Um, did he?"

"Of what exactly?"

"Um, it does not matter. I could tell you the answer, and you could think about what it means, but it is not the answer you came here for."

"I thought the deal was I get answers?"

"Unfortunately, for some questions there will be no answers. Ask whatever you like, um, within reason, and I will endeavor to answer, within reason. Remember, I can spend only so much time with you before I am forced to attend to, um, my other duties."

He placed some gum in his mouth and began to chew. "Begin."

Echo felt unprepared. His mind was empty. "I'm not sure where."

"Sure you do. Um, just tell me the first thing on your mind."

"Am I here, now? I'm still confused about when this is."

"That is your first question?" Sonnet lamented. "Um, I've already answered that one. It's, um, a month or so later. Consider the opportunity you have here, Echo. Um, ask me something profound."

"Okay, well…how can I find happiness?"

Sonnet laughed. "Um, that's not something I can provide a definite answer for, unfortunately. I can prescribe certain pills that will, um, release chemicals in your brain that will induce a sense of happiness, but it will be fleeting, and, um, lack a sense of personal fulfillment. Finding happiness is different for each individual. Um, for example, for me, it is my work. For you, um, that is something you will have to discover on your own."

"I don't even know what I'm looking for."

"It is less important that you know what you are looking for, than, um, that you recognize what it is when you find it."

"That's actually a pretty good answer."

Sonnet grinned. "On to the next question then. Um, remember we have only so much time."

The mention of the word *time* jogged Echo's memory. "Is there a connection between time and the mind?"

Sonnet thought for a moment. "The perception of time is not universal among all beings. Time is, um, an idea. As an idea we created, it can seem to have unusual properties that could be called, um, unnatural due to our own limited understanding of it."

"That's half an answer, Sonnet. You just sidestepped the question. There has to be a connection between time and the mind. What about things like rubber bands?"

Sonnet's grin faded. He cleared his throat readying his answer.

"Um, suppose that there is a connection between time and the mind. What does it mean? What is the nature of the connection? Um, we don't know ourselves. There have been too many coincidences for there not to be a connection. The foundation of science is in repeatable, discernible results. An, um, impossibility under current conditions. The question that always arises is: Am I perceiving actual reality-altering events or, um, is it merely a localized event within the brain? Um, as disturbing as this may sound, we have gathered a significant amount of data that suggest some alteration of the brain has occurred as a direct result of the, um, phenomenon's presence."

Sonnet paused. He chewed, then continued speaking. "Um, consider that the human brain is composed of approximately seventy-eight percent water, ordinarily unaffected by gravitational forces. Um, now consider the effects of gravity in the sky. The ocean-like waves originating from the phenomenon. These waves affect the human brain in a subtle, but, um, measurable way. Your brain, my brain, every human being's brain, is slowly rippling. The distortion is minor, but, um, the question must be asked: How is this influencing our everyday lives and perception? It has always been interesting to note that rubber bands are consistently oriented around events of personal trauma. When an individual describes a rubber band, it is easy to dismiss it as a brief episode of mental delusion or, um, a temporary psychotic state. When more than one person shares the same rubber band experience, we, um, we find that there is no reasonable answer at all."

"So you have no idea what a rubber band is?"

"Um, I'm afraid not."

"Is this brain-rippling thing causing people to go insane?"

"Correct, though slowly."

"Great. How can I trust what I see? How do I know what's real?"

"Um, because you are immune to the effects. Everything you perceive is taking place in the common reality we all share."

Echo half-laughed. "I don't even know if I believe you. I mean, I've seen things that make no sense at all. What about things like time lightning or instant replay?"

Sonnet put a fresh stick of gum in his mouth. "Um, we did an experiment not long ago. We gathered around, um, thirty random individuals into a sealed dormitory. A wrist-mounted device capable of delivering a lethal injection by remote was attached to each of them. We spent months observing them, um, waiting for one of them to enter a rubber band state of mind. The theory we wanted to test was if the mind was really traveling back to an earlier point in time, then, um, if we killed the body in the present, would the mind continue to live in the past?"

"What happened?"

"Eventually one individual entered a rubber band state. We initiated the lethal injection, and, um, well, um, they proceeded to completely disappear."

"What?"

"Um, it was as if the person had been erased. While we could, um, remember the person, all records and data vanished. It was as if we had created a paradox."

"That's impossible."

"Um, is it?" Sonnet sat up in his chair. "What is possible? Um, what is impossible? Only what we say as humans? It is extraordinarily arrogant of us to assume the rules we made up to explain how the universe works were to be obeyed universally. Um, consider the phrase 'It breaks the laws of physics.' Um, what does that mean? That it breaks our rules? The rules we made up? The rules we applied to everything and hold fast to like religion? We made them up. We did the best we could do, and, um, they generally worked to explain everything we know. But, um, then nobody saw this, this thing coming. For all our rules, we had to realize that we were wrong and have been wrong since the very beginning."

"What do you mean by 'wrong?'"

The office door suddenly flew open. Bombast barged into the room. He looked at Sonnet, then at Echo. Sonnet slowly stood up, straightening his rumpled shirt.

"Um, that's all the time I have, Echo."

He looked at Bombast and left the room. Bombast asked if Echo could walk, then grabbed him by the arm before he could answer and hauled him out the door.

CHAPTER 20

AN INDUCED COMPLIANCE PARADIGM

———

Bombast marched down a long office-themed hallway practically dragging Echo along with him. Echo stumbled, trying to keep up with the
big man's fast pace. Bombast huffed as he went, determined to get Echo
to their destination quickly.

"Mister, I don't know how you survived out there. You are the weak-
est candidate yet."

Echo started hopping to keep pace. "Wait, what does that mean?"

"Answer time is over."

"You can't answer one question? A big guy like you?"

Bombast jerked Echo to one side of the hall and pressed him up
against the wall.

"Mister, in case you haven't noticed, this world is coming to an end. Frankly, I have more important things to worry about. Understand?"

Echo nodded.

"There you are! Fantastic! And to think I was going to come to you," a friendly female voice said from behind the big man. Bombast turned, saw who it was, and saluted. A middle-aged woman dressed in a military uniform with tightly pulled back red hair smiled warmly at Echo.

Echo read her name. "Rapport?"

She laughed. "Now, now, that's Rapport. The 't' is silent."

Rapport exchanged a glance with Bombast. He nodded and marched down the hallway. She fixed Echo's collar in a tender manner, smiling at him.

"Are you feeling all right now?"

"No. I'm confused and scared, like I don't know what the hell is going on."

Rapport looked at him warmly. "Oh, there is nothing to be scared of. Everything is going to be just fine."

Echo felt something strange about this woman. "I, I'm not sure if I can believe you."

Rapport smiled again. She rubbed his arm soothingly. "Oh, you." She laughed. Her words seemed preplanned, friendly by design, and strangely devoid of any personal details. She reminded Echo of a cruise ship activity coordinator.

"Are you ready for a quick tour?" she chimed.

"I really don't have any choice now, do I?"

"That's right!" She said happily, patting his shoulder. "You have absolutely no choice at all. Now, let's remember the rules: If anybody says anything that's, well, that sounds a little crazy, you just let it go, and don't worry about it. If anybody grabs hold of you for any reason, remember to relax. Don't do anything to escalate the situation, and I'll take care of it."

Echo nervously laughed. "Am I in any kind of danger here?"

"How do you define 'in danger?' Is that before or after you get hurt?"

"Before."

"Great! That's a goal we can work toward together!" She smiled again. Her teeth looked larger than the mouth they had to fit into. Her smile reminded Echo of a horse. He smirked. She patted him on the shoulder.

"That's the spirit!" she said.

She took Echo's arm in hers and led him down the long, empty hallway. They turned left. Then right. Walked for a few minutes. Then turned a few more times until Echo lost track of the path they had taken. The sound of Rapport's high heels clicking, echoed endlessly in every direction. Around every corner was a security camera tracking their movement. Rapport patted Echo's hand. She smelled like lavender and vanilla. She kept looking at him and smiling.

"I hope you don't mind, but we had to confiscate your fondue pot."

"What? Why?"

"We have a lot of cheese. We are the government, after all."

"And did the government take anything else?"

"There was a hard drive full of music. We had to impound it due to some copyright violations. We could give it back, but only if you have written permission from the copyright holders." She smiled.

Echo sighed. "Anything else?"

"The boys thought you had an awful lot of underwear."

"Well, shit happens."

"Oh my."

They arrived at a security door. It buzzed. Rapport pushed it open and led Echo into another labyrinth hallway that looked exactly the same as the previous hallway. They walked past a weight room.

"Are you going to train me for my mission?"

"Mission? My word, that sounds important. There is nothing to worry about, Echo. We're just asking you to take a pleasant little drive."

"Oh, yeah, I mean, it's only to the end of the world, right?"

He tried to slow down, but she pulled him along, smiling the entire time. They passed a weight room again. He felt like they were going in circles.

"Don't you think I should get a little bit of training? What if I run into a ninja? What do I do then?"

Rapport laughed. "A real ninja?" She laughed again. "Chances are you would be dead before you realized you were facing a ninja."

"What about a gun? What if I need to protect myself?"

"You're going to give yourself an ulcer with all that worry. Everything is going to be just fine. You have to trust us. We have your best interest at heart."

"I don't think there is any circumstance in which I would believe that the government has my best interest at heart."

Rapport frowned at him as if he had been naughty. She stopped suddenly in the hallway.

"Don't be such a worrywart. We've gone through a whole lot of trouble to make sure you will get to where you need to be on time. We tuned up your car. Made you special ID badges and security cards. We even upgraded all your food."

"But what about a gun?"

Rapport shook her head. "Guns only provoke violence, Echo. If people find out you are armed, they could get scared and hurt you. You're not the only person out there who is afraid." She patted his arm. "I'm so excited for you. You have such an amazing opportunity ahead of you. You're going to be a pioneer. It's wonderful."

"Lady, I appreciate the amount of smoke being blowing up my ass, but—"

"And here we are!"

Echo looked around. "But we've passed by this wall at least twice."

"*And* here we are!"

She swiped a security card against a door Echo hadn't noticed before. The door beeped twice before Rapport opened it. Shouting could be heard right away from inside. They stepped over a toppled file cabinet packed full of handwritten notes and into a brightly lit warm room. Unshaven wild-haired scientists ran out of small offices and into other offices filled with computers. Math was written everywhere, across every available flat surface. Every office had a whiteboard filled with equations and question marks. Equations decorated the walls like graffiti in a truck stop bathroom. Some of the equations that had been proven wrong were marked out with obscene doodles and four-letter words. All the scientists maintained a sense of urgency, a frantic pace of figuring. Most of the scientists were so wrapped up in their work, they failed to notice Echo. A couple did, however. One burst out of his pile of old papers and computer tablets and rushed toward Echo, nearly knocking down another scientist.

"Whoa! Hey! Hey you!" the man screamed. "You can't reverse entropy no more than you can turn salsa back into a tomato! Tomatoes broke our math, you fucker!"

Rapport gently calmed the man. The man looked thoroughly deranged. As Rapport tended to him, another scientist ran up to Echo and grabbed him by the collar of his jumpsuit.

"Brain damage!" the man screamed with a Scottish accent rolling his r's with his tongue. "We all have brain damage! That's why none of us can remember clearly what life was like before this began! We didn't forget! It's just gone! Is this real? Is it? Mass hysteria! None of this is happening! And it never did!"

The man began to laugh insanely, shaking Echo back and forth as he screamed about brain damage again.

Echo called for Rapport. "In danger! In danger here!"

Two soldiers appeared from behind Echo and sedated the scientist with a quick injection to the neck. They had to pry the unconscious man's hands off of Echo's clothing before dragging him out a door. Echo watched as Rapport dealt with a group of unruly lab coats demanding toilet paper and lollipops. Echo almost laughed at the absurdity of their demands.

Another scientist saw Echo's grin and threw down her clipboard with a shout. She ran over to him accusingly.

"You don't think we work hard enough? That this is easy? Oh, I know what you're thinking! Just build a time machine! Then we can go back in time and fix this before it ever began! Genius! Maybe we already built a time machine and somebody went back in time and caused all this to happen! Maybe we did this to ourselves! Maybe we should have set the bar lower. Like domesticating bears! I could go for a bear steak right now, couldn't you? Let's go shoot some bears and eat them! Quick! Before we run out of bears!"

Rapport pulled the woman away from Echo. The woman began to beat on Rapport and grab at her hair. Rapport struggled to maintain her friendly composure until a soldier was able to pull the woman off of her. Rapport took Echo by the arm.

"We can't go through here right now." She forced a smile. "They're brainstorming. Isn't it wonderful?"

They exited through a different door into another identical hallway. Rapport locked the door behind them and let out a sigh of relief.

"Phew, how 'bout that? Creative types can be pretty kooky sometimes."

"Are you fucking kidding me? They're out of their minds!"

"Yes, yes, they are," Rapport said. Her hair was pulled out of place and a red welt was growing on her forehead. She looked exhausted. She tried to smile, but the magic was gone.

"We thought you should see that."

Echo could hear screaming, like a murder was being committed behind the door.

"Why would anyone want me to see that?"

There was a tremendous crash behind the wall. Rapport tried to pull her hair back into place.

"It's becoming increasingly difficult to hold this place together. Doubt, grief, and despair are undermining all our efforts."

The door thumped hard, causing them both to jump away from it. Rapport looked at Echo, her face bearing a fatalistic gaze.

"There is nothing for you here. Forward is your only option."

"Forward? To what? The whole world is like that. There is no place left to go."

"That's exactly the point."

Alarm klaxons started to wail through the hallway, making it impossible to hear anything else. Rapport touched her ear to listen to a hidden wireless device. She screamed over the klaxons something Echo couldn't make out. She grabbed Echo by the arm and forcefully walked him down the hallway to an elevator, out of which poured a squad of soldiers with cattle prods and syringes at the ready. Rapport held a yelling conversation with one soldier, apparently the one in command of the squad. Afterward, the soldiers ran down the hallway. Rapport pulled Echo into the elevator with her. The door closed, silencing the alarms, and the elevator began to climb.

Echo let a second pass. "What's going to happen to those people?"

"If they are too far gone, we take them to the hospital."

"Hospital?"

Rapport put her hand on his shoulder. "That's where we salvage what we can."

"Like a lobotomy or something?"

Rapport seemed completely frazzled. She looked at Echo. Then looked away. Then looked back at him with determination.

"It's called deep cognitive hypnosis. It's a long process that takes—"

"Let me guess…about a month? Did you really think I expected anything less than to be completely fucked over? That's the story of my whole…" His words stopped there.

The elevator doors whipped open. Bombast stood in front of them, waiting. He pulled Echo out by the arm and led him past the plastic plants, through the staging area, and up the pneumatically lifted metal stairs to the surface of the Think Tank. They passed through the forest of white buildings and stepped out onto a wide-open tarmac. The sun shone down into Echo's eyes, blinding him. Rapport held her hand over his eyes, blocking the glare out. Bombast had no time for her kindness and yanked Echo along. The Audi was parked nearby, aligned with the road he had driven in on. A group of lab coats were wiping it down with towels. A few stray drops of water glistened in the light, indicating it had been washed recently. Bombast hauled Echo over to the vehicle by the arm. Rapport tagged along behind them.

A large black box was bolted to the top of the car's roof. It had a blinking red light and looked exactly like the one Echo had seen in the post office bathroom. The sight of the grotesque cube disgusted Echo. He should have been worried about his mind and how fucked it was. For some reason, though, that did not seem as important as his car.

"Come on, guys! Did you have to put that big ugly thing on the outside of the car? You know, German engineers designed this vehicle to be efficient and beautiful. You meatheads have ruined the aesthetics."

Bombast was flabbergasted. He shot a look at Rapport; she shrugged. He yanked Echo toward him and gestured angrily with a pointed finger.

"Mister, these men busted their asses to have this thing ready for your escape."

"Oh yeah, my escape! I mean, how can I stay here when there is no salad bar?"

"Mister, that's a pretty piss-poor attitude you have there."

"It's hard to change who I am, but I'm always open to suggestions. How about you tell me what you want me to think, and then, I'll think about thinking that way! Is that a deal?"

"Don't be a prick—we already have a deal."

"Do we? What part of that deal involved mind-fucking?"

"Right." Bombast seethed. "Mister, there is no deal you can make with anyone that won't involve being screwed in some way. The real question is, what amount of screwed can you live with and still feel like you made out all right?"

Echo took a step back and looked at Bombast. "Divorced?"

Bombast grit his teeth. "Six times."

Echo raised his eyebrows. "Damn."

Echo took a deep breath, then exhaled, letting go of his anger. "Look, I just want to get out of here. I mean, this has been more fucked up than I ever could have imagined."

"Mister, we want you to leave, too."

Bombast walked Echo around the car pointing out the new chrome exhaust tips they had added. He opened the driver's side door of the Audi and forcefully pushed Echo inside. Echo glanced into the backseat and realized something was very different. He turned again to take another look. The backseat had been removed entirely to accommodate a new storage space made of sheet metal, painted black, and welded to the frame of the car so that it could never be removed. All his belongings had been organized into labeled plastic bins that had been installed directly into the storage space like drawers. Echo noticed they had also added a roll bar. He suspected any number of other hidden modifications had been made. There was no telling what new secrets the car held.

"I haven't even finished reading the manual yet, and now you guys went and changed everything."

Bombast snickered. "Life's a bitch, isn't it?"

Rapport groaned disapprovingly.

Echo looked behind him again. "You realize this can't be a sedan without a backseat, right?"

Bombast grabbed the door. "Watch your fingers!" He slammed it shut.

Echo rolled the window down. "So how screwed am I?"

Bombast grinned. "I think you made out all right." He turned and walked away.

Rapport came beside the door and kneeled down close to Echo.

"It's been great having you here. You seem like a fun guy." She laughed. "Try to listen to yourself more closely from now on. It's going to feel a lot like intuition."

Echo sighed. "This sucks."

She smiled. "Not everything we did was self-serving. Who knows? If you meet a ninja, you might actually know what to do!"

Echo sighed again. "I can't wait."

Bombast wandered over and leaned through the window, crowding out Rapport.

"Sheep can go wherever they want to go, but only the shepherd can lead them to Shangri-La. Mister, we're the government; trust us, we won't lead you astray."

Echo looked at the two of them, appalled. He started the car. They stepped back. He put his head down for a moment and felt a shallow anger brewing inside. They started waving good-bye. He could not believe the audacity of these people. Echo slowly leaned out the window and gave a curt wave. They smiled and waved again. Echo waved back, and then he floored it.

CHAPTER 21

ANOMALY ROAD

The Audi sped up the on-ramp at full throttle. The windows were down, and the road ahead was clear. Echo was alone, and he had been since he left the Think Tank. He was not sure how much time had passed; it felt like several days, but it was probably longer, based on the distance he had traveled. It made no difference to him; he no longer cared. He picked up an old CD he had taken from a gutted electronics store, pushed it into the car's CD player, and listened as "Nowhere Man" by the Beatles began to play. He was glad he had found something that he liked. The lyrics seemed to resonate with him. He turned up the volume.

He thought of the Think Tank. In the time since he had left, he had not felt any differently. He still thought the same way, or at least as far as he could tell. He wondered if the real conspiracy was not that he had undergone some kind of secret hypnosis, but that he had never had the procedure in the first place. Maybe the only thing they had actually done was give him reason to believe he might be under the influence of mind control, and his own wild imaginative paranoia would do the rest.

Everything he had been shown, told, and seen was part of the conspiracy. All of it was meant to reinforce certain ideas. Their odd behavior, the rushing him out the door…it seemed so neat and tidy. Where had Sonnet been? He had disappeared. To where? Probably to orchestrate the entire production.

Echo's eyes narrowed. "That douche bag."

The Audi raced up a steep hill and weaved around a lone crushed can of soda on the road. At the crest of the hill, he slowed to a stop. He could see a gray darkness miles away on the horizon. Black specks hung in the air amid what appeared to be a massive wall of sinister thunderstorm clouds. This was the edge of the abyss, and those black specks were actually gigantic slabs of the planet that had been torn up by the forces at work. He was already closer than he wanted to be. The CD had moved on to more cheerful tracks, but the music suddenly felt intrusive, and he abruptly turned the player off. The radio crackled with empty static. He found it comforting and decided to leave it on.

He could see an unmanned roadblock up ahead. It was the first of many warnings meant to deter those foolish enough to drive toward the abyss. It was only a couple of orange-striped sawhorses with blinking lights. An ominous sign warned of "increased chances of temporal anomalies" beyond that point. Echo had seen these before during his first trip to the end of the world. He knew the pattern. Each successive roadblock would grow increasingly more elaborate and overtly threatening until he reached the fully manned fence at the border. He was excited to see it again. Then he questioned his own intentions. Were these his feelings? Is this what he wanted to do? Or was it what they wanted him to do?

He picked up the ID badges given to him at the Think Tank and looked at them. One of them was covered with holographic stamps, and a gold-plated microchip in the shape of the presidential seal inlaid into a glossy black plastic frame inscribed with a bar code. There was a photo of him on it that appeared to have been taken while he was unconscious. The other was made of titanium, police-like in design, with the insignia of the Think Tank command acting as the shield. His name was engraved on it—his real name he no longer used—and it had been misspelled.

"Those bastards," he said bitterly. "Nobody cares."

He drove around the roadblock and continued on. He wondered about his motivation for going. He wondered if his desires were his own anymore, and if they ever had been. Where was he really going? And why? He asked himself over and over again. He grew angry over thoughts and feelings that he felt were hidden and intangible. He struggled to understand his own reasoning and relentlessly questioned himself about it. He realized that there was nothing else left for him. He knew this would be his final destination. He told himself this, but inside, buried beneath the darkest recesses of his mind, the truth was it was a chance to hope that he would find what he was looking for in the only place he had not yet looked.

"And what will I do with myself if nothing is there?" he asked. He heard no answer. He heard only the static of the radio.

CHAPTER 22

A BRAVE FACE

The sky flashed with a bright white light that seemed to be everywhere. A siren sounded, and everyone at the checkpoint stood still. Echo listened to the siren reverberate through the turbulence caused by the time lightning, knocking it out of sync. It sounded strange, as if he heard the end of the siren before it began, the middle of the tone having been lost in a fold of time. He closed his eyes. He could feel the border fence stretching out before him in each direction. It loomed over him, oppressing his desire to pass beyond its gate. The fence walls were built on wheels, like pieces of a movie set, waiting to be moved or in the process of being moved. The border was constantly advancing forward to stay ahead of the destruction of the abyss.

"Contact!" a soldier yelled from a guard tower as he pointed to the northern edge of the storm cloud wall.

Echo opened his eyes to see what it was. A jagged arc of lightning ripped down from the sky about a mile away and stopped, frozen in place. A lightning stalk had formed right before his eyes. He was disappointed it had happened exactly as he had expected. Like normal lightning halting the moment it touched the ground. He was not sure what he had expected it to look like. He wanted something more. Something not so normal. Not so expected.

The siren slowly wound down and was followed by an announcement that the time lightning phenomenon had ended and it was safe to resume normal operations. Echo walked around his car to get his water bottle for a quick drink. The air was dry and filled with static. A buzzing whine could be heard coming from no discernible direction. The loudspeakers crackled as they switched back to playing music to drown the noise out. The deep voice of Johnny Cash crooned across the gate.

The border was positioned just under the cusp of the cloud wall, a bank of dark thunderstorm clouds that were stacked seemingly to the edge of space. It was very dark just beyond them, almost night-like. The very distant horizon seemed to be pitch black. It made the hairs on Echo's neck stand up just looking into it. He had been waiting patiently under the stormy ceiling for the last two hours while the soldiers checked his credentials. It was very quiet there, apart from the continuously playing music. The soldiers rarely spoke, even to one another. They were vigilant and alert to their responsibilities...driven, it seemed, by the stability duty offered. Only the commanding officer carried on a conversation with Echo. A man who had torn the name tag off his uniform and had come to be known as Dual-cool, so named because he was a marine who had qualified as both a diver and a parachutist. Two things he would never do again.

Dual-cool was a tough one to figure out. In his mannerisms and actions, he was everything expected of a marine. In appearance, however, he was covered in tattoos and body piercings from head to toe. Dual-cool's face had been etched with the portraits of every person he had lost since the end began. Rosary chains connected his nose piercings with those in his ears, and a small cross dangled between his nostrils. He wore no shirt, apparently satisfied with wearing only a sleeveless tactical combat vest, as if prepared for battle even though there was no enemy and there would never be a thing called an enemy again. His arms were covered in names, places, and religious doctrine. He was a walking memorial, an outer projection of deep internal pain. Echo was shocked when he first saw him and thought for sure he had run into a band of cannibals. His opinion changed with the friendly sound of Dual-cool's voice. Whatever tragedy this man had gone through had nearly destroyed him. But he had endured it and would now remain steadfast to the end.

A loud rumble rolled out from the abyss. It sounded like a mountaintop had slid into a rock quarry. It was a deep grinding roar, thunderous, destruction on a scale unimaginable. The specks hanging in the sky were much more easily seen now. Islands the size of whole city blocks tumbled slowly through the clouds. Floating chunks of rocks drifted between them trailing the scattered remains of countless human things. These islands often crashed together like icebergs. The mechanism for planetary destruction, as Dual-cool had told him, was a powerful force surrounding the abyss that tore the ground up at the edge and tossed the bits into the sky, where they would collide together and break down. Then they slowly floated over the horizon and into the abyss itself. Beyond that nobody knew what happened.

The scrapping sound of thunder rolled across the checkpoint once again. Dual-cool stormed out of a command trailer mounted on top of a flatbed truck. In his hands were the ID badges the Think Tank had given to Echo. He marched over to Echo unmoved by the sounds of thunder or the Patsy Cline tune being pumped out of the speakers.

He handed Echo his papers in an abrupt manner. Then Dual-cool spoke again with the voice that sounded like the most generous and kindest man in the world.

"Everything checks out, Mister."

"Can you call me Echo? I just go by that."

"Yes, sir, if that is your preference. Everything checks out, Echo, though we did see in our records that you have approached a checkpoint before."

"I was curious."

"Many people are, but I can assure you, there is nothing to see out there but the face of oblivion. I should warn you that beyond this border there is no policing force. Should you run into trouble, we are not authorized to attempt a rescue operation under any circumstances. The border is large, and we have barely enough men to cover its entire length as it is."

Echo looked into the darkness before him. "What kind of trouble can I expect? Do I need a gun?"

Dual-cool grinned. "The rumors of cannibalism are simply untrue. In all the time I have manned this border, I have never once seen such a thing or read a report about an incident occurring. The rumors of vampire cults, the mobile church of the dark alliance, alien savior spacecraft rendezvous points, and the deli run by Jesus are all decidedly false. What you may still encounter are groups of people scared out of their minds, scavengers who might be interested in your vehicle, and gamers who are determined to play *Conundrum* until the very end. You will probably see bodies, depending on where you go. Dead humans do not decay in this environment. I'd advise against exploring locations where people would gather for suicide, such as schools, gyms, churches, shopping malls, movie theaters, bars, and franchise restaurants known for their family atmosphere. As morbid as it sounds, birthday parties were the prime choice for parents when poisoning their children."

Echo was aghast at Dual-cool's frankness. "That's terrible."

"It happened. Many times. I feel I should inform you of the reality that you will face out there. The very least I can do is provide you with the knowledge to avoid the worst of it. You will not need a firearm. Carrying one will only invite more trouble than it will prevent. I can offer you some pepper spray if you would like some form of deterrence."

"I think I'll take you up on that."

"Can I assist you in anything else?"

Echo's stomach growled. "Well, I was planning to forage for some food in there, but I guess that's not such a good idea, is it?"

"No, sir, it's not something I would recommend. We can provide you with additional supplies if you feel you need them."

"Actually, the Think Tank stocked me up pretty good. I'm just paranoid they put something inside the food they gave me."

Dual-cool's hardened gaze softened a little. "I understand what you mean. The use of pharmaceuticals in the general population has become extreme, and in my opinion, out of hand. I can have what they gave you tested and verified for purity. My command is not under the Think Tank initiative, so I can offer an independent perspective, if you are willing to trust me. I can also provide you with MREs from our stock as an alternative...Those are meals ready to eat."

Echo nodded. "How long will the testing take?"

"We have a XR-282 deluxe particle detector we sweep over the food, and that's it."

"And that works?"

"All modern drugs are laced with a trace radioactive substance that is easily detectable. Time dilation prevents the radioactive marker from reaching its half-life, and because cell division has come to a near stand-still there is little chance of mutation and cancer growth from their use. This has been the standard since shortly after the abyss formed."

"They knew all along from the very beginning this was the end, didn't they?"

"That assertion is correct; however, the formation and goal of the Think Tanks are legitimate, though no one ever planned for them to suc-ceed. With only nineteen percent of the planet remaining, it seems safe to assume they won't."

"Holy shit. I can't believe that much is gone."

Dual-cool's face remained resolute.

"It's not over yet. There is still time enough to live. If you are willing to live life, life will live for you. Remember that. It is only our minds that allow ourselves to be defeated by this darkness. Only your mind. Stay strong, believe in something, and you will live through anything."

Echo understood this more than he was willing to admit. "Thanks, Dual-cool. Thanks for everything."

Dual-cool saluted. "You're a brave man to undertake a one-way mission. You honor us with your sacrifice."

Echo laughed nervously and saluted back in a sloppy manner. Up until that moment, even though he considered his trip into the abyss to be his final one, it had not seemed real. He now realized that he would not be returning. His body broke out into a sweat. He sipped some water, trying to look casual. Dual-cool ordered a soldier to find the XR-282 for a food inspection. Another soldier was ordered to gather additional fresh supplies for Echo. The air rumbled ominously with the sound of rocks grinding. Echo leaned against his car feeling slightly tired from a distant depression creeping up on him. In the corner of his eye, he could see soldiers gossiping, pointing toward him, and shaking their heads as if hearing he had been condemned.

CHAPTER 23

IN THE END

An hour passed by on the road. The car hummed steadily toward oblivion under a darkening sky. The highway was said to be unbroken and clear all the way to the edge. Fate had always granted Echo a measure of convenience most would be jealous of. In the rearview mirror, the horizon glowed brightly in a thin line, like light beaming though the crack at the bottom of a closed door. Everything outside the car had turned to shades of gray. He could see burned-out buildings razed for their supplies long ago next to more recently abandoned structures that were pristine in appearance.

The soldiers had offered him a selection of music before he left. They found that certain songs drowned out the high-pitched whine better than others. He had politely declined the offer. To him, the sound was no worse than the radio static he often listened to. It was strangely monophonic. A constant ringing in the ears. No one knew what it was. One theory was that it came from supersonic turbulence created by particles of dust being sucked away into the abyss. Another theory was that it was the effect of gravitational forces vibrating the atmosphere. There were other theories. There were always other theories. The world had stopped, and everyone everywhere finally had plenty of time to think. If they chose to.

The darkness was as black as night within the second hour, and the sliver of daylight in the rearview mirror had disappeared. Echo's greatest fear was getting lost in the dark. It was not a natural darkness that blocked out the light. It was as if the darkness hung in the air around him like a black fog. Even with the high beams on, the road ahead was limited to just a few feet of visibility. Infrared and night vision did not function properly in the fog. Light did not travel far in it. It was as if the darkness absorbed it. The blackness behaved in the same manner as India ink thrown into a tank of water. It swirled around him, breaking, forming, coming, going, engulfing. He had been told he could breathe it, but he dared not get out and try. He feared becoming caught up in it. He feared drowning alone within the nameless void.

Dual-cool had given him a device that pinpointed the direction back to the border. It was the only thing that worked in the darkness. A compass was impractical with most of the planet gone. Global positioning systems were blocked by the currents in the upper atmosphere, or from the destruction of the satellites. No one knew for sure. The device measured signal pulses sent out by a transmitter at the border fence. It was a little black box with an LCD screen showing an arrow. Time dilation prevented it from calculating distance. Whichever way the arrow pointed was the way back. Useful if a person is in a vehicle. On foot it was possible the user would be chasing a horizon he could never reach. The closer a person was to the abyss, the slower time became, so that a perceivable minute could pass for the walker walking, while hours passed for the soldiers at the border. With the border moving forward at a walking pace every few days, only speed could overcome the discrep-

ancy, theoretically at least. Another theory based on inconsistent obser-
vations. A rule that had been made up simply to resolve certain fears.

The inky darkness swirled outside the Audi. The density and strange
directions it flowed in created the illusion he was no longer moving,
even though he could see the road speeding beneath him in the headlights. He drove on top of the painted lane-divider lines because they
were easier to see in the muddled soup. He could hear the occasional
sound of sand or dust blowing against the exterior. Once in a while, a
rock would be thrown up into a wheel well, with a sharp bang. He could
see nothing, and he worried about what might be out there on the road.
He had already decided to not get out if he got a flat tire. He would
turn around and drive on the rim until he reached the border. His palms
sweated as he gripped the steering wheel, waiting for something unex-
pected to emerge from the darkness. He imagined a hitchhiker appear-
ing in front of him suddenly. The sky rumbled loudly. He wondered if he
was underneath the crushing chunks of earth, if he would be smashed
by falling rock. Goosebumps ran up his arm. He felt cold at the thought.
He touched the window, and it was cold. The chill he felt was real. He
turned on the heater.

Another hour passed by on the road, and it was growing harder to
see ahead. He could make out only a tiny portion of the asphalt speeding beneath him. He slowed down, even though it was the last thing he
wanted to do. He felt he had no choice but to slow down or risk wreck-
ing the car. He was in too far now. All around him, the black ink stag-
nated. It no longer moved or swirled but hung thick and motionless. He
was cold and afraid. At no time did he even consider turning around. He
knew there was no going back. He had to push through, even if he never
returned to the light. He had to know what this thing was that waited
ahead. Even if he could never tell anyone about it. Even if he could never
understand what it was he was seeing. This would be the answer.

More time passed, although Echo had no idea how much. Fear gripped his mind, but still he drove on. He desperately wanted to know why he kept driving forward into the darkness. A thunderous crash pounded overhead. He instinctively ducked inside the car. Nothing fell from the sky, but it was incredibly loud and continued to be loud for a few minutes.

"Hypnotic bullshit!" he exploded, finally succumbing to panic.

They must have put something in his head! They must have! Why was he doing this? He was just driving along as if he had to. Was he doing it for them? For himself? What did he hope to find at the end of the world? Did he think he would attain some form of satisfaction from confirming with his own eyes that the world was being destroyed? He could never go back to the light and live, knowing what was coming. Had he gone so mad that he actually expected to find Cayenne? She was not even real, and he knew it. He had shaped his life around dreams and desires that could never be achieved or fulfilled. He was a fool. He screamed at himself every combination of profanity he knew. He used every hateful word he had ever heard to tear himself apart. He was pathetic. He punched the roof. He hated himself with such fury, he hoped his heart would rupture from the stress of it.

"Fuck you! Fuck you! Fuck you!" he screamed until he was hoarse and tears rolled down his cheeks.

Suddenly, he saw a cobalt blue light piercing through the darkness in front of him. It seemed to glow and it was just ahead. He slowed down a little to wipe his eyes. Is this the end? he asked himself. He sped up, curious to see what it was. He had exhausted his outrage. He had nothing left in him. His breath wavered as he grew excited to see what the blue light was. His head was clear. He was calm, accepting of his fate and the choices he had made. It would be okay now. The dark blue light grew more intense. He slowed down, afraid he might drive off the edge of the world. Then suddenly the car broke through the wall of black fog, leaving a swirling trail of ink behind it. The highway ramped up just ahead. It appeared to be the beginning of a bridge overpass. The peak of the bridge had been sheered away, leaving only the ramp. Echo cautiously continued toward it. He could see in the dark blue light that there was a small town or city surrounding the highway. The city sat half falling over the edge. Parts of it floated in the sky on slabs of ground. Everything was bathed in blue.

As he slowly took the car up the broken ramp, the source of light came into view. It was the moon. It was closer than he had ever seen it or ever thought possible. He could see the depth of its spherical form, a perfect naked roundness hanging in the sky. The moon filled his view, and its presence overwhelmed him. He stopped and turned the Audi's engine off to stare at it. There was no sound. Even the whine was absent. Echo opened the door cautiously. He sniffed the air, but smelled nothing. He stepped out of the car and felt heavier than normal. He looked back at the wall of black fog. His eyes followed its height upward. The magnitude of what he saw left him speechless.

High above, thousands of chunks of debris were spinning slowly, grinding silently as they were pulverized into dust. The dust swirled down past the moon, catching its light, forming delicate threads of silver that coalesced into a massive cloud the moon seemed to hover above. The cloud spun with a ferocious hurricane-like movement, its silver essence dissolving into the bottomless gaping maw of a surrounding inky darkness that blotted out the stars. This was the abyss…a black void of unknown origin and motivation. The silver cloud boiled without a hint of sound to match the fury of its struggle against the darkness. The moon blocked Echo's view of the eye of the storm preventing him from seeing into the center of the abyss. The size of the darkness was easily many times larger than the entirety of the planet Earth. He could see a faint glow at the distant edge, as if hidden behind it was the dawn of a new day.

He carefully walked to the very edge of the broken overpass ramp that hung over the abyss. He could hear his footsteps so clearly that it made him uneasy. The moonlight illuminated everything in a cobalt blue. Echo could see the end of the planet like a rocky coast without an ocean. He kneeled down at the edge and peered over. Rubble floated far below, looking the same as it did high up in the sky. He could see that the planet was being eaten away from underneath. There was not much of it left. He and everyone else lived on a slowly shrinking island of light. The silver hurricane cloud appeared almost majestic under the moon. Its violent motion was softened by its quietness. The size of the abyssal maw behind the cloud made him wonder if the moon would be consumed too, but it appeared to float harmlessly over the danger. It seemed odd that nature would spare it. Then again, maybe what he was seeing was not natural at all.

Beep! Beep! Beep! Ka-ching! Echo stood up suddenly at the sound. The black box on top of his car had unlatched itself. He remembered why he had come here. He walked over and carefully lifted the box off the roof. He laughed a little thinking how he was taking care not to scratch the roof of his car when all around him flew destruction. He set the box down at the edge of the ramp, where it had a clear view of the turbulent abyss. He sat down on it to watch the movement of the silver cloud. A sense of tranquility entered him. He felt comforted by the presence of the moon, that it was there seeing him off. He felt affection for it, as he would for a good friend. It soothed him and gave him a sense of security. These were old feelings he had not felt in a long time. He felt he should stay a while with the moon. He decided to have a picnic at the edge of the broken ramp. He wanted to spend time with this old friend, because he knew after he left he would never see it again. Just this once, just this one last time, he would sit down and enjoy the moon.

CHAPTER 24

TO KNOW AVAIL

It was silent. Even the floating rocks ripping away from the planet made no sound. It was eerie, but also comforting. The air was chilly, but not as cold as it had been while passing through the black fog. It reminded Echo of a spring night. He watched the moon, the clouds, the chaos, all of it moving together while he ate. He had traded away all the food given to him by the Think Tank after the test results proved inconclusive. The military rations he had replaced them with were made with real ingredients he had not tasted in quite some time. The water tasted cleaner than usual too, but he barely noticed either as he sat there.

The light of the moon was bright yet soft. It was as beautiful as it was awe-inspiring. He consumed the meal in a matter of minutes. He threw the water bottle off the edge of the overpass ramp and watched as it was taken up into the sky like a leaf caught in an updraft. He knew then that just a few feet in front of him there was no gravity. He felt heavy where he sat and figured that as long as there was ground below him he would be safe. He looked at the blinking black box that sat beside him. He considered tossing it off the edge, too, but decided against it. The box would meet its fate where he left it. He surveyed the clouds, trying to see where the bottle had drifted. He could not find it. It was gone forever.

He gazed at the moon and decided to speak.

"It's nice to see you again…" he mumbled.

If he was going to speak to this space object, he knew he had better use his voice. The moon had been worshipped as a goddess by humans since the beginning of history, and it deserved to be spoken to clearly and loudly. Its presence demanded that of him. He cleared his throat and shouted, "IT'S NICE TO SEE YOU AGAIN!" He felt as if the moon were watching him now, its attention called by his small voice. He took a deep breath and sighed.

"I guess this is it, isn't it? There is nothing else."

He flicked a pebble off the edge. He watched as its momentum slowed to a halt, and it gradually tumbled into the sky. He felt the hairs on his neck stand up.

"You know, when I look back at everything, from this perspective, it's as if I built my life around things that never mattered to begin with. I feel bound by my contradictions. I don't want to know people, but I'm lonely as hell. I tell myself love has no place in my life, but I feel like it's the one thing I'm missing. I don't believe in it, but I wish for it. I guess everyone hides behind a mask. You never meet a real person; you just meet who they pretend to be. Everyone out there has been so hurt, they can't stand the thought of being hurt again. It's worse than ever, too. I mean, I call myself Echo Gain. That's not my name, but I wanted it to be. I wanted to be this thing I never was and never could be. I never actually became anything else, though. It's still me. I can't stand that. I hate myself sometimes, and I hate other people all the time. I know that's not true. I wish I had a good friend, but I can't stand the thought of being let down again. The more they know you, the more they can hurt you."

He leaned back on his elbows and stared at the moon.

"Then I wonder if I'm angry because they gave up on me, or because I gave up on them? And there is no answer. Just like this. For some reason, I thought I'd find something here. I mean, I know I found you, and it is really good to see you again, but I guess I felt for certain I'd find something here that could...I don't know, I really don't know. I wanted to find happiness. I guess I don't know what that is. I've heard what it is for different people, but I don't know what it is for me."

He stopped talking. He felt a thought leap into his mind with such a jolt, it caused his heart to skip a beat.

"There was this girl, or maybe there *is* this girl. I can't be sure, because I don't know if she was real or just a dream. There was just something about her. She's the only person I can't forget, and I've tried. I know I liked her, but its hurts to say that, and I wish it didn't. I always kept an eye out for her, just in case she was real. I had to believe in something, even if it was a lie. For what it's worth, it feels good to think about her; at least I have that. I just wish that I had—"

His eyes traced over the heavily cratered surface of the moon, realizing for the first time how worn down it appeared.

"I guess we all have our scars. Some are more visible than others..."

He stood up and dusted himself off. "And I guess that's it."

He turned away from the moon intent on taking a nap in the Audi. He looked out at the wall of black fog, expecting it to be right where he had last seen it. It had moved. It had pulled back, revealing a mile of landscape in the same way low tide reveals hidden treasures on a beach. Echo grabbed his binoculars from the passenger seat and began examining what the low tide had revealed. He wondered when the black fog would return. He knew it must have gone out fairly recently, meaning he might have time to venture down into the abandoned city to see what he could find. He saw an exit ramp just beyond the bridge overpass. He could use that to get into the city. As long as he got back on the highway before the black fog returned, he would not be lost in it. He had nothing else to do, and the pristine structures he saw through his binoculars indicated that the area had been evacuated rather quickly. This meant there was no telling what he might find. He wanted to find something. He hoped for anything.

He hopped in the Audi and started it up. He rolled down the window to wave good-bye to the moon and drove away. He did not drive very fast this time. He wanted to keep looking for a destination. He wanted to pick out a building that he could explore. It was to be a treasure hunt. He kept driving a little, stopping, staring at the buildings lined up along various streets, and considering which had the best prospects. There were no cars, no lights, no papers blowing in the wind. It was very clean, very empty, and he felt this was a place he belonged. He sped down the highway to the next exit ramp and suddenly saw an orange light coming from a building. He could see several cars parked outside of it. He stopped the car, got out with his binoculars, and ran to the edge of the highway for a better look.

It was a coffee shop with a few people inside. Echo's first thoughts were of the warnings Dual-cool had given him. He felt afraid at first and then angry. For the briefest of moments, the edge of the abyss had been his and his alone. He was excited to explore it knowing he was the only person there. It was safe. It was his sanctuary from everything he had known. No people at all. Absolute emotional neutrality. Now he saw people. Not the mutants or suicidal fanatics he feared. These people appeared to be scholarly. They were reading books, painting, and entertaining one another with cheerful small talk near an espresso machine. One of the painters turned from her canvas and told a joke. Everyone laughed. What right had they to be happy? Echo seethed. He hated them for it. He turned to leave, intent on returning to the daylight and finding some isolated corner where he could hide. He just wanted to be alone, but to leave would mean he was condemning himself to loneliness, that in some sick way he preferred to endure this pain instead of going down there to see who they were.

He made a fist. He had to go down there. There was nothing else for him to do. His thoughts hung in his mind like orders commanding him to overcome his fear. He must do this or he would regret it forever. He traced a path from the exit ramp to the shop. It was just a couple turns. Easy to get to. Easy to get away from if he needed to. He searched through the supplies the soldiers had given him. He found the pepper spray and clipped it to his belt. He dug out the red sledgehammer from the trunk and put it close by where he could grab it. He practiced reaching for it. He stood near the car, reached in, grabbed the sledgehammer, and swung at the air angrily with the intent to kill. Then he jumped in the car and started it. He did this several times until he felt confident he could escape. If things turned sour, he would use the spray and his pocket knife to get out of the shop. Then he could use the sledgehammer if people pursued. Once in the car, he could follow the street all the way to the edge of the abyss. Even if the tide came back in, he would be able to find his way back onto the highway. He felt ready now.

He drove down to the coffee shop, being careful not to run the engine too loudly. The shop was easy to find. It was a warm orange light shining in a world of cool blue. The parking lot contained an RV, a motorcycle, a beat-up old station wagon, a pick-up truck, and a Honda Civic that looked much like the one he used to own. He pulled into a parking space at the end. The lights from the Audi beamed in through the shop windows, drawing the attention of the occupants inside.

As soon as they saw him, they rushed out the door carrying baseball bats, golf clubs, a copper skillet, and a steel folding chair. Echo put the Audi in reverse and started to leave. An unarmed barista ran out from the crowd with her arms waving to get his attention. She was followed by two other baristas. They yelled at him to wait. He ignored them and pulled out to the street. Then he stopped, realizing something was odd about the angry mob. He considered the absurdity of the crowd; some were still sipping their lattes between angry ranting, others smiling as if it were all good sport. The scene seemed superficial. The car was now aligned with the street. He could speed away should things go badly.

An auburn-haired barista ran over to him, while the armed patrons stayed huddled near the shop entrance. She slowed and walked over to the driver's side. Echo reached for the pepper spray as she leaned in through the window.

"Don't run," she said. "We don't mean to scare you away. We're just afraid of you. We don't know you."

"Oh, I know him!" a familiar voice said. A barista with jet-black hair and glasses walked into view. Echo's heart raced from just the sight of her.

"Cayenne?" he yelled in a panic.

She quickly made her way to the car, smiling nervously. The auburn-haired barista made room, and Cayenne poked her head through the window. Echo stared at her awestruck.

"Is this real? Is it really happening? What the fuck is happening? What the fuck is going on?"

"Chill out, Echo. Sheesh!"

"Who are you?"

"Cayenne!" she said with a laugh.

"Are you sure?"

"Yes."

His heart pounded. What was this? She smiled at him. His throat tightened.

"How can you be here?"

She shrugged. "Because I am, just like you."

"But I don't understand."

She smiled. "I think you should come inside."

CHAPTER 25

ENTROPY'S ESPRESSO

———

Echo talked. They listened. He sat on a barstool at the coffee shop counter and poured out the long story that had led him to their doorstep. He held nothing back. Cayenne stood close behind him; he could feel her there. She put her hand in his back pocket, and his voice cracked. He cleared his throat. The gathered patrons smiled and encouraged him to continue. He found it easy to recount his most painful memories to them. He had nothing to hide here at the end. He told them everything, and they listened graciously as if they already knew his secrets. He even shared with them how he knew Cayenne. They smiled and nodded, not hinting in the slightest if they thought he was crazy. He felt nervous, but okay. When he finished speaking, they served him a cup of chamomile and mint tea to help calm his nerves.

Cayenne put her chin on his right shoulder and wrapped her left arm around the other. She hugged him. He felt a strong urge to break out of her grasp and push her away, even though he longed for such intimacy. It was true he had known her for a long time, but she was also very much a stranger. He remained frozen in place, torn between conflicting fears and desires. He gulped and nervously fiddled with his tea unsure of how to respond with so many people watching.

A man who stood stiffly nearby ordered a plain black coffee and took a seat on the stool next to Echo. He was dressed in a custom-tailored charcoal gray business suit with a rattlesnake head bolo tie, a shiny belt buckle large enough to deflect bullets, snakeskin cowboy boots, and a dusty-white country western hat. He was too burly to pull the look off, even with the sculpted horseshoe mustache. He unbuttoned his suit jacket, trying his best to look at ease and casual.

"The only thing worse than lying to each other is lying to ourselves," said the man. His voice was hardy, stern, deep, and conveyed being in charge.

"Echo," he said, tossing the ID badges on the counter, "do you know *why* you are here?"

Echo knew it had to be because of the hypnosis, but if he said that the man might not offer his own explanation.

"Well, it's like I said. I was just driving by; I felt a little thirsty, a bit tired, and I thought, how about some coffee?"

"Echo. This is the end of the world, literally the end of the goddamn world. Are you going to sit there and try to bullshit me?"

No, he was not going to. "I was sent here, wasn't I?"

"Sure. They sent you here."

The man sipped his black coffee. He winced from the bitterness and had to shake it off. He let out a long breath.

"Echo. Every choice made in life is decided by the potential rewards and punishments we might receive. You do 'x' so that you can avoid 'y' and achieve 'z.' If you're provided with logical motivations and reasonable discouragements, you can be convinced to do just about anything, and goddamn it, you'll think it was your idea all along. The government is subtle and patient. Anything too obvious is designed to be that way. They sent you and Cayenne here because you two get along nicely and you both wanted to be here. You both hated the world and most other people. That's exactly the type of personality that could accept leaving and never coming back. "

Echo slowly shook his head. "So I'm here to do what? Cuddle with Cayenne?"

She laughed and buried her head in his shoulder. Echo pulled her hand out of his back pocket.

"Cayenne, can I have a little space? Please?"

She pulled away with a sigh. His feelings were mixed, strange, and unfamiliar. He turned back to the man.

"So I was manipulated by hypnosis and"—he looked at Cayenne—"and other reasons, to come here and do…what?"

"To join this crew."

Crew? Echo thought suddenly. He looked around the coffee shop as if taking in its details for the first time. Everything about the shop looked like what a trendy hipster-attracting coffee shop would be expected to look like. It was lit with warm orange lights, affable faux-wood walls, an oddly shaped couch in the corner, space for artists to set up easels, copper espresso machines, a small stage for poetry readings, and assorted tables cleverly shaped like puzzle pieces. All these components were to be expected in such an establishment. It was the other things that raised suspicion.

At every entrance was a strange glowing sign with a pulsating symbol that resembled a spiral of arrows. The sign marked that the coffee shop was a government-designated time shelter. The outer walls of the shop were plated with a substance that resembled carbon fiber, but wasn't. Behind the poetry stage was a large screen that showed what seemed to be a timer that sometimes counted down and sometimes counted up. The shop's floor was covered in black metal grating. The tables and chairs had magnetic feet, as if the designer expected gravity to be lost. There were other things, too, like breaks in the wall that appeared to reveal complex machinery behind them, and randomly scattered buttons and control panels that glowed as if on standby. All of it together made no sense realistically, but with a little imagination, he began to wonder if the coffee shop was actually some sort of spacecraft.

"Is this some kind of…spaceship?" he asked.

The man laughed. "The bastards never approved those. This is something different…" He looked Echo in the eye. "They call me Pylon, by the way."

Echo stared at the cowboy hat. "The name just doesn't fit."

Pylon chuckled. "Well, sure, you don't know me well enough to see why it fits. I'm named after my integrity and strength of character. I was specially picked for this operation. It's the last mission I'll ever have, and one that will last for as long as we all survive."

"Wait a minute. Survive? Survive what?"

Cayenne slouched on the barstool to his other side. She held the bridge of her nose in the same manner Echo did when he was frustrated.

"Oh come on, Echo, you know this thing is about to fly right into the abyss, right?"

Pylon drank his coffee and winced. "Sure is. Right through the pooper."

A rush of paranoid thoughts flooded Echo's mind.

"That's crazy. This looks like some low-budget, made-for-TV sci-fi movie set. You people are all part of some kind of weird caffeine-powered cult that built this thing to fool yourselves into believing there is some way of avoiding the end of the world. The reality is we are all fucked."

Pylon shook his head. "Is that the reality you want to live in, Echo? A paranoid close-minded world that has no room for imagining that something impossible just might be possible? That's not you. I know that's not you, goddamn it. You're not a close-minded coward."

"How can I believe anything you say?"

"How can you doubt with such conviction?"

Cayenne tugged on Echo's shirt for him to calm down. He shook his head "no." He looked at her and felt extremely conflicted. He was angry with her in a distant way that was buried beneath the feelings he felt for her. He ran his hand through his hair and snapped a suspicious glance at her.

"Am I here because of you?"

She seemed flattered. "Maybe," she teased. Then she said more quietly, "But not in the way you think."

Echo grinned. "You *know,* don't you? This isn't real, is it?"

"Oh, please! Why do you keep saying that?"

Pylon slammed his hand down on the counter. "All right! Time for some tough love."

Pylon grabbed Echo by the arm, and a big burly hand slapped him hard across the face. The other patrons gasped. Echo was stunned. His lower lip trembled from the shock of the violent act. Pylon slapped him again. Then again. He demanded that a barista give him a fork. He held Echo's hand down on the counter and jabbed the fork into it. Echo yelled. Then Pylon ordered Cayenne to kiss him hard on the mouth. Echo was just about to cry when Cayenne grabbed him by the shoulders, yanked him toward her, and kissed him so hard that their teeth knocked together. Then she let go. Everyone watched him. He rubbed his hand and licked his lips. They tasted like Cayenne…warm, and slightly sweet. He felt many different things all at once.

"I'm dead; there is no other answer."

Pylon snarled, and pounded his fist on the counter, rattling his cup of coffee.

"Get out of your head, man! You're alive, and no matter what crap you keep trying to pull over what is happening around you, the fact is you're here. This is now, goddamn it; don't fight against opportunity when it's in front of you! What are you afraid of?"

"I'm afraid that I'll wake up and this will all be gone. That none of this is real."

"That is goddamn ridiculous! Have you ever not known when reality was real?"

He considered that for a moment. "No. I guess I've always known the difference."

"Good. Trust that feeling. You know what is real and what is true. Even if it's confusing—and it often is in the face of entropy."

"But this coffee shop is a spaceship!" He let out a nervous laugh. "How can I get behind that idea? It's crazy!"

"Echo. This is not a spaceship. It's a vessel that has been designed to manipulate the forces of entropy so that we can travel through spacetime in a nonlinear manner. This is not a time machine. It's not going to travel by any conventional means of understanding. Look, how do I explain this to you? Any normal person out there right now would be driven insane by the way this coffee shop is going to travel. There are very few people in the world that have the right kind of brain, or what have you, to sustain an event that could very well be trans-quantum temporal goddamn dimensional in nature. To survive something like this, you have to have an imagination, be open to new ideas…strange new ideas. Do you know why you were asked to bring that black box here? That thing is gathering telemetry for us. It's the final data before we go in."

"But it's all so convenient. So impossibly convenient."

"Sure it is. Get over yourself."

"Think about it! Think how completely improbable it was for that Think Tank, which I chose at random, to discover a 'special' person like me, and send me here."

Pylon grit his teeth with irritation. "Echo, listen. If you put a block of cheese out, and you wait long enough, you will attract a mouse. Those Think Tanks are the cheese. It's impossible to determine who is immune and who isn't by any normal means. We didn't need a nation-wide screening to find people. We just had to wait long enough, and the people we were looking for found us. You took a risk, Cayenne took a risk; it's the same story for everyone else here."

Echo squinted his eyes at Cayenne.

"Weren't you the one who told me to go to that Think Tank?"

She seemed suddenly flustered. "Oh, come on! You would have ended up there anyways. I mean, just where do you think that white room was? Grr! Could I have been any more obvious that I knew what was going on?"

"That was at the Think Tank? So I was remembering the future! But how?"

Pylon reset his hat on his head. "There is no future, Echo. All time exists simultaneously. The linear perception that there is a past, present, and future is an illusion created by our minds. Time has no direction except the one you give it. It's the present here and now, *now*, because you want it to be now, got it?"

"Fucking crazy shit!"

Cayenne rolled her eyes. "Really, Echo? I mean, really? You think you can find a smarter way of expressing yourself other than cursing?"

He grinned. "So *when* was the white room?"

"That was the waiting room between examinations. Sheesh."

"I knew it! They did screw up my head!"

Pylon's patience was being tested. "What do you want to believe happened, Echo? That a month was spent trying to program your brain to go somewhere you didn't want to go, or that they evaluated you and subconsciously revealed the location of the only means of escape off the planet?"

"You make it sound like I had a choice in coming here."

"Sure you did. The government can show you the road, but only you can decide to travel it. They gave you the incentive and know-how; the rest was up to you."

Pylon sat back against the counter. "This world is over, Echo. They can't save it. Even if they could, everyone is too far-gone mentally to go back to the way it was. There were never enough resources to build a spaceship. They couldn't launch one anyway. Conventional thinking no longer applies. We had to think outside the box. So they came up with this. It's not a spaceship or a time machine, but it can go places."

"Yeah? Where will we go? Another Earth? Another today? Or how about tomorrow?"

Pylon finished his coffee with a disgusted gag. "Sure. Anything is possible. Fact is, I don't know."

"You don't know?"

"I know we will be the third one to launch. The first was a super-market, the second was a library, but both of those were large buildings, and there was some concern about maintaining fifth dimensional structural integrity while transitioning between realities. Resources were running low, so they decided to build a coffee shop. When this landmass crumbles, we will launch into the unknown—to die or to travel, we don't know—but we hope it works. We think it will."

"Great. So my choice is to stay here and ride a coffee shop into the pit of oblivion or return to what remains of the world and live another thousand years until it ends?"

"It's not going to last another thousand years, Echo. The world is dead. It's not a planet anymore; it's just a shell. The only thing left is a seven-mile thick layer of crust that could shatter at any moment. The last estimate I read said that there was no more than ten years left until it imploded."

"So, again, convenient. Oh! I made it here just in time! Oh! You can't go back! Oh! And there is a beautiful brunette who can't help falling all over you! This is absurd. You realize that, right? I bet the real answer is that I'm still unconscious back at the Think Tank. I never woke up."

"Really? You selfish fucker!" Cayenne stood up. "I think it's more that you are afraid to be happy. And you are looking for something, any-thing at all, to be wrong. You are trying to find a problem where there really isn't one. Now you are trying to create one. Can't you accept that sometimes things just fall into place? That things kinda have a way of working out? You can't run away from the possibility of being happy just because you're afraid. Sheesh. Take a chance!"

"On what? On this? On you?"

"On yourself!"

Echo slowly shook his head. He tried to take it all in. He wanted to accept it, but he could not. He felt betrayed and manipulated. Befriended and desired, conflicted and confused. There was no answer. There was no choice. He felt pressured, like he might explode. But there was another option: He could choose to self-destruct. He would leave and throw it all away. That way he would not have to deal with it at all. They could have their fate, and he could have his own. One of his own choosing, made of his own actions. He looked at Cayenne, angrily. He loathed his desire to be with her. It meant everything to him, and he hated himself for it. She could see his mind exploding with all the wrong ideas. She reached out to him. He swatted her hand away and walked out the door.

CHAPTER 26

THE WARM EMBRACE OF OBLIVION

It was cool and quiet outside the coffee shop. Echo took a deep breath. The black ink cloud loomed over the street like a pyroclastic explosion from an erupting volcano falling in slow motion. It swirled and flowed against itself. It was as black as the cast of a shadow at midnight; shapeless, and creeping. Occasionally a piece of floating debris would catch a highlight of blue from the moon. Echo stared into it marveling at the sight of this thing that had no name and that no one could understand. He sat down on the curb next to where the Audi was parked. He put his hands in his pockets. He heard small footsteps behind him. He knew it was Cayenne. He felt bad about swatting her hand away.

"I'm not angry at you or anything. I'm just frustrated in general...I didn't mean to hit you."

She smirked. "Hit me? You mean that weak limp-wristed slap? Oh, please. That's the kind of thing I'd expect a child to do. Not a man. And you are still a man, aren't you?"

Echo grinned. "Sometimes."

She looked him up and down, her mind churning with thought.

"Come here," he said to her. He took a hand out of his pocket and patted the space next to him on the curb. She sat down next to him. She looked a little anxious. There was space between them.

He glanced over at her. She was fidgeting with her hands. Her knees were drawn up to her chin. She was almost a little ball. He smiled and spoke softly.

"Have you ever watched someone else watching TV? Or playing a video game? Have you ever gone to the movies and watched other people? They just sit very still, staring. You know what they are experiencing: It's a whole other reality in their heads. They escape into it. In their mind it surrounds them, but in real life, they are staring at something. Blank. Ignorant. Expressionless. Imagine that everywhere you went people lived out their lives like that. That vacant look of being somewhere else far away. That look is what I see in people everywhere I go. It's like everyone around me is watching the same movie, playing the same video game, and I'm watching them. I don't understand people. I can't relate to them, and I don't get them."

Cayenne chipped at her black nail polish. She blew a flake off her finger. "I didn't mean to yell at you."

"That's okay. You were right. I am selfish. I think I am, but then, I don't know. I think about the different things I've experienced, the choices I've made, and all the choices that were made for me." Echo looked up at the ink-covered sky. "It's just weird."

"What do you mean?"

"I mean, this is everything I could want. I can have you."

Cayenne jumped in. "Oh, come on! It's pretty arrogant of you to think you can just *have* me. Even if it is the end of the world and I'm flirting a lot with you. And I do like you. And I do want you, too. And I suppose, in a way, it was predestined—well, depending on how you look at it, I guess…Oh, for heaven's sake, Echo, I'm just as single as you are. But it really doesn't work that way. You know? A relationship is something two people have to build. Together."

Echo put his head down. "Relax, Cayenne. That's not what I meant."

"Oh, please! I know you, Echo. You've always talked like a guy who's never been in a relationship before or even had a real girlfriend. Sheesh. It's more than just sex. More than just chemicals in the brain. It's mutual, something you kinda share together with each other. Haven't you ever experienced that?"

"No. When you put it that way, I guess I haven't."

She looked at him stunned. "But…that's so sad."

"I know." He avoided her gaze. "I don't tell anyone how lonely I really am. How empty my life is. First of all, nobody wants to hear that because, no matter how much they say they care, people really don't give a shit about any other problems but their own. Second, women get scared when I tell them that I'm lonely. They look at me like something is wrong with me instead of understanding I'm a human being."

"What if I told you I was the same way?"

"What? Lonely?"

"Yeah…"

"I find that hard to believe," he said coldly. "You're too pretty."

Echo felt like a jerk for saying that. There was silence between them. He could say something to fix it, but he had no idea what, and it was already too late. He knew where that had come from: that part deep inside him that hates people just to keep them from getting too close.

"That came out wrong," he said apologetically.

She bit her lower lip. She had nothing to say to him.

Echo took his hands out of his pockets and sat back. "I must have lived for thousands of years now. Shouldn't I be older and wiser?"

She looked at him through the corner of her eye. "If that were really true, everyone would be wise, but they're not. People are just as horrid as they have always been."

"You mean me, don't you?"

"I mean everyone."

"Right. I'm the jerk here. I know I am."

"Oh, come off it, Echo, I never expected you to—"

"You can fuck off with your expectations! I'll only let you down. I'll only be strange, and crazy, and lonely, and depressed. I'm sorry I can't be much else than that." He stood up.

"No, wait! That's really not what I meant."

He looked hurt and disgusted. "I find that hard to believe."

He walked over to the door of the Audi and opened it. "You know I thought I came out here for some fresh air, but I think I really meant to leave. I'm going."

She stood up, frustrated with him for acting so dramatic. "Really? Where? There is nothing out there, and you know it."

"Anything is better than staying here."

"You don't really mean that. You want to be here."

"What makes you think that?"

"Because you came here."

"Three words: deep cognitive hypnosis."

"Oh, fuck you! That's such a weak excuse!"

"No, fuck you!" He slammed the door shut.

The Audi started up with a roar. Cayenne ran over to the driver's side window.

"Oh, come on, Echo! Don't be that way. Don't leave."

"Why not?"

"Because I want you to stay."

"Because *you* want me to stay? Or because I'm *predestined* to stay?" he said cynically. He shook his head. "Cayenne, you are the only reason I would stay. I don't give a fuck about any of those people or their coffee. If you want to be with me, then get in. Let's get out of here. "

"I can't."

"Then…I guess this is good-bye."

Echo hit the gas hard, forcing her to yank her head out the window. He pulled away, then turned down the moonlit street and sped into the darkness, leaving the coffee shop behind. After a few blocks in the cool air, he felt calmer. He kept driving without looking back. He knew she was watching him leave, and that bothered him. He felt more lost than ever. He wanted to forget the coffee shop. He hated that it was possible he had not found it on his own, that he had been subconsciously led there by hypnosis. He hated that there may not be any hypnosis at all and that his arrival was somehow inevitable. Most of all, he hated her.

"Enough!" he shouted, forcing the hatred out of his mind.

He was tired of hating. He felt as if he had spent his whole life hating. He used hate to hide his fear. Hate had protected him, and its safety had ruined him. Now it was easier to push the world away than to let one person into his life. He was afraid of her and the feelings he felt when he was around her. Who was she really? He had no idea. No idea at all.

As he drove, the sky grew darker. The tide of the black cloud was coming in, and soon he would be surrounded by it. What was he doing? Why was he doing this? He slammed on the brakes. The car screeched to a stop. He got out. It was much colder than in front of the coffee shop. He paced in front of the headlights, holding his head. Then he realized he had felt warm there because of Cayenne. He threw his hands in the air, angrily. Black streaks of ink were rolling forward far above him. This is loneliness, he thought. The darkness. It made him mad. Why was it that loneliness was associated with the cold and darkness? Was that how it really felt? Or was it just what he had been taught to feel by society? What if solitude was a vision of a beautiful beach and sunny skies? Would loneliness still feel the same? He made a fist. The girl! The girl! The girl! What was going on inside him?

"How can I escape, when I can't even escape from myself?"

He sat down. He felt tired. He knew it was the depression. He felt sick. Sick of the conflict within him. The air was growing colder. He could see his breath in the headlights. He laughed a little. He was such a fool. He could hear his heart beating. What was he going to do? There was no running away this time. He had run out of choices. This would be the end. Why was it so difficult to accept her?

"Am I that afraid?" he wondered. He sat for a few minutes, then answered his own question. "Yes. You're afraid of being happy." He smiled. "That's why you never found it. You never wanted it in the first place. You're afraid to lose your pain."

He had to go back. He knew he would never see her again if he did not. Before, Cayenne was just a dream. A person who may or may not exist. He knew she was real now and that if he let her go he would regret it forever. This scared him more than anything. He sat there watching the sky fall onto him. He closed his eyes.

"If I could have anything I wanted. If I could do anything I wanted. What would I do?"

He took a deep breath and waited for the answer. It came in the form of Cayenne yelling at him. "ECHO!"

He opened his eyes. He was sitting on a barstool in the coffee shop. He felt as if he had just woken up.

"How did I get here?"

Cayenne was standing near the window as if she had been watching the street. It appeared that she had been there for some time. The Audi was parked in its space again. Echo stood up, his head pounded, and he felt dizzy. He took a step, stumbled, and fell. A big hand scooped him up and placed him in a chair at a table. Pylon sat down at the table with him. He held Echo's hand. Pylon's hands were huge and warm, like giant oven mitts.

"You're here because you want to be here, same as the rest of us."

Echo rubbed his eyes to get used to the lights of the coffee shop again. Cayenne brought him black coffee. He took a sip. The bitterness caught him off guard, causing him to let out an involuntary hack. She rubbed his back.

"I thought you were really gone," she said.

Echo frowned. "So...was I? What happened? How did I get here?"

She pulled a chair up next to him.

"It kinda has to do with the connection between time and the mind. It's complicated, but its real. You're here *now*...and I'm sorry."

Echo pulled his hand out of Pylon's grasp. The guy had a hell of a grip. They exchanged an awkward look. Echo turned to Cayenne.

"I overreacted. I was just...afraid."

Cayenne reached out to him. She hesitated for a moment, then gently ran her fingers through his hair. Echo tensed up, struggling to accept her affection. Pylon grabbed one of Echo's hands again.

"You need to relax. You need to breathe. Like this…take a deep breath in, hold it, then let it out. Breathe in the sunny ions, breath out the tar."

Echo looked at Pylon suspiciously. "Who told you that?"

"Some guy I met once."

"Fat guy?"

"Sure was."

"Weird."

"How so?"

"I think I knew the same guy."

Pylon grinned. "Are you doing okay? Do you want to be here?"

Echo took a deep breath, then let it out. "Yeah, yeah I want to be here."

Pylon looked relieved. "That's good. I think it might be too late for you to leave anyway."

The coffee shop shook. Echo could see debris floating outside. "Are we moving?"

"We're about to go over the edge."

Echo panicked. Pylon put a big hand on his shoulder and motioned for him to breathe. All Echo could do was let out a nervous half-laugh.

"What about my car and my things?"

Pylon was amused by the question. "They're all coming with us. This place generates its own gravity well. It's good for two things: One, everything inside it will be held down and two, anything outside it will be deflected. The parking lot is within our sphere of influence, as it were. Everything but that goddamn RV is coming with us. We're like our own self-contained world here."

"How do you fly this thing?"

"There is an automated control center in the basement."

"Automated?"

"Sure." Pylon chuckled. "I'm pretty sure it is. All I know is, it does my taxes."

Echo's eyes widened. Cayenne intertwined her fingers with his. His voice cracked.

"Just where are we going, then?"

Pylon lit up with excitement. "That's the best part. We don't know. We'll find out when we get there, I guess. But don't let that freak you out, Echo."

Echo was committed now, and whatever the outcome, he was sure it had to be a better experience than what he was leaving behind.

"Great. Is this one of those 'the ending is just the beginning' deals?"

Pylon laughed. "No, it's more like a continuance. Think of us as explorers searching for a new home we can colonize to propagate our species."

He put his hands down on Echo's and Cayenne's shoulders, and winked.

"Will we start to age again?" Echo asked.

"Don't know. Our temporal abeyance could be permanent."

The coffee shop rumbled again. Pylon barked some orders to one of the baristas, walked over to the espresso machine, and began turning knobs on it. A cheerful computer voice asked them to prepare for departure. The patrons of the shop started cleaning up their areas and stowing their belongings in cabinets. Echo noticed that the large countdown clock was fluctuating between zero and negative one. Cayenne moved her head in front of his. She looked into his eyes. His stomach felt funny, causing him to smile. Her gaze melted.

"Come on," she said, "we can get a good view over by the window."

"But it's covered in black fog."

"That's going to disappear when we fall in."

"Fall in?"

"Into the abyss. Sheesh. Don't worry, we'll be safe inside the shop."

She stood up and took his hand in hers. He pulled her back down.

"I *am* worried, Cayenne. I don't even know how I got back here."

"But you want to be here, right?"

"What does that mean? What does what I want have to do with anything?"

"Everything!" She smiled. "You wouldn't really be here if you didn't want to be here. That's the way it works. You create your own destiny. Time doesn't create it for you. It just records the choice you made at whatever point you made it."

"But I—"

Everyone gathered by the windows as the coffee shop began to teeter back and forth. Nothing inside the shop moved. Pylon checked a control panel next to the espresso machine. He pompously announced that the gravity well was now fully functional and that Earth's gravity no longer held any affect on them. While no one inside the shop could feel the violent rocking, they could see it through the windows. The fog lifted as the precipice the shop had been sitting on was torn apart by the abyss. The shop clung to the edge, defiantly, while the world around it was siphoned away. Echo watched as the highway near the shop broke apart. He realized that this really was the end.

"We are actually going into that thing, aren't we?"

Cayenne hopped excitedly. "For real! It's going to be sooo cool."

Even as Cayenne stood near him and squeezed his hand, old fears of doubt started to creep into his mind. He took a step back.

"This is pretty crazy. I don't know—"

Cayenne interrupted him. "Oh, Echo, don't go there. What really matters is what you do from this point forward. Which, by the way, is completely within your control, whether you realize it or not. I know that sounds easier than it is, but the moment today becomes tomorrow, what happened yesterday will no longer matter."

She mouthed the words silently, making sure she had said it right. "You know, the choices we make affect each other, too. It's not just what we decide alone that determines our fate. It's what we decide together."

"But what if—"

She put a finger on his mouth to quiet him.

"Come on, Echo! There is no way you can account for all the variables in life. Just worry about the here and now."

"You do realize that in a moment there won't be a here or a now, right?"

She pulled his head down to her and kissed him gently on the mouth. At that moment, answers no longer mattered. Happiness was not something he had to find; it was something he had to allow himself to have. He hugged her tightly. The moon appeared outside the window suddenly. He took her hand, and together, they fell into the abyss.

RECOMMENDED READING

As with all science fiction, some real-world science inspired this work. While there are currently no definitive answers to the makeup of time, the universe, and the nature of our reality, there are many dedicated theoretical physicists who are attempting to answer those questions through math and science. Their work is exciting to read, with fascinating philosophical ramifications to consider. *In the Sanctum of Entropy* plays with the possibilities of those ramifications in a manner that stretches the truth for entertainment purposes. If, however, you would like to learn more about the real science touched on in this novel, I recommend the inspiring works of the following authors:

From Eternity to Here: The Quest for the Ultimate Theory of Time by Sean Carroll

www.preposterousuniverse.com

The Elegant Universe and *The Fabric of the Cosmos* by Brian Greene

www.briangreene.org

Thank you for reading.